AF433132

PAGE AND SCROLL PUBLISHING PRESENTS

Names: Theyson, T.P. 1986 - Author
Title: PANIC / T.P. Theyson
Description: First Edition | Page and Scroll Publishing 2025
www.tptheyson.com
301 Mt. Holly Rd. Unit 55
Stanley, North Carolina 28164

For anyone struggling to put down the bottle.
I believe in you.

PANIC

T.P. THEYSON

&

FROM THE WORLD OF *PANIC*
OUT OF THE DARKNESS

CHAPTER ONE

An abrasive vibrating sound rattles my skull as it shoots through the interior of my car, filling every empty space, making me jump as I blink my eyes, my mind free falling from floating in nothingness. I pull back to reality from a world of daydreams. A world that isn't full of darkness and death; a world devoid of broken bones and torn flesh. The sound is so intense it makes my teeth feel like they are about to shake loose from my head before I see that I have drifted into the oncoming lane on the old, cracked, four lane freeway; one that still has rumble strips in the center of the lanes instead of just on the sides. Horns blare and lights flash as oncoming traffic heads directly towards me. At the sight of a campervan on a collision course with my car, I inhale a sharp breath, grabbing the steering wheel hard, my knuckles turning white as I yank it to the right, over adjusting, making the tires squeal as the car swings back over the rumble strip into confluent traffic to more horns blaring from behind me. I almost graze the guard rail, making me have to yank the wheel back to the left to compensate as my rear end sways back and forth, the car in the lane next to me laying on it's horn. Centered back in my lane, my heart hammers, adrenaline pumping through my veins as I take a deep breath, steadying myself and rolling down the window, hoping the fresh air that blows my jet black hair around my face helps me to stay alert. I quickly abandon the idea however, as I roll the window back up, blocking out the hot, humid southern air that fills the inside of my car, making it feel like trying to breathe through a wet blanket as it carries the smell of roadkill and pollen into my Civic. I glance over to the right and the woman in the car next to me holds up her middle finger, letting it hover in front of a face of disgust. I sigh, questioning for not the first time, why I am even here as I turn forward and slow down so the woman can pass me and drive away. To further punctuate how displeased she is with me, as her car pulls in front of mine, her hand shoots out of her window, once again showing me her raised middle finger topped with an orange, almond shaped, fake nail. I look at the stick figure family, stickered on her back glass. A husband, herself, a kid and seven cat stickers stand next to a sticker that says IF YOU CAN READ THIS, GET OFF MY ASS, staring at me as her car speeds away.

10

I roll my eyes and say to myself,
"Southern hospitality at it's finest."

My heart rate slows as I feel my nerves start to calm, the adrenaline flowing through my body slower. I can't help but think about how I've been drifting off more lately, my mind trying to dissociate; to pull itself into another reality altogether. One where my parents and brother didn't brutally die in a car accident a year ago.

Whenever I think about that day, the sounds of their screams come roaring back to me, tearing through my brain, sharp claws ripping through the gray matter of my mind. I absentmindedly reach up, my fingers sliding over the scar on my neck that rests there like a thick worm laying dead on my skin, a gift given to me so that I can never look in the mirror and not associate myself with death. A constant reminder of the loss I have suffered. Realizing what I am doing, I pull my hand away, straightening my back, glancing into the rearview mirror, my eyes focusing on the raised red line that starts below my right ear and runs down my neck disappearing under my shirt collar. A blaring neon sign emblazoned on my flesh that I see every day that screams at me that I have no one. A vacancy, advertising the hole in my heart that will never again be filled. Everyone looks at it, even though they try to act like they don't and in everyone's mind, I instantly become "the girl with the scar". Someone who has been hurt and is wounded. I shake my head, trying to aim my thoughts like a gun, to keep them focused on what is happening here and now, but as hard as I try, they slide back to that day.

When the car crashed, time had slowed down. I had later thought to myself while stuck in the mangled vehicle, slowly dying, that you didn't need to reach the speed of light to time travel. In fact you didn't even need to get close. You just needed to shoot your body into an unexpected traumatic situation and seconds could feel like days. Maybe physicists have had it wrong the whole time and it is really about making your thoughts travel faster than light, not your body.

An 18-wheeler, the driver having drifted off from being on his fifteenth hour of driving, desperate to make a deadline given to him by an employer whose last concern is the safety of their employees, crossed over the broken lines into our lane and sideswiped our car, making my father yank the wheel in the opposite direction in an attempt to try to get away from the truck who had already sheared off all the paint and some of the metal from the drivers side of the car. We quickly found ourselves encased in a moving metal

death trap in the form of my father's 1973 Delta 88. The family car we had grown up with, transformed into a coffin filled with gasoline and screams as we drove directly towards the guard rail, blocking traffic from a deep ditch next to the freeway. The massive piece of metal could have proven to be the one thing that saved our lives, but in a spot of cruel fate, a drunk driver had run into the rail a week prior, knocking the end loose, making the metal rest against the ground. I was told later by an attorney for the city, as he sat in my hospital room; trying to work out a deal with me, that it was on the job list for city workers to come repair, but with their backed up log, they weren't going to get to it for at least another month. He told me this with a look on his face, like this explanation would just make everything better. Like I would realize the extremely inconvenient position I was putting him in and say,
"Oh, Okay! All is forgiven!"

I stared at him, offering no response and with a shrug of his shoulders he was the precursor to how everyone else would react. My family dying was looked at by others as just a spot of bad luck; an unavoidable, unfortunate series of events. Something that people could read about in their newspapers, safe at home with their kids and their mugs of coffee; shaking their heads with a frown and think, *how unfortunate*, expecting me to pull myself up by my bootstraps, conquering the next stage of my life to give the story a happy ending. To everyone else it was simply a case of wrong place, wrong time, but for me, it was not a moment in my life to rise from the ashes, a phoenix reborn.

It was absolutely and utterly apocalyptic. It was the final bomb that sends chasms shooting through the ground, buildings falling, and people screaming out in pain and fear. It was the end of myself. It was not a trial to make me stand tall and profess that it had not killed me, only made me stronger. It was an all consuming darkness that ate my fucking soul and drank my tears, never letting go.

When our car hit the rail, it emulated a ramp, launching us ten feet above the ground. The Delta turned 180 degrees in mid air, coming back down on the guardrail with a slam. Sparks shot out from under the vehicle as the impact severed the metal rail like a gray bone being hit with a giant hammer. When it did, a massive piece of metal entered through the driver's side window, skewering both of my parents who, cruelly, did not die instantly, but after ten minutes of incredible pain. I still remember the moment their screams faded, crying out to me and my brother that they loved us both before their heads lulled to the side as the rest of their blood drained from their bodies, leaving my world in silence, despite the sirens of the ambulances outside of our car. I screamed out for Michael, my brother, who, because of the way the car had come to a stop on its side, was above me in the back seat, held by his seatbelt; something by design that is supposed to protect us, now a chain, binding both of us to this ball of metal filled with the stench of blood and death. When he responded, his voice came back as level and calm; my big brother, the one who could brave any situation, who could be a guide through any tragedy. I felt so relieved that he was alive, my mind telling me that somehow, we would be able to carry on through this together. My relief; the feeling of still having one person left in my life was not destined to last long. Michael had survived the crash, but when the fire department tried to get him out of the car, his seat belt snapped and he fell face first against my window. The impact and the way he fell broke his neck, killing him instantly. As Michael laid there in the car, lifeless, I stared into his vacant eyes, my reality, every single thing around me breaking and turning black; my brain diving into a hole too deep for me to ever climb out of. One where I didn't cry, I didn't scream, I just laid there, waiting for death to reach out and wrap it's cold fingers around me so that I could fall into the void of nothingness, this absolute nightmare coming to an end. My heart beat slowed, I parted my lips, and with one last breath, I let go of my life, allowing myself to be consumed by the darkness.

What felt like only seconds later, my eyes shot open as my mouth gasped like a fish out of water, gulping air to fill my lungs against my will. I had survived. Some told me I was lucky, a phrase that would follow me forever, but I didn't feel lucky; I felt cursed. Cursed to walk this world alone, an empty husk devoid of any real emotion. Just wasting air that could be inhaled by someone who actually wants to live.

I was told that a shard of metal had flown through the car and hit me in the neck, making me lose consciousness and almost bleed out, but medics had stabilized me on the scene, air lifting my body afterwards to the nearest hospital. Most days I wish they hadn't done that. I wish I had died with my family and not attended three funerals at the same time, watching three coffins get placed into a plot together in front of three headstones, while I sat silent in a new, black Versace dress that I burned after the funeral so that I would never have to look at it again.

I am alone now, living in a void. There is an energy that surrounds me. One that does not let anything joyous or bright filter through. I don't leave the house, I don't talk to friends, food doesn't taste the same; I haven't even laughed in a year. I have found that there is a place that exists between life and death. A place where everything is gray and meaningless. There is no key; no door to knock upon. There is no road that leads there, no guide to show you the path. The only way to find it is to truly give up. To lose all faith and desire in every single thing that surrounds us. This is not depression. It is a primordial creature that gave birth to misery and sorrow. It has found me and shown me the world for what it truly is; nothing but pain.

As I start to drift away from reality again, my thoughts overtaking me, a memory breaks loose of my mother once telling me that when she was a child she had bumped into a table in her grandmother's hallway, knocking over and shattering a lamp. Her grandmother wasn't upset, but when

my mother suggested that maybe they could fix it, my grandmother shook her head. She told her the antique lamp would never be able to be replaced. She told her,
"There are some things in this world that are so special that once they're gone, they will never make a miraculous return and we just have to face that. All we can do is appreciate the time we had with it."

My mother would repeat that bit of wisdom to me throughout my childhood when there was something I lost or broke that couldn't be replaced. I never once thought it would apply to the people in my life instead of inanimate objects. Just like the lamp, my whole life shattered that day when my family was yanked away from me, but I couldn't face it. I couldn't just appreciate the time I had with them. I had no concept of how to even begin letting go.

In the months after the accident, our family lawyer helped me file several lawsuits on my behalf. First against the city for the guard rail not being repaired based on the fact that it could have saved our lives instead of destroying them. Second, against the fire department on the basis that they did not secure the scene correctly, leading to my brother's death and finally, we sued Five Farms Food Supply, who owned the truck that was headed to drop off pallets of food supplies at a Tres Amigos Cantina in Kolme, another hours drive from the lake.

After being released from the hospital, I found myself unable to recover the motivation to participate in the corporate rat race that the people in power have tried tirelessly to convince us is so important. We are led to believe we are worthless unless we work ourselves to death to support their goals and endeavors and I just couldn't muster the energy to participate anymore. So when I had called into work so many times that I had been fired, the money, I suppose, was welcome, but just like everything else, I found it hard to care.

When all was said and done, I walked away with three million dollars after taxes and the payoff to my lawyer. You'd think that would be worth something, but to be honest, I'd give it all up for one more day with my family. I know that sounds cliche, but it doesn't make it any less true. Three million is nothing compared to the chance to take the time to say goodbye instead of having someone you love be here one minute and then gone the next, ripped from your fingers that reach out trying to hold onto them.

After the money was deposited into my account, I quickly learned that giving someone who has deep depression three million dollars is not the best idea. I almost immediately sought out methods of self medicating to cover my pain. Things that would pull my mind away from the reality of my world; things that even for a short time could help me forget. After falling into heavy drinking for months, I woke up one morning, having driven my car through my own mailbox the night before, wreaking of liquor and bad decisions. I rolled over, my head feeling like it was going to burst as I wiped the stale tasting drool from the corner of my mouth. As my eyelids slowly closed, the remnants of the alcohol in my system pulling me back into sleep, an alert pinged from my phone on the bedside table. I decided to leave it alone, happy I hadn't lost my phone while drunk, voting to check it later. When another ping came; then another, I let out an aggravated growl, rolling over, picking up my phone to see I had three messages.

The texts were from my friend Luna; a friend that despite trying to check up on me, I hadn't spoken to in months. I squinted my eyes, trying to focus on the words broken into entire paragraphs filled with concern, telling me that she was worried about me and that she didn't mean to pry, but that the staff of Lookie Lou's, the bar she works at, was talking about how out of control I was the night before and that the owner, Lou himself, doesn't want to see me in there for a while. She went on to say that she wishes I would lean on her in this "hard time" and that it is unhealthy for me to just drop off of the map and turn inward, as she put it. She finished the message by saying that if I didn't feel like I could talk to *her*, she knew of a therapist that came highly recommended if I needed to talk to someone less invested. I was angry at first. Angry that whenever people are prying, they tell you that they aren't trying to pry, but that night as I sat at my kitchen table, performing my nightly ritual of getting black out drunk, my eyes kept drifting to my phone. Eventually, with tears in my eyes, I called Dr. Lindsey Hartgrove and left a slurred message.

The next day, she called me back, telling me she had a cancellation, freeing up an appointment for later that day. I reluctantly agreed and found myself in the elevator of her building, three hours later. As I sat in her office, Doctor Hartgrove watched me, perched upon her imported Italian leather chair, surrounded by soft colors and non threatening decor. The objects placed around the room screaming that she is open minded and progressive. Things like a statue of a Indigenous god standing next to a book about religious history. An eye of protection above the door and a "Love Wins" sticker on her water bottle. The temperature was a perfect seventy two degrees and the clock on the wall said "Take your time".

She stared at me over her glasses, legs crossed, a high heel dangling from her right foot as I felt the urge to have just one pull of liquor in my system. After we talked on the phone, I had made sure to skip my usual shot in my morning coffee, wanting to show up to my appointment completely sober, but as I felt myself start to shake and sweat, I wondered if that was a mistake. It took about ten minutes before she asked me how much I had been drinking since the loss of my family.

In our third session, everything in the room the exact same except for Doctor Hatrgrove's choice of a pantsuit instead of a skirt. She told me that through self medicating, I had established negative patterns that were not allowing me to climb out of the pit of despair I had fallen into. She said I needed a shock to my system. Something that would drastically change my outlook on life so that I could start the healing process. As I walked out of her office, the cool air blowing clouds in over the mountains, I walked straight to the bar, downing shots with beer chasers, muttering to myself how full of shit Doctor Hartgrove was.

When my family died next to me, we were headed to the . Not *our* lakehouse; as we didn't own it, but we always called it "the lakehouse" as we went there every summer for a week-long family vacation when Michael and I were growing up. Having moved out of our parent's house long ago, we hadn't been there in years, but our parents had arranged to have a reunion, as they called it. They claimed that with everything going on in the world, we could all use a week away from electronics and bad news flooding our TV's and social media platforms to, as they said, take a minute to ourselves. Both my brother and I couldn't disagree with their reasoning, so when the time came, we had met at our parents house with hugs and laughter, packed the car with our bags, food, and supplies and drove for two hours, just to have it all go drastically south before we even hit the bridge to cross the lake.

———————————   ———————————

When I woke up the next morning after my appointment, laying next to a man and woman I had no recollection of, in my bed. I went to the kitchen, hungover and on the verge of

throwing up the eighteen chicken nuggets I had eaten at three in the morning. As I poured a cup of coffee, making excuses for why I couldn't go get breakfast or see, who I found out were Jack and Jill (no I'm not kidding), ever again, telling them I wasn't going to be in town much longer, I was struck with an idea. Grabbing my laptop, I made another split decision. If Doctor Hartgrove wanted me to shock my system, I knew exactly how I was going to do it. A couple of internet searches later, I decided that I was going to buy the lakehouse. My searches revealed the house was currently on the market for the first time in a long time so I downed three advil and called my lawyer, asking for advice. He told me he would get people he knew on it and before the day was over I got a return call telling me that the owner was being stubborn. He was willing to sell, but there was one condition. They wanted one million dollars for the home and surrounding property that was listed at $750,000 and valued even lower. My lawyer, always on my side since he made a huge chunk off me during the lawsuits, started rambling off what a ridiculous offer that was and how we could work on talking them down or maybe find a different property I would like. I could feel his silent shock over the phone line when I interrupted him and said,
"Tell them it's a deal."

He instantly tried to talk me out of it, telling me once again that it was a ridiculous price and that he could get them to bring it down and all I said in reply was.
"I want it. Tell them it's a deal."

22

It took a while to get things ready, the house needing some repairs that were found during inspection. When all was said and done, I did a wire transfer for $970,000 to the seller and the lakehouse was mine.

———————   ———————

I come out of my thoughts and memories as I glance to the side, a spot next to the freeway where a section of guardrail is new and shiny compared to the other half that is worn and gray. Sitting to the right of the rail is a white cross, one *I* did not place there with a wreath of fake flowers hanging from it. I shake my head at the audacity of the type of person who assumes that everyone is of the same religion as them, taking the liberty to mark a place of loss, *my* place of loss with a cross. I turn my eyes away from where it all happened, a single tear forming in the corner of my eye, dropping and leaving a trail down my cheek. I wipe it away, inhaling a deep breath, the sounds of screams returning to me again, filling my ears as I relive my family's death before the bump in the road makes me jump as my car drives across the bridge that goes over the lake.

———————   ———————

The sunlight dances off the water as boats and jet skis fill the lake that flows underneath the overpass made of concrete and steel. I feel like a ghost driving over this bridge; something haunting the lives of everyone I come into contact with. My brain has dissociated so heavily that a lot of times I find my short term memory is at a loss; forgetting things that have happened less than ten minutes prior. I wonder as I watch a boat sail towards the bridge if that is what it is like to be a spirit. If a wandering specter can never remember the things that happen and that is why they inhabit the same space, trying to live the same life, over and over, winding up frustrated and angry, lashing out, the way I do. I feel like I died back at that guard rail, the new piece of shiny metal, my tombstone, and I shouldn't be here now. I am just drifting. No purpose and no will to carry on.

Seeing the place where my family died brings with it the need to stop at the liquor store before the turn off for the house, my mind telling me to just have a couple sips to take the edge off. As I sit at the red light feeling that unscratchable itch, the click of my turn signal, a ticking clock counting down while I try to make a decision, I feel myself getting jittery as I imagine the sound of the cap breaking away from the safety seal. The room temperature liquid sloshing into the glass as the bottle makes a glug, glug, glug noise. The first sip, the second pour, the amazing blanket that covers my thoughts, making them fade into the recesses of my brain as I slowly kill myself with drink. A car horn blares behind me, making me look up and see the light has turned green. I push the feeling down and tuck it away, pulling out of the turn lane and heading home.

CHAPTER TWO

I pass nothing but forests full of trees, partly orange and red, partly green, the weather not deciding if it's ready to be fall or if it wants to grasp on to the lingering heat of summer. Dead leaves coat the ground amongst wild growth, covering every inch of exposed dirt. I take a chance, far away from the freeway at this point and roll down the window to inhale the nature that surrounds me, breathing it in deeply, letting it act as the glue to fill all the broken pieces of myself that I am trying to hold together. A cool breeze breaks through the humid heat of the afternoon, cutting it down the middle like a knife, finding my window. Pine and fresh air fills my car, but there is something else; something lingering in the shadows cast by the forest. My nostrils twitch at the smell of rot; wet leaves and something worse lingering underneath. I try to ignore it, letting the sunlight shine on my face and the beautiful scenery fill my mind, but I can't pull away from the sense that I am always surrounded by death. At this thought the smell of decomposition takes over, making me feel sick before I roll up my window and turn the air on high, inhaling the cold air conditioning.

I regain my composure as I pull up to a stop sign, faded to a light red from years of sunlight. My eyes drift up as I notice the three small bullet holes in the metal. This is something that might make most people feel uneasy, thoughts of people riding around in the backs of trucks, shooting guns off in the middle of the night, but since the holes look like they're from a small caliber like a .22, I write it off as bored country kids with nothing to do, finding a way to get into trouble.

I sit at the stop sign, the car idling as I turn my head right, then left, looking both ways before pressing slightly on the gas pedal to pull forward. I immediately slam on the brakes as a classic, orange Chevy truck flies by, laying on their horn the entire way. I turn my head left, looking as they drive away, exhaust billowing out of their tailpipe and see the driver's middle finger shoot out from their open window, held high in the air. My adrenaline pumps hard as I sit still, looking at the second middle finger given to me today, questioning myself about what just happened. Did I seriously just not see the truck coming, or worse yet; did my mind not register it? I sigh and look again twice down the long stretch of road, before pulling forward and making my turn. After driving for a few more minutes, I come around a curve where I pass a line of nine mismatched, rusty mailboxes lined up together on the side of the road. I make a mental note that my new mailbox, an orange one with paint flaking off of it next to one shaped like a pig with wings sticking off the side, is included in that group and I'll have to walk or drive down there to get my mail. At the thought, I feel my shoulders make an involuntary "who cares" shrug, knowing I probably won't check my mail for a couple weeks, if ever. I know it's the depression making things like that happen, but just like G.I. Joe used to tell us when we were kids, knowing, truly is only half the battle as it's not something I can just turn off. I am aware of why I do things like drink myself into oblivion at any given chance, but I still do them and therein lies the problem.

It feels like the sunlight surrounding me physically fades as my thoughts turn dark. I think for a second I must be imagining it, but when I look around I see that as I've followed the road, the trees have grown denser, blocking out the sunlight, making my surroundings more like my mind, my car thrown into shadow as different shades of dark green, so thick the sunlight is unable to penetrate through them, fly by the window. I come around another curve and the trees open suddenly, making me squint as bright light floods the car once again and I slow down, turning my blinker on and looking to the left at the long driveway that leads to the house I've arrived at a year too late. The home that is now mine. I turn left and ease towards the lakehouse.

I pull past two apple trees, one placed on each side of the entrance into the gravel driveway. The apples are small, underdeveloped in the heat and I wonder if they will grow, producing fruit to be eaten or if they will be more like me, rotten and shriveled, falling from a place of beauty to decay and turn rancid. The stones make crackling noises underneath my tires as I approach the massive home looming before me, the windows on the front reflecting my car coming closer, like the giant eyes of a monster, watching its prey advance, a tiny creature unaware of the danger that lurks, gazing at its next meal. The house is what some might describe as a "modern cabin". This means it is indeed built of logs like a cabin would be, but that it is a lot bigger than one might imagine a cabin. It is two stories with massive windows on the front and back. It has four skylights, two fireplaces, and is 4,100 square feet, making it much more house than I will ever need, but my mind is already made up. I, in my own fucked up way, want to finish the family trip one way or another. I want to go to the happy place we were all headed to a year ago. I want an ounce of the joy we felt here for so many years to puncture the shell of depression that surrounds me and I want it to make me feel something; anything. My therapist constantly talks about closure and I guess, in my mind, I hope being in this happy place will help me stop being a depressed drunk, destroying my own life because it no longer holds any value for me *or* if that doesn't work, it will at least allow me to become a recluse, drinking myself to death in my empty house without people constantly telling me they're worried about me, offering their unsolicited advice on a silver platter made of condolences, using my family's death as a conversation starter. At this point, I feel indifferent to the result and either outcome is fine with me.

As the thought comes and leaves my mind, I pause, asking myself if that's really true. Have I truly lost all concern for my own life or are the long fingers belonging to depression puncturing the shadows, reaching out and wrapping themselves around me so that I cannot think clearly? I know what my family would want for me and I do truly want to give it a try. On the few occasions that I break through the darkness, I know they are the reason why. I sometimes have moments of clarity where I know my parents and my brother would want me to carry on. They would want me to be happy in any way that I could. I don't believe in all that mystical shit that they are walking with me, leaving footprints beside mine in the sand or whatever. It's just that sometimes I care that that is what they would want…and sometimes, most times; I don't.

The gravel stops crackling as my tires bounce onto the paved part of the driveway that starts halfway up from the house. I look to the right, seeing the massive, tan shipping

container that has been dropped off for me by the moving company I hired, the name and logo of "Two Guys and A Truck", huge on the side in faded green paint. It is full of my family's things, and I know I will have to sort through it at some point, but I am not even close to being ready to face that task. Luckily, instead of paying the rental fee for the container for the next year, I bought it outright, so it can sit there for the rest of time if I want it to. I look away from my museum of death contained in its own metal shell and halfway down the paved driveway, I stop the car, staring out of my windshield at the house; *my* house. Something that used to be a focal point of life, now one of death. I feel my pulse rise as my brain tells me that I'm not ready for this. I should turn around and head back to Ashton with it's bluegrass clubs and breweries on every corner. If I leave now, I can be there in a few hours, inside my favorite cafe, an orange double decker bus, turned into a coffee shop, parked right on the corner of the street, an irish coffee with extra Bailey's in hand, the crisp mountain air coming through open windows, mixing with the smell of fresh ground espresso beans, while a buzz creeps into my head. I can sit at my favorite table on the upper level and call my landlord, get my old place back and forget about this nonsense. Then maybe I can-
WHAM!

A short, shrill scream escapes my mouth as a bird slams into my windshield hard enough to put a small crack into the glass, leaving behind a red, oblong splotch of blood; it's body hitting the hood and falling off of my car onto the ground. My heart hammers as I slowly release my grip on the side of the passenger seat, moving forward slowly, inspecting the texture of the blood on the glass, a thick, dark clump sitting off center in a light red circle, starting to capitulate to gravity, threatening to drip down the windshield. I open my door and step out, looking towards the front of my car for the body. I hesitantly move forward and see the brown bird laying on the cement with it's little feet curled and sticking up in the air. I take another step forward, crouching down to look at the poor creature with red staining on it's neck and chest. Another memory enters my mind of my father telling me on our first camping trip, when a raccoon stole my graham crackers, leaving me crying and upset, that we were the ones intruding on the animal's territory, not the other way around. I reach out, wrapping my fingers around it's delicate body and stand, holding it out in front of me, watching the wind blow through it's feathers. Even though there was nothing within my power that I could do to stop this from happening, my heart feels full of guilt as I try to use humor to cover my sadness.

"Well, that can't be a good sign."

I suck in a breath as the bird's eyes open and it twists it's neck, making it's head turn all the way upside down, then swings it's head forward like a snake and lets out a hiss.

"Fucking shit!"

I drop the bird as I jump back, letting it's body fall towards the ground, but before it hits, it spreads it's wings, flapping

them rapidly and flies away. A heavy sigh escapes my lips as I run my hands through my hair, wishing I had stopped at the liquor store for that drink.
"I'm too sober to be dealing with this shit."

I get back in my car, turning on my windshield wipers that leave a red line of blood, smeared across the glass. As they return to their dormant position, with an ear piercing squeak of dry rubber on a dry windshield, the thought enters my mind that this is too much blood for that tiny bird to have survived, but the notion leaves me as I shift my car into drive, following the paved driveway as it curves around the side of the house to the bottom of the back where a two car garage sits under the rest of the house. I reach over to my passenger seat, digging to the bottom of my bookbag and find the classic style garage door opener that was given to me with the keys by the realtor at closing. I click it and a rumble comes from inside as the garage door to the left starts to open, a system of chain and metal wheels being pulled along a track. When we were here as kids, Michael and I used to click the button affixed to the wall on the inside, run down the stairs and roll under the door before it closed in a game we called, "don't get crushed". I can almost hear our little voices, laughter mixed with screams when the door finishes moving, and I blink, coming back to myself. I pull forward, coming to a stop inside the garage as my brakes give a small squeal. I reach forward, placing my fingers on the key, still in the ignition and pause. The thought enters my mind about just closing the garage door and letting the carbon monoxide do it's

32

work, but then I roll my eyes and sigh, knowing I'm too much of a coward to try a second attempt at killing myself. The first time, three weeks after I left the hospital, I tried to do it with pills, only succeeding in making myself sick, throwing up undigested Advil PM all over my bed and myself before falling asleep, waking up twelve hours later, covered in dried vomit. I turn off the engine and the noise dies out in the small space. I open the car door and when I push it closed, the sound echoes off the cement floor and walls. My eyes glance over to the white french door fridge in the corner, a staple of the house. I walk over and pull open the doors. In summers past it would be stocked with syrupy delicious sodas like Surge and Pepsi, but now, I stare back at nothing but carbonated water in a variety of flavors; something the seller obviously didn't care enough about to take with them. My eyes land on a pomegranate Redbull nestled into the back, hiding behind a row of pineapple water and my heart gives a small beat of joy, my body eager for any substance at this point. I reach over the water and grab the skinny can, lifting and taking it out of the fridge, letting the doors close on their own. I pop the tab on the can and lift it to my lips, taking a long sip, letting the caffeine and taurine take hold of me. My body feels satisfied to have a chemical running through it, but only momentarily as I feel the itch creep back in. The feeling that's always there, the need to be inebriated and not in control.

I push the feeling away, letting the nagging recede into the back of my mind as I crack my neck, releasing a sigh of regret that I didn't stop at the liquor store. I leave my things in the car except for one small orange and black duffle bag and my bookbag, walking up the wooden, unfinished steps from the garage. I grip the handle of the door at the top and twist, opening it into the large kitchen space where we all used to play board games at the island and cook meals together. The space smells too clean like bleach and lemon, not lived in like it always had before. Some of the updates that were demanded for such a high price tag stare at me already, like granite countertops and a smart fridge that tells me when I need to restock something. The place looks good; even better than I remember and even through my deep depression that I now live in constantly, I can admit that it is really nice.

Coming home to a fully furnished, massive cabin full of natural sunlight would make most people feel lucky to even be standing in such a space, but I know that the only reason I'm here is to lick my wounds or to wallow in self pity. Which I will choose; to be determined. At this moment, this house feels like nothing more than a period to end the story of my life. At best, a rehab center I've paid almost a million dollars to place myself in. At worst, an empty space, devoid of love and people, just like my heart.

I walk from the kitchen into the familiar living room filled with leather chairs, a matching couch, an easel and stool placed by the window and a hidden television that needs a switch to lower into view. The fireplace is covered in river rock, extending from the floor, five feet up. The exposed chimney stands tall, crawling up the wall all the way to the vaulted ceiling. As I look around, something on the glass top coffee table catches my eye and I pick it up, seeing that it is a note left on thick card stock. I turn it over and see in beautiful handwritten cursive, *Welcome Home.* I roll my eyes.

"The realtor."

I toss the card back onto the table, watching as it lands. I stare down at the glass; a new piece from when I was a kid, as I remember when I was five years old, I was bored, sitting in the living room while my dad and Michael were fishing down at the dock. My mom was in the shower upstairs and I decided to create a game for myself. I started jumping from each piece of furniture, determined not to touch the ground or I would lose the game. I went from chair to chair, then the couch and then onto the coffee table. I made my rounds again and again, laughing to myself until the third time around, when I jumped on the table and the large piece of glass shattered underneath my weight, sending me falling to the floor as I went through it. I looked around the room, in shock, my mind trying to catch up with what had happened as my mom ran in, in her robe, to see what the noise was. When she saw me sitting on the floor, surrounded by razor sharp glass, she let out a scream, making my dad and brother come running. My dad approached slowly, not wanting to startle me and make me move as I sat inside the frame of the table, two foot pieces of glass surrounding me, threatening to cut me open. In the end, it would be the first time I was told by a doctor that I was "lucky". A jagged piece of glass sat less than an inch from my neck, but all I ended up with was seven stitches on my foot, preventing me from getting in the water for the rest of the vacation.

The memory fades, a photograph slid back into plastic as the album is closed. I look around the room, fully realizing that every inch of this house, every splinter and fiber holds personal memories. Memories I will have to confront or do my best to forget. Something else grabs my attention from the corner of the living room. Next to one of the massive windows is a triangular shaped liquor cabinet, snuggly fit into a corner where two walls meet. I don't remember this being here, which means it must have been added fairly recently. The shape of it is too perfect and I know it was custom built to fit the space. I mosey over, glancing at the glass front, seeing that there is only one bottle left inside. I glance back at the realtor's note on the coffee table and speak to it like it is a gateway to making the realtor who represented this house hear my frustration.
"Left me a note, but couldn't leave some new booze, huh?"

I open the door and pluck out the odd shaped bottle, looking at what was so bad, the owner decided to leave it behind. I grimace, my face falling into one of disgust as I read, Goldschläger. Memories of teenage years, sneaking into the woods with a stolen bottle of liquor come flowing back, the taste of throwing up cinnamon and the laughter that came afterwards, when life was simpler. Just as soon as I act disgusted, I look at the bottle again that is almost

completely full and shrug my shoulders as I say to no one but myself,
"Whatever."

My brain has been pulling at me to have a drink and it's going to get what it wants. If the liquor gods didn't want me to drink, they wouldn't have let the old owner leave this here for me, right? Half convincing myself that this is fated, but also knowing that my half assed attempt at a plausible excuse is nothing but pure bullshit, I find an old mason jar in one of the cabinets and pour two fingers, golden flakes dancing around in the booze as the bottle makes the glug, glug, glug noise I fantasized about earlier. I still feel a bit of my hangover lingering from the day before and as I lift the glass jar, I say something my college boyfriend used to whenever we would go out drinking multiple nights in a row. "Time to grease the pipes!"

I throw back the glass, pounding the liquor, my mouth and throat lighting up instantly, filled with cinnamon flavor. I follow the burn with a huge sip of my Redbull, that I instantly regret as I find out first hand what pomegranate mixed with cinnamon tastes like. I retch, the drink threatening to make a return, but steady myself on the counter, taking a deep breath and letting my gag reflex settle. When my stomach's somersault has concluded, I look down at the bottle and say,
"Thought you were going to get me, huh?"

When you are hungover, the first drink is the hardest, but once "the pipes are greased", it all goes down much easier. I pour another two fingers and shoot it back, the second shot already going down more smoothly than the first. As I set the mason jar on the counter, my eyebrows raise and I examine the bottle, turning it in my hand.
"Hmm. Not as bad as I remember."

The sun comes out from behind a cloud and I glance out of the windows looking out onto the back of the property before I pour a double into my glass this time, taking a sip as I reach into my bookbag, pulling out my camera and walking across the large rug in the living room to the sliding glass door that leads out to a raised, wrap around porch going around the entire back of the house. The view is admittedly unbeatable, the house sitting directly on Aima Island Lake with Mount Aima in the background, appearing blue from this distance. I hold the camera up, peering through the viewfinder before snapping a picture, pulling the camera away from my face. Another thing suggested to me by Doctor Hartgrove was to find things to occupy my time, leaving less space for my mind to wander. Having exactly zero hobbies to lean into, I went with one I had in highschool. I loved the feeling and smells of the darkroom; the excitement of watching your photos develop and reveal themselves to you. It was truly my refuge; a way to get away from everything going on in my life and just embrace the silence. Lindsey told me in her office that she has seen significant improvement on substance abuse and dependence when people lean into a hobby, so I dug out my old camera and paid a company to come turn one of the spare rooms in my new home into a dark room before I moved in, in another attempt to fix myself. I chuckle as I lean on the porches railing with my elbows, sipping my glass of liquor. I raise my mason jar to no one and say, "Not working too well so far."

I take another sip, my throat burning less than my guilt. I thought telling myself that it was time to go cold turkey before leaving my old house to drive down here would motivate me. New start, new me bullshit, but now I'm standing here, liquor already giving me a buzz, thinking about how it's been less than one day since I said I was done drinking. I didn't even make it a full twenty-four hours.

The guilt eventually fades as each sip makes me feel better about my decision. I lean further over the railing, looking at the water that flows up against my backyard, a private dock, the same one that has always been there, looking like it consists of nothing but splinters held together with super glue, jutting out into the crystal blue surface. As I watch the water lap at the shore, the liquor tells me another good decision would be to go for a swim. I slide the back door open and go back inside the house, setting down my camera and retrieving my bathing suit from my duffle bag. I strip in the living room, leaving my clothes on one of the chairs and pull on my black one-piece. The schnapps makes the short amount of time a blur and seem faster than it is as I find myself walking down the grass hill towards the sand that surrounds the edge of the lake, my mason jar now filled to the brim with Goldschläger in hand. The grass feels soft on my bare feet and when I walk onto the old wooden dock, decades of memories fill my head. My father and mother holding me and my brother on their shoulders to play chicken; a game where you try to knock the other person from their carrier's shoulders and into the water; the nights filled with the smell of cooked fish filling the air as we grilled out, fireworks, and naps on the deck. This was the place that had and would always unite us, which is why when my dad called, saying it had been too long since we had been here, I instantly agreed, visions of warm summer nights filled with fireflies and jars of apple pie moonshine honeycombing my brain. The decision to put my life on hold to go on a family vacation was the easiest one I'd ever made. My boyfriend at the time however, didn't understand. I told him how excited I was to get away and spend time with my brother and parents, but the only thing he responded with were questions about why he couldn't tag along. I tried to explain to him that this place, this destination, is a core family memory that no one outside of the four of us have ever been privy to. No grandparents, no cousins, no friends. It was always just us. He got so jealous and we fought for the whole night with him giving me an ultimatum between him or my trip. It's never a good idea to give someone a choice rooted in finality, but he continued to be importunate, so the next day, despite his apologies, I told him to not call me anymore, closing the door in his face and on our relationship.

I leave the past again, pulling myself back to the here and now as my brain ping pongs from what was and what is. As the images of my life before fade, I stand on the edge of the dock, staring down at my reflection in the water. I have lost a vast amount of weight since the accident. First from eating through nothing but feeding tubes in the hospital, but then, after, from the will to only drink myself into oblivion, not eat. My ribs jut out like a primitive xylophone has been stuck under my skin and it's not hard to admit that I don't look good. In fact, I look absolutely sickly, but as I start to feel completely drunk, my palliative of choice flooding my bloodstream and saturating my brain, I find that I don't care. I don't care about anything anymore.

I leap off the dock, jumping into the lake and the cold temperature of the water shocks my system, making me shoot up, taking in a breath of air as I break through the surface. I didn't think about the water not being warm and as I tread water, shivering in a lake, my body feeling like my veins are filled with ice, the situation becomes a perfect example of where I'm at in my life. Drinking and not thinking. I swim over to the dock, the liquor helping my body feel warm as I grab my mason jar from where I set it and sling back more booze. My teeth stop chattering and I decide to stay in, swimming through the crystal blue water, my body growing more used to the temperature by the second. Another flashback kicks it's way into my brain, a slide show of pain and torment, of the swimming races my mother and I used to have. Sometimes she would slow down to let me win and even though I knew she was doing it, I appreciated that she was doing it to make me feel good. That was just her nature. She was always kind and wanted everyone she came in contact with to feel that warmth radiate off of her so they would know they were welcome. I can see her in my mind, a distant specter made into flesh and I worry how long it will be before the corners of my brain are stretched to their absolute capacity, dislodging old retrospections to make way for new memories, leaving my mind's portrayal of her behind. I worry how long it will be before I start to forget her face. I crave so heavily to feel her loving touch just one more time. A tear falls down my face and I instinctively reach up to wipe it away, making water splash into my open mouth. I cough and hack, deciding I've had enough of the lake for one day as I turn to head back to shore.

I feel something quaggy brush up against my ankle as I yelp, yanking my leg up, making the water splash around me. I paddle, stationary for a moment, looking down and turning my head from right to left, trying to see past the reflective surface for what could have touched me, but find nothing. I start to reassure myself that it wasn't anything when I feel it again. Panicked about what is circling me underneath the lake's crystal veneer, I start to swim towards the shore. I don't even make it three feet as what was a light touch before, becomes something more horrifying, grabbing me, boring into the skin of my ankle. I can't help but think that whatever is wrapping around me feels like fingers as it digs harder into my flesh and pulls me beneath the water.

CHAPTER THREE

I shoot above the surface, coughing and choking, trying to get away from whatever pulled me under. I flail, trying to work against the alcohol inside me that makes my movements chaotic, swimming as hard as I can, which is as strong as someone who took one summer of swimming lessons at camp between making lanyards and friendship bracelets when they were seven. I look behind me, seeing if whatever grabbed my ankle is following me through the water, but still see nothing as I reach the dock and climb the ladder as fast as I can, banging my shin on my way up.

I breathe hard, gasping for air, laying on the cold wet wood of the dock as my blood mixed with lake water drips down the side of my leg. I sit up, looking out at the lake, my nerves starting to fray when I see a gray, dead face float above the surface of the water. I gasp, scooting back and closing my eyes tight. I know this isn't real. Ever since I woke up in the hospital I've had problems with hallucinations stemming from trauma caused by the accident. Laying in my hospital bed watching my bloody mother and father sit in the chairs across the room, staring at me was just the start. I'd see bugs in my food, blood on my clean hands, and crashed cars on the side of the road where there, in reality, was nothing. Attempting to pull my dead brother out of the path of a city bus and almost being killed was what led the state to force me into involuntary admission into a psychiatric hospital to, in their words, "protect myself and those around me".

After being released, I went out and had one of the biggest benders of my life. I can't remember everything that I put into my body, but the next morning I felt like I'd been hit in the head with a hammer; twice. I pushed through it and kept forcing my memories to fade into the back of my mind, drowned in drink, for a month straight, until I wound up in Doctor Lindsay Hartgrove's office. From the moment I walked through her door, I regretted ever calling her, but I do have to hand it to her; no matter how difficult I've been for her she has stuck with me since the start and that's why I have kept her as my doctor even though I have moved away from Ashton.

44

One of the ways she told me to deal with hallucinations is to close my eyes and tell myself it's all in my mind until I start to feel calm. She said that my brain needs a minute to catch up to reality. According to Doctor Hartgrove, I can create a safe space of darkness to reset and take the time to separate reality from fiction. With my eyes still jammed shut I repeat,

"It's all in my mind. It's all in my mind. It's all in my mind."

I slowly open my eyes, blinking as my pupils adjust to the sunlight. I look out over the water and feel relief flood through me as I see that the face in the water is gone. I rub my hands over my face, inhaling through my nose and out of my mouth, making a sniffing sound.

With a sigh, I stand, backing up a couple of steps, bending over to pick up my jar, downing the rest of the liquor inside with shaky hands. I stare at the water, waiting to see if the face comes back, but when it doesn't, I break my gaze and turn, walking back to the house drunk and deflated. I am currently in a vicious cycle, according to Dr. Hartgrove, of self medicating, but she will not prescribe me medication until I stop self medicating. All I know is the booze makes the "not real shit" go away…sometimes.

The walk back to the house is far less enjoyable with my heart still thumping and the grass now sticking to my bare feet, making them itch. My brain is swimming, despite my desire to no longer be drunk. When I get back inside, I head upstairs, into the hallway bathroom, turning on the shower and taking off my bathing suit, dropping it onto the tiled floor with a wet slap, where I leave it sitting in a puddle, like a dead slug, curled up in its own mucus. The lake water feels dirty on my skin now. It feels tainted and itchy. It takes three rounds of heavy scrubbing before my body starts to feel clean. Halfway through my shower the image of the face in the lake flashes through my mind with the realization that some of that water got into my mouth and I gag, bracing my hands against the shower wall and breathing hard to stop myself from throwing up.

After my shower, I sit on the closed toilet, wrapped in a towel as water dribbles down my calves and pools around my bare feet. I take a deep breath, rubbing my forehead with my hand.

"She was not real, Melissa. Get a grip."

After another ten minutes of convincing myself that I didn't just see a dead person in the water, I head back downstairs, pulling shorts and a hoodie out of my duffle bag. Once I'm dressed I walk over to the kitchen, opening the freezer door and taking out the entire bottle of Goldschläger that I left in there before walking down to the dock. I walk through the living room, the sensation of feeling my bare feet move from hardwood to carpet then back onto wood again as I walk to the back door, opening it to head out onto the back deck, taking a seat in one of the deck chairs, leaning back to let the mountain view be my entertainment instead of watching dead people that aren't there, floating around in the lake. I take a drink straight from the bottle and close my eyes, inhaling the fresh mountain air. An eagle passes overhead and it reminds me of a story my father told me once about the Norse god, Odin, father to all of the gods. He stole the mead of poetry, a drink that had been made from dwarves murdering another god and turning him into the alcoholic beverage. The mead ends up in the hands of a giant and Odin tricks the giant's daughter into letting him have a sip. Well, he downs the whole thing and turns into an eagle, flying high into the sky to Asgard, the land of the gods. The giant turns into an eagle too and chases him, but Odin, noticing this, sprays some of the mead out of his ass into the giant's face and escapes. I think about how my mother slapped my father on the arm, claiming the story was inappropriate, but I loved it, always wanting more of the amazing stories my father would tell. I lean back and think about the story of Odin, a constant character in stories my father would use to make me go to sleep and it still gets the job done as I close my eyes and everything fades away as my last conscious thought slides through my muddy mind. No matter how many gods there are or where they're from, they've all abandoned me.

I wake up, the sky dark, full of white dots. Usually, I might take a moment to take in all the beauty that is the night sky here, so far from the city's light pollution that the stars overtake the view. Instead, the vastness of the sky makes my stomach turn as I feel instantly sick. I sit up in my chair as hot vomit shoots up my throat and out of my mouth onto the deck with a sickening splat. I throw up until there's nothing left and then my stomach dry heaves multiple times before my body calms down. I raise my hand, wiping my mouth with the back of it, leaving a streak of hot stink on my skin. I stand almost losing my balance and gagging as the smell of stomach acid mixed with cinnamon hits my nostrils.

"Fuck."

I hobble to the sliding glass door and reach to open it when a loud noise comes from beside me. I freeze, my hand outstretched, hovering in mid air. Even after coming here every year since I was a child, the noises that come from deep in the dark still make sweat drip down my back and send me into flight mode. Going against my instincts, I turn slowly, walking back to the edge of the deck that wraps around the side of the house, peering over like one of the characters you always yell at in a horror movie to run and forget about investigating what may be lurking in the shadows. Images of hockey masked killers, chainsaw wielding murderers and monsters of all shapes and sizes crawl through my mind as I tell myself that I'm not being stupid and instead am being responsible. There have always been reports of bears and coyotes out here and if they are hanging around, I need to know what I'm dealing with. None of the exterior lights are on and the woods below the deck loom, only outlines visible. I squint, determined to find what made the noise and scare the shit out of myself, instead of just heading inside. Another loud crack makes me jump back before leaning back over and squinting harder into the darkness. I am about to give up when the moonlight hits something very large moving through the trees. I lean even further over the railing, gripping the edge so I don't fall over and break my neck. I try to see what woodland creature is below me when the noise of glass breaking makes me turn wildly, almost making me piss myself. The Goldschläger bottle lays broken on the deck, having fallen from its resting place on the arm of the chair. I release an exasperated chuckle, completely over things scaring the shit out of me today. I take a deep breath and tell myself I need to go to bed when something affixed to the wall next to the glass sliding door catches my eye. I walk over and see a metal box with a red button, covered by a plastic cover. I lift the casing and rest my finger against the button, not sure of what will happen when I press it. I push down and hear a loud "thunk" sound come from behind me, making me turn to see that four extremely bright, outdoor spotlights have illuminated the woods and cleared area leading to the lake, behind the house. No sooner have the lights lit up the backyard, when the loudest howl I've ever heard comes from trees behind my porch. This time I don't stop to investigate, but do a weird terrified run, like my whole deck is covered in legos and I am trying to avoid every one. I slap the red button, making the lights turn off and the plastic cover fall closed as I slide open the glass door hard and leap inside, sliding it closed and locking the small lock on the handle that truly can't keep anything out, but makes people feel more secure. I stare through the glass, like a werewolf is about to hop up on my porch. Breathing heavily, I suddenly realize how drunk I still am and my stomach turns again at the thought. I run to the kitchen sink and somehow throw up again, even though I'd felt like I already emptied the entire contents of my stomach on the porch. I turn on the faucet and wash the sour smell down the drain. The one benefit of being so drunk all the time that you forget to eat is that there aren't chunks of food in your puke.

As I lean down to drink from the tap I glance towards the sliding door and a pair of eyes looking through the glass make me leap backwards and grip the kitchen counter. After righting myself, I see that the "eyes" are just a reflection of the lights mounted on the wall directly above me. I scold myself loudly.
"Melissa, what the fuck?! Fucking relax!"

I walk over to the leather couch, laying down, my body now covered in sweat from being terrified twenty times in a five minute period. Slowly, I feel the liquor pull me down into darkness, to the land of dreams. The leather is forgiving and the couch feels plush and worn in, in the best way. I sigh as my heavy eyelids start to fall closed, despite my efforts to keep them open. Before they shut completely I glance at the window where a face stares back at me.

CHAPTER FOUR

My eyes shoot open, the sun blinding me with a massive headache chaser directly behind it. I squint, raising my arm to act as some kind of cover from the abrasive light peering in through the windows. With my eyes covered, I lay back down on the couch, a ball of misery from drinking so heavily last night. My inner dialogue sets in, starting to berate myself, but I shut it down instantly. I know I have a problem, but at the moment, I don't care.

The throbbing ache in my head, like someone installed subwoofers in my brain and are currently playing Army Of The Pharaohs on full volume, outweighs my weak attempt at making myself feel guilty. Thirty minutes later, after dozing off and waking back up, I try sitting up again, the still present pain in my head racing to the front of my skull, making it feel like someone ran a truck into my forehead. The irony that I would pick that analogy is not lost on me and I feel angry at myself as I lay back down asking internally why I keep doing this to myself. My internal argument starts like two demons on my shoulders. One who likes to drink and one who *really* likes to drink. I realize that the symbolism is supposed to be an angel and a demon, but I don't think angels exist and even if they did, mine packed it's bags and left that day on the freeway. I go back and forth between telling myself that I need to stop drinking, but on the other hand, I have convinced myself multiple times that the only reason I feel guilty about drinking is because society has convinced me that I *should* feel guilty and not because I actually do. If I'm being completely honest, I think minding your own business is the greatest virtue of all and one more people should participate in.

I reach over, grabbing my phone off the coffee table and, having given up on trying to participate in social media months ago, open up my search engine page that has suggested articles. The third one down catches my eye, titled: Native Birds and Their Metaphysical Meanings. Usually I would roll my eyes at something like this, but the bird from yesterday has me feeling curious and I click the article. I scroll through things like Cardinals, Bluejays, Hawks, and even Vultures, but see nothing resembling the little heinous thing that suicide bombed my car yesterday. I click back and scroll up to the search bar, typing in, *birds that hiss.* I look through black vultures, burrowing owls, chickadees, and then I see it. The Eurasian Wryneck; the exact bird I saw yesterday. I hold down on the bird's name, copying the words so I don't have to try to type them out and I return to the search bar. I paste in Eurasian Wryneck and am influenced by the first article I saw, so I add the word, "symbolism" to my search. The results populate and I click the first article. I read about how the bird was used for love spells, but also to bring someone back to a place after they had left. I pause reading, my eyes raising and looking around the room in the house I have just come back to. I turn back to the article, scrolling down when my eyes freeze at the words: *The Eurasian Wryneck has been used in old world spells to jinx an individual, the word itself being believed to come from the bird's scientific name, Jynx Torquilla. It is still believed by some cultures to be a sign of a bad omen to see the bird and even worse if one is held in your hand.* I close my eyes, sighing and dropping my phone next to me on the couch. I have to remind myself that I don't believe in things like that, but I think everyone, including myself, believes in it at least a little bit. I start to feel anxious that I have been cursed by someone; some person who has manipulated my perceived reality to destroy my family and tear me apart bit by bit. I rack my brain for who I could have made an enemy of that would do something so vile, but come up with nothing except that I am just being paranoid. I roll over and close my eyes, letting my hangover push me back into dreamless sleep.

After another hour spent laying on the couch in self inflicted agony, the light from the windows has shifted, growing duller, making me crack my right eye open, realizing it's sometime past noon. I slowly raise myself from the couch, making it to a standing position, looking like a zombie coming back to life. My guts turn and I purse my lips, internally telling my stomach to relax while I wait for it to settle before taking a step towards the kitchen, deciding that I'll see if the previous owners left anything else useful around. I open the kitchen cabinet and see exactly what I was wishing for. A bottle of Advil. Feeling like I manifested the pills, I grab it, popping the top off and turning it upside down, over my hand, but nothing falls out. I turn it rightside up, looking down into the bottle and see it is completely empty.

"Cool. They just left me their trash, apparently."

I drop the bottle on the counter and it bounces with a clacking sound before rolling to a stop against the backsplash. I open the other cabinets but find nothing but empty shelf space. I pick up my mason jar from the night before and wash it out before filling it with water, chugging the whole thing. The water isn't quite cold and tastes like metal making me smack my tongue against the roof of my mouth after drinking the tainted liquid. Despite the taste, my body instantly craves more and I fill it again, raising the glass to my lips when I stop. My gaze falls on the window that faces the side of the couch and a drunken memory comes back to me like a long lost picture found in a junk drawer. A face in the darkness; eyes staring at me from behind glass. I stare at the window trying to remember if it was something that was actually there or another figment of my imagination, triggered by trauma, fueled with an excess of alcohol. That's the problem with having hallucinations. It makes it very hard to determine whether memories of things you saw are actually real or created entirely by your mind. Pouring copious amounts of alcohol on top of that can balance your brain *or* it can make it worse. Everytime is a gamble; one that I am obviously willing to play the odds at.

Unable to decide if there was someone watching me through my window the night prior, I let it go; drinking the rest of my glass of water and setting the empty jar on the counter before grabbing my keys, going out the door in the kitchen, and back down the stairs to the garage. I click my key fob, unlocking the locks of my Honda with a beep, then freeze. There are three large scratch marks along the whole side of my car. I look to the right and see that I left the garage door open, making me rub my hand across my face and expel an exasperated growl. As I lower my hand, the memory of the thing creeping around in the woods comes rushing back; the ear piercing scream, and me running inside from the deck practically shitting myself. I stare at the trees, the brush and thick growth, growing in between them making an opaque screen, hiding whatever lives in the

forest surrounding my house. A rustle at the base of a tree grabs my attention, then one at the top of another, a third comes and fear starts to creep into me once again. I am about to retreat back into the house when a squirrel comes popping out of the woods, a foraged nut in it's mouth. It stops on my driveway, standing up on its hind legs and turning its head back and forth, examining me. I look back down at the scratches on my car.
"Well that's not from a squirrel."

The car isn't special to me, per say. All the things that I have that are special are sitting in that storage container in the front yard. The one I refuse to touch. The car is another thing I bought with what I consider to be blood money, paid from the death of my family. What does piss me off is that it's literally six months old and in less than twenty four hours a bird cracked the windshield and something came into my garage and fucked up the paint. I stare at the scratches that are long and deep, running my fingers across them before shaking my head and sighing,
"Whatever."

I pop the trunk of my car and unload the boxes inside, sliding them against the wall. Sitting on top of one is a burnt CD with Vacation Mix written on top. I feel a pang in my heart as I stare down at it. Dad always made mixes for our trips out here. Originally they were on cassettes and then CD's as he adapted with the times. I pick it up, turning it over to look at the track list written on the back. Dad was always one to enjoy all types of music, not close minded to any particular genre. You wouldn't know it by his sweaters and khaki pants, but he had a bit of everything in his collection. Black Flag could lead into Foggy Mountain Boys, then shoot you out onto The White Stripes, just to move on to Slaughterhouse and end with Left to Suffer. I get in my car and slide the CD into the player. As I pull out of the garage I see the sun is still out, despite my wishes for the opposite. The blue sky is devoid of clouds with the temperature high and the humidity higher. I fumble my sunglasses out of the small storage bin that sits above the rearview mirror and slide them on my face before reaching down, turning the air conditioning on full blast as I drive out onto the remote road, back towards the main one to take me into town. As I pull up to the stop sign, I press play on my radio and A Day To Remember chants out, "DaDa-DaDa-Da-Da-Duh-Duh, LETS GO!"

The song is loud and makes me scrunch my face as I reach out to turn the radio off, but stop, deciding to leave it on, just turning it down a bit to make it less like getting bullets shot directly into my temples. As I start to turn, I glance in the rearview mirror and see a Chevy truck coming down the road behind me. Not just *a* Chevy truck, I realize; *the* Chevy truck. As far as I can tell it is the exact same one that almost tore off my front end yesterday before the driver gave me the finger. Great, I think to myself. This asshole must be one of my neighbors. I don't want people's attention, be it good or bad. I just want to be left alone. The literal last thing I need is one of my neighbors holding a grudge against me and in turn, fucking with me to make themselves feel better about their shitty life. I keep my eyes on the mirror as the truck comes closer and closer, showing no intention of slowing down.

Without warning, my radio switches from the CD player to AM radio, static flowing through the speakers of my car. I jab my finger at the radio button, my eyes moving back and forth from the rearview mirror to the radio controls. As I sit, half turned in the middle of the road, I press the power button over and over, the sound refusing to cease, when I jump in my seat as I hear a voice, low and scratchy say, "*Melissa...*"

I look back up in the mirror, the truck suddenly right behind me as the volume on my radio skyrockets and the voice coming through the AM station yells,
"*WATCH OUT!*"

I let out a shriek and slam my foot down on the gas, my tires squealing as I swing around the turn, another car screeching to a halt and laying on its horn. I look up into my mirror again and see the Lincoln that I cut off moving once again, pulling up behind me. Feeling relief at having a car in between me and the Chevy, I come to the main road and stop, staring ahead. If I go straight, the road in front of me will take me to the liquor store. If I make a right, I can go to the market and get things I actually need. I hesitate, imagining the old world Greek demons sitting on my shoulder again; each holding a bottle of booze labeled XXX, laughing at my addiction and inability to make a decision. A blaring noise pulls me back to the present, making me feel bad for first cutting this person off, then making them wait behind me at the stop sign. I look up into the mirror and the Lincoln is nowhere to be seen, having turned off the road before the stop and instead, Chevy dickhead lays on his horn.

"Alright! Alright!"

I yell to myself, since he can't hear me and I turn right.

The radio crackles again, but this time when I hit the volume knob with my hand it turns off. I don't have the capacity to even think about what just happened with a voice speaking to me through my radio and I swear I can physically feel my body disassociate, pushing the thought to the back corner of my mind to sit with everything else I don't want to think about.

I watch behind me as the person driving the truck slams on the gas, his tires making a small squeal as they grip the hot pavement. I quickly glance into my mirror, wincing as he also turns right, speeding up and staying directly behind me as we both enter the four lane freeway. Without realizing, my foot instinctively presses down harder on the gas, making me pick up speed as I try to get away from the local psycho. I drive for a few minutes before I see a Super Everything coming up on my left. Looking down, I see that my speedometer is on the shy side of 100 and I quickly release the gas pedal, allowing my car to start to slow down. I look behind me again at the Chevy before switching lanes, easing to the right. I watch as he follows suit, doing exactly what I wanted him to do. I speed up again, passing cars before slamming my wheel to the left, flying into the other lane to put distance between me and this asshole. I move into the turn lane, coming to a stop. My eyes flick back up to the mirror, making me turn fully around in my seat as I hear the screech of tires and horns blare as the truck cuts off the other drivers, making them slam on their breaks in the middle of the freeway. As they pull into the lane behind me, I feel my stomach flip as the thought passes through my mind that whoever this person is, they want to do more than just scare me. Despite my air conditioner being on full blast, I feel sweat start to form on my forehead as last night's alcohol threatens to make an unwelcome return. My eyes flick back and forth between the traffic light, still lit up red, and the truck idling behind me, trying to make out any of the driver's features, but the glare of the glass from the sun hanging in the sky is too high and I can only see a dark silhouette. A shadow person; internal fears manifested into physical form. Every second sitting here, trapped between the red light and a crazed redneck makes me feel sicker, my mouth tasting sour, bile threatening to come up like a burst dam. The tick, tick, tick of my own blinker counts every second, matching the yellow light that flashes on and off next to his left headlight, that he has decided to use at this turn, probably more out of wanting to taunt me than actually following traffic laws. The seconds crawl by and just as I feel the tension is going to make me scream, the light turns green and I try to gas it, hoping to speed through the turn and lose him in the shopping center's parking lot. I swing around the

turn looking in my rearview mirror as he lags behind. I yell out a victorious,
"Hah!"

Still keeping an eye on my mirror, I turn quickly into the shopping center and take the long way around to Super Everything by driving behind all the buildings where the dumpsters and grease traps are kept, passing smoking employees and a group of kids skateboarding, before turning out into the parking lot by a Siren's Song Coffee. My eyes drift over the drive through line full of people willing to overpay for things like a Trenta low fat, soy, decaf, macchiato latte. My eyes follow the brick building up to the now famous logo of a siren from myth holding a coffee cup and I admittedly think about getting a pistachio cold brew, but decide my nerves are already frazzled enough without drinking enough caffeine to make me feel like I have wasps crawling in between the lobes of my brain. I move past the line of cars, turning out into the open parking lot, looking around and seeing if I see the Chevy cruising the rows of parked cars, thinking about what I need to do if he is here and this situation takes a turn.

I drive down one row of parked cars, then another, still looking around, not convinced that I'm safe. After five more minutes of spotting nothing I finally relent and pull into an empty spot that has another vacant one in front of it. My brother used to call things like that "small miracles". Little victories of things working out just the way you want. Pulling through, I press my foot on the brake, shifting

into park and taking a breath. I turn off the car. and start to open the door when despite the engine being shut off completely, the radio comes to life again, squealing, then falling into static. A screech comes from behind me as the Chevy comes to a stop and I slam the door closed, fumbling with the lock button, staring into my mirror at the silhouette of the person inside staring at the back of my car. All I can make out is broad shoulders and a truckers hat on top of their head. After sitting for a few seconds, they slam on the gas, making the tires burn out, leaving a cloud of smoke with the rancid smell of burnt rubber lingering behind. Another crackle from the radio makes me look down at it as the same ghostly voice comes through the speakers.
"Help us, Melissa…"

This time I full on punch the radio splitting the skin of my knuckle, making blood drip down my hand as I yell at it.
"SHUT UP!"

It turns off instantly and I sit back, allowing the silence in the car to surround me like a comfort blanket, offering me a single moment of peace before I leave the confines of this protective metal shell and put myself back out into the world. Breathing hard as I wait in my car with the doors locked, I see the Chevy in the distance, turn out onto the main road and my breathing slows, my nerves starting to calm. I wait another five minutes before unlocking the car door and tentatively easing out. Even though I just watched them drive away, when I get out of my car, I look around, making sure they didn't double back, tricking me into

getting out and exposing myself. When I see the coast is clear, I quickly walk towards the entrance to the store, past a flower stand, a wooden sign hung over top with Fir Tree Flowers, in orange paint, being run by an elderly local woman. My footsteps slow as the scents of Mountain Laurels, Flame Azaleas and Eastern Redbuds hit my nostrils, making me turn and look at her entire set up. She smiles at me and I force a smile back, continuing to quickly walk past when I hear her say,
"I saw what that man did to you out there."

I stop, turning and saying,
"People can be so wild sometimes, right? Just road rage I guess."

The smile fades from her face and she points to the parking lot, none of the kindness from just a moment ago gracing her voice as she says,
"Not there."

Her finger swings to the left, pointing off into the distance and she turns her head slowly, looking at me with eyes that have completely glazed over.
"Out there."

My eyes follow where her skinny finger, bone barely covered in skin, is pointing and land on the highway, cars rushing by at high speeds as people leave and enter Aima Island, completely oblivious of the blood that steamed off of the pavement a year ago. My heart pounds in my chest, the edges of my vision fading into darkness. My ears fill with a rushing sound as I get sucked into watching the traffic fly by. A blur of colors, horns blaring, tires slowly disintegrating, ready to blow at any moment, causing a pile up. Families dying and children screaming.

I see a Delta, just like the one my father drove, come down the road, four people inside. Suddenly an eighteen wheeler slams up against the side of the car and I close my eyes as the sound of crunching metal makes me shake with fear. Even with my eyes closed I see blood rushing down the highway, drowning everything in it's path. I stand at the bridge over the lake holding the dead, brown bird in my hand. I look down at its little body, wind ruffling its feathers. Then the jinx bird opens it's eyes and twists its head to look at me, but this time when it opens its beak instead of a hiss a bleat comes from the small black chasm that is its mouth.

My eyes fly open, as it takes my mind a moment to catch up and realize where I am. I turn and the woman is no longer pointing at the road or even looking at me. She is trimming the stems of flowers and placing them in water, tending to her stand. My eyebrows furrow as she looks at me and smiles like it's the first time she's seen me. I shake my head, trying to decide if I just had another hallucination or not. In the past year, after screaming at a woman inside a department store because she looked like my mother, I've learned that it's better to just go about my way instead of questioning someone on if what just happened actually happened. I turn, glancing back once more, my eyes landing on a small figurine of a deer's skull with antlers next to her cash box, before turning my back to her and walking into the store.

As the automatic doors slide open, the cool air rushes out from inside Super Everything, hitting me, making me feel somewhat refreshed. I head to the bathroom, washing the blood off my hand and splashing water on my face. When I come back out, the smell of produce and packaged products fills my senses; but truly, what makes me feel better is something I've grown to usually dislike; human interaction. But being around other people so that whoever was driving that Chevy can't come after me is quite comforting at the moment. I walk to the line of faded red, plastic shopping carts, pulling one out of the line while I continue to take long breaths through my nose of the cool air being pumped into the entire store, exhaling through my mouth to calm myself, all while wondering if I've made a terrible decision moving here.

My mind is a hive of bees, thoughts buzzing through, one after the other, as I walk aimlessly up and down the aisles, convincing myself that whoever is driving that orange truck is just some country asshole who has chosen to fuck with me because of that first day when I almost pulled out in

front of them. In all actuality they probably wouldn't have done anything if I'd have actually given them the opportunity. As the thought grows, I start to go on the offensive, talking shit *now* that I'm alone in the store wrapped in a metaphorical safety blanket.
"Even if they had done something, I would have beat their ass",
I chuckle to myself.

They're just some mountain hillbilly trying to scare me, out of some misguided, misogynistic, bullshit sense of being a local versus an outsider. Well, fuck them. If they come around again, maybe I'll just show them who they're fucking with.

The thought of the most likely outcome of that situation, being my demise or serious injury, breaks through my "tough girl" facade. The truth is I've never been in a fight in my life. This admittance to myself makes my face sober, even if my body can't as I still swim through my hangover like a fish in wet cement. My mind pushes the thought to the forefront that no matter what their motivation, in our modern time when someone wearing a cross around their neck will kill you just because of the way you look or who you love, it's scary to have someone act the way they were. If the type of people who live on Aima Island turn out to be the same kind of people that believe they are protecting children by walking around a library brandishing guns so a drag queen won't read them a story, those are not people I want to press back against, if I'm being honest. I was

already aware, and have been since I was a child, of the town mentality being a bit behind the times, having been here so many times before over the course of my childhood. Like lots of small towns, most of the people are friendly, but there is always some group that seem like they live for nothing else but to treat other people like shit. Miserable little maggots that crawl out of the rot every now and again to remind us all that they still exist, to our collective disappointment. Let's just say things like gender identity are not something the "good people" of Aima Island are familiar with. Sometimes small towns produce small minds, but I am determined to not make assumptions about everyone while I start this journey to really try my hardest to start my life over. I stop in the middle of the aisle, rolling my eyes at myself. I always get all mushy about quitting drinking and starting my life over, when I'm hungover. I give myself an elaborate speech, then get drunk and if I'm being honest, I know today isn't going to be any different. A man breaks my inner dialogue as he walks by wearing a tank top with a rebel flag. I glance at him and silently read the words on his shirt; Heritage, not hate. As he walks by, I roll my eyes and say to myself,
"Fucking idiot."

I guess I won't be able to stop myself from judging *some* people.

Since I have given myself the quitting alcohol speech, I decide it's time to grease the pipes and get rid of this headache. I grab two bottles of wine off the shelf, placing them in my cart that has a rickety wheel that has come loose, spinning in circles as I push the buggy forward. I move past the rest of the alcohol, looking at products aimlessly as I suddenly can't remember what I came here for. I decide that since I am already here, I might as well get something to eat, but the problem with that is when you no longer care about eating, it's hard to get excited about spending time cooking food. Most of my meals come from a can or a package that I've nuked in the microwave, despite having raved for years on the dangers of using microwave ovens, and so I grab some corned beef, realizing I don't own a crockpot, then head to the electronics aisle and put a crock pot into my cart. I head back over to the grocery section and find the produce. I get everything else I need for dinner and start to make my way towards the register, the safety I felt from being in a crowd fading, already feeling like I just want to be alone in my home, away from everyone, especially after the kid sitting in his cart while his mother squeezed avocados made eye contact with me while he dropped a major load, grunting while his cheeks turned red; how wonderful.

I walk by the beer section, glancing down the aisle that the store has lit beautifully, placing hardwood laminate on the floor only to make people feel better about feeding their addictions as if getting shit hammered and making bad decisions is glamorous. According to the commercials that have been around since we were little, featuring beloved characters, we're supposed to believe that with these brown bottles or aluminum cans come impromptu beach parties, roof top romances, and having a great time with ska bands showing up in hawaiian shirts, instead of the reality of tears, fights, breakups and vomit. When I was a kid and beer commercials were more prevalent, we all loved the frogs that were mascots for a national brand. Everyone liked Spuds Mackenzie and Joe Camel too. I suppose *everyone* loving them is the reason those companies were forced to get rid of them.

I look down at my two bottles of wine, telling myself that I don't need more booze before continuing forward and getting in line to check out. I promptly step out of line remembering I need to buy a broom and dust pan, to clean up the broken bottle still sitting on the porch, little gold flakes most likely glued to the wood by this point, I'm sure. Down the aisle from the brooms I see bedding and decide to pick up a sheet set with a blanket. I scoff,
"For what bed, genius?"

This is a problem I know I can fix as I reach into my back pocket, taking out my phone and logging onto Amazon to order one of those mattresses that comes in a bag and expands to three times its size when you open it. I am in luck as the bed says it can be delivered today if I order within the next thirty minutes, as I have met the amount needed to be spent to make this happen. I click purchase and put my phone away. Buying the bed brings on a sense of domesticity and I find myself able to separate from my troubles and depression for the next hour. I fall into the stores trap of endless shopping and end up buying a lamp, a

cutting board with one of those Ginsu butcher knives that can cut through a shoe, a bookshelf, some books for said bookshelf, plants, and after parking a cart and filling a second one, arrive at the checkout. They say spending money can be therapeutic and this "therapy session" just cost me ten times what my normal therapy does. As the mohawked cashier rings up my hardcovers of Ninth House, The Silent Patient, and American Gods, she notices a second cart full of items waiting to be loaded onto the checkout conveyor, making her raise a pierced eyebrow, dyed green to match her hair. She directs her look at me and I give a little smile.
"Just moved here."

She says nothing, her eyebrows falling back into place over a face that is filled with metal and disinterest. I look at the tattoo over her eyebrow that says Hellbound in a confusing, twisted script as she grabs more items, sliding them over the scanner with a *BEEP*, then placing them into plastic bags that will eventually end up half buried in the dirt of a landfill. For a split second I make myself feel guilty over that fact, telling myself for the millionth time that I need to invest in reusable bags that I don't forget in my car's trunk every time I come into the store. I look up from my thoughts about "saving the planet" and see the cashier has her hand, decorated in at least seven rings, outstretched. I'm not sure if she has said anything and so I say,
"Sorry, what?"

She gives a half roll of her eyes and says,

70

"I.D.? For the alcohol?"

I shake my head.
"Oh, yes, of course."

I reach in my bag and pull out my I.D., handing it over. She scans it with her eyes that give a slight twitch, making me think there is a problem before she nods once, handing it back to me. I don't bother to place it back in my wallet and just drop it back into my bag. I try to break the silence while my billion items are being rung up and ask,
"Are you having a good day?"

All I get in response is another single nod, making me give up any attempt at friendliness. Bagged, my purchases take up even more space somehow and three carts are filled with white bags that have "Super Everything: Have a SUPER day." written in orange above a giant orange thumbs up. The cashier holds out my receipt and asks,
Do you need help loading your groceries, Melissa?"

My eyebrows furrow at the use of my name and I ask her,
"I'm sorry, have we met before?"

I finally see emotion cross her face as her cheeks gain color, her dimple piercings surrounded by a bright red hue, making her look instantly abashed, like she has made some kind of mistake. Her eyes flick to the side before coming back to me.

"Um...no? I saw your name on your license. Melissa Monos, right? I just notice things like that."

I consider this, the situation still striking me as odd, but the excuse, I suppose, being good enough. I think about the fact that growing up in a large town like Ashton has made me distrust people in general. I look into her eyes and offer a half smile.
"Oh, right."

I glance over to my carts and then back to her.
"Help would be great."

A look instantly crosses her face like no one ever accepts this and regret that she even asked me makes itself apparent. I don't know how she expected me to take care of three carts myself, but she sighs, flipping a button that turns off the light that shows that her check out lane is open and turns, grabbing one of my three carts, turning it, and walking towards the exit.

Outside, the heat hits me once again, making me feel like I wreak of liquor. As I feel droplets of sweat evacuate from my pores, I seriously regret not taking a shower before leaving the house. Luckily, one of the things I got was cucumber body wash and I make a mental note to shower as soon as I get home, for myself, not because of anyone else. My check out girl calls out to two guys wearing the trademark orange polo of Super Everything, leaning up against the side of the building having a smoke break and they throw down their cigarettes, heading inside to retrieve the other two carts. They are quicker than we are and almost instantaneously return outside, pushing the overloaded buggies across the parking lot. They join us at the back of my car and I press a button on my keys, making the trunk pop. We start to load the bags, eventually needing the backseat, the floor and the passenger side of the front as well. Once everything is in, I pull out my wallet, thanking the three of them and holding out twenty dollar bills for each of them. Suddenly they don't seem so annoyed that they had to help me, instead thanking me and walking back to the store, the boys punching each other in the arm and laughing while the girl rolls her eyes and tells them they're both morons.

I climb into my car and sit there for a minute, feeling better that I am actually taking steps to turn the lakehouse into *my* house. Sure I got fucked up last night and gave myself a scare, but I have done something responsible today. I say to myself,
"Small miracles."
Reaching forward to turn the key and head home.

A knock comes from my window, making me jump and whip my head to the left. Standing there is one of the guys that just helped me load all of my things into my car. I raise a palm to my chest, taking a deep, comforting breath before I roll down the window and he says,
"Sorry, I didn't mean to scare you."

I force a closed lip smile as he continues,
"I just noticed these scratches on your car and was going to tell you that my uncle owns a body shop. Could probably fix it up for you for a good price."

At first I'm not sure what he's talking about, the incident with the Chevy making me forget all about the scratches on my car. Suddenly it clicks, my mind bringing it to the forefront as I lean halfway out of my window, looking at the scratches that I found on my car this morning, left by something unknown, but big. My eyes drift back up to the teen in his Super Everything uniform as I settle back down into my seat.
"Oh…okay, what's the name of his shop?"

He smiles and says,
"Aima Island Paint and Body."

I return the smile and say,
"Got it, thanks. I appreciate it."

He taps the roof of the car twice, the southern symbol of "have a good one, now" and says,
"Yup, you have yourself a great day."

I watch as he turns, walking away and I roll the window up, put my car in drive and pull away. Despite having a car full of groceries, I almost immediately ditch the plan to cook myself a meal, my stomach feeling like a car battery full of acid. My hangover has made my head start to pound and all my body craves are the drunken rule of three; grease, meat, and cheese. Once on the main road I put on my turn signal, pulling off the road and into the drive-thru of a Tres Amigos Cantina where I buy six tacos; three carne asada and three firecracker chicken, nacho fries, and a large Cheerwine.

Thankfully there is no sign of the Chevy on my way home, but that doesn't stop me from looking in my rearview mirror at least one hundred times and keeping my eyes peeled at every stop. I hesitate again at the turn for the liquor store, but am able to convince myself to not stop, based on the fact that I already bought wine at Super Everything *and* I now have so many things to put away. This reasoning would have been sufficient, but I internally also mention to myself that I should definitely be good on alcohol since while I was shopping, I circled back and got a 12 pack of Lonely Beaver beer, even after telling myself I didn't need it. I guess the fancy aisle did make me feel better about my addiction, plus the fact that Lonely Beaver Brewery is located in Ashton and I justified it by saying that I wanted a taste of home. I'm sure Super Everything paid some scientist dickhead to run studies on what would draw alcoholics into the beer aisle before they installed it in every store in America. Maybe when I crack the first one, I'll find myself at a rooftop party with a dog in a Hawaiin shirt and a smoking camel in a leather jacket, a ska band playing in the corner.

After what feels like a longer drive home than the one to the store and still no sign of Chevy asshole, I pull into my driveway, driving down and around into the garage. When I get out, I look out at the woods again, my curiosity still peaked about what kind of animal could have been stalking around my house. I make a mental note to contact Mount Aima Paint and Body about getting the scratches on the car fixed before walking outside onto the driveway, looking around for any sign of what could have made the marks on my car last night. And I mean, I look for *anything*. Scat, fur, a claw that came loose when digging into metal, anything at all.

With a lack of clues, I quickly give up, turning back towards my garage and freeze. In the mud next to the pavement is the biggest hoof track I've ever seen. I crouch down, examining the print stuck in the now dried mud. I don't recognize it, but instantly ask myself why I *would* recognize it and reach into my back pocket, pulling out my phone, and opening a search page. I click the camera icon and it activates my phone camera. I center it on the print and click the shutter button. My phone thinks for a minute before bringing up results. The first is deer, but that's definitely not right. The second is moose, but this print is even bigger. After scrolling and finding nothing, I stand, going back into the garage and press the button on the wall to make the door close. The system is loud, probably from the 90's, but when the door closes, silence, once again, fills the garage. A kind of silence that feels stuffy like the space has been filled in and the lack of sound is in itself, something audible. It starts to feel liminal, making me feel trapped, so I reach in and click the button, making the garage door open again. As it opens, I reach into my trunk grabbing two bags with each hand and stand up to full height, dropping the bags to the ground instantly when I see a man standing in my garage entrance.

CHAPTER FIVE

I scream, falling back against the car and almost going completely into the trunk as he raises his hands in surrender and says,
"Woah! Woah!"

My eyes take in the person in front of me. Khaki shirt, dark green pants, campaign hat. Finally my eyes land on the badge affixed to his chest and I let out a sigh of relief as he takes two steps forward into my garage.
"I am so sorry. I didn't mean to scare you."

The amount of things scaring me that aren't meant to scare me has grown to it's absolute limit, but when he reaches out a hand, I take it, allowing him to pull me out of my trunk and up to full height. He releases my hand and bends down, picking up the bags that I dropped.

"I'm sorry for the scare. Can I help you take these inside?"

I don't want him in my house to be honest. Just one day in Aima Island has given me a lifetime's worth of human interaction, but he has already picked up the bags, so I relent.

"Sure."

I grab two more bags, one in each hand, the plastic handles digging into my skin as we both ascend the stairs, me in the lead and the Sheriff following close behind. I have never been a law breaker, unless you count my recent bouts of driving under the influence, but cops always make me nervous; especially when they show up to my home unannounced. I think it's just because I don't like to be in the proximity of someone who in an instant could drastically change my life without me being able to do much about it. As his steps echo behind me on the wooden stairs, the hair on the back of my neck stands on end. This man is a complete stranger, not only invading my private space, but about to enter my home.

Little bouts of conversation happen between us as we make six trips to get everything from the car into the house, making me wish that I had paid extra to have an elevator installed, but mostly silence abounds between us, making the situation feel more and more uncomfortable. When

we're finally done, the kitchen floor sits full of items in plastic cocoons, waiting to birth themselves and become part of my home. I decide that before I unpack everything, I will feed the urge tugging at my brain, making my skin start to crawl and reward myself with a beer. I ask the Sheriff if he wants one, realizing he's on duty after I ask and slapping my forehead.
"Sorry, force of habit."

He smiles and with the smallest southern touch to his voice says,
"Oh, well that's alright, it's not that serious."

 His wording strikes me as odd as I literally can't think of anything being more serious than being a Sheriff on duty. He reaches out a hand, taking the bottle from me and says, "One never killed anybody."

I have an invasive thought present itself, telling me I should tell him about the sixty nine people that died from drinking tainted beer in Mozambique, but I keep my mouth shut as I twist the cap off my beer. The sweet symphony of the pressure releasing from under the caps makes my mouth water. I want to down the whole bottle, but not wanting to show my alcoholism in front of the Sheriff, I turn the bottle up slowly, taking a sip.
"So, is there something I can do for you?"

80

He looks like he has suddenly remembered this isn't a social call and turns the bottle down quickly, clearing his throat.
"Well not exactly."

He spreads his hands apart, one still holding his beer.
"We're just a small community here and I heard word that this place had sold to an out of towner and wanted to stop by to say hello and introduce myself."

He purses his lips, lifting his free hand to point at his nametag pinned to his shirt.
"I'm Sheriff Smith. Since we only have a few hundred residents here, if you ever have any trouble, I'll most likely be the one who shows up."

I nod and say,
"Good to meet you. I'm-"

He holds up a hand and says,
"Don't tell me, don't tell me."

He taps the side of his forehead like it's going to shake the answer loose, while he draws the next part out as if the sounds are returning to his mind slowly as he says them.
"Meliiiiiiiissa…..Melissa Monos, right?"

I find that I'm really starting to feel uneasy about the people of Aima Island for many reasons, but especially for

knowing my name. It leaves me with a creepy feeling I can't shake, like I'm being watched.
"Yes; yes that's right, but how did you-"

He smiles again, his eyes moving down and to the side, bashful.
"I admittedly took a peek at the deed for the house."

He holds up his hands again, in mock surrender, showing he's not a threat. As he sees my eyebrows start to furrow, he rushes to explain.
"It's public record of course. I respect people's privacy."

My mind internally tells me that he's not doing a very good job of respecting my privacy currently, but I force another dry smile onto my face and say,
"Of course. Good memory."

I turn the bottle up, finishing it in a matter of seconds and toss the empty into the trash bin with a clunk as it hits the bottom. The sheriff's eyes follow me as I grab a second bottle, twisting off the cap and tossing it onto the counter. As I drink my second beer, my eyes look out the porch doors at the water and then I remember I need to clean up the broken glass from last night. I look between the mess sitting on the wooden planks of my porch and the bags surrounding me on the floor, suddenly feeling overwhelmed by the tasks that await me. The sheriff's eyes follow mine to the mess on the back porch.
"What happened there?"

82

My head jerks back as he looks at me with one eyebrow raised.

"Oh, I just dropped a glass out there."

He purses his lips as one eyebrow joins the other, climbing up his forehead. He lifts his bottle, finishing it's contents before he stands, walking over to the counter and setting his empty on top of it.

"Well, it seems you've got plenty to keep you busy. I'll let you get to it. Just wanted to stop by and offer a friendly hello."

He starts to walk towards the front door and stops.

"Oh, and I almost forgot."

He turns around reaching a hand behind his back, pulling something from his back pocket. He holds it out for me to take and says,

"I took the liberty of bringing you your mail. Hope you don't mind."

I do in fact mind, but do not see any purpose in telling Sheriff Smith that his idea of respecting someone's privacy is seriously askew, so instead I simply take the mail, setting it on the counter and plaster on, what I hope is the last fake smile of my life.

"Thanks."

He turns again, retracing his footsteps towards the front door.

"Yup! Just fulfilling the serve part of "protect and serve"."

He stops at my front door and I watch as he grips the handle, pressing forward to apply pressure before unlocking my deadbolt and opening the door, seeming very familiar with the layout of my home. He turns, lifting his right hand and tips his hat towards me.
"Stay out of trouble now, Melissa Monos."

The door closes and I release a sigh of relief.
"What the fuck was that?"

After I hear his cruiser crank up and pull away, I feel true relief, taking a moment to process that the Aima Island Sheriff was just in my house, drinking my beer, trying to let my brain catch up with the day and everything that has happened. I look around again at all the bags surrounding me and the next sigh that comes is the type of exasperation you feel when a daunting task is making you feel tired before you've even begun.

I decide the first order of business is sweeping up the broken glass on the porch. Once that is done, I can put away the things I bought at the store. I take the broom and dustpan from my mountain of purchased products and open the sliding door, being careful to avoid the broken glass. The sun begins to set, my whole day practically consumed as I start to sweep up the glass that jingles as it slides into the dustpan. As I bring the broom forward to get the last of the mess, a jagged piece of glass falls through the quarter inch space between the boards, falling to the ground below. I let out an aggravated sigh, debating with myself if that piece belongs to the abyss that is the underside of the porch, but decide that if I leave it there it will be the first of many decisions that lead to the dilapidation of this home and more than likely there will one day be a reason that I need to go under the porch. Chances are when this happens, I'll have long forgotten about the piece of glass and I will most likely have been drinking. This equation will result in me putting my hand down on the ground right on top of the forgotten piece and slicing right through my palm; so even though I really don't feel like it, after I go inside and empty the broken glass into the trash can, making the rain of shattered Goldschläger bottle ring out as it collides with the empty beer bottles that linger at the bottom of the can, I bang the dustpan against the side to make sure there are no small pieces of glass lingering, then take my broom and dustpan down the garage steps to the underside of the porch. As I walk out of the garage door, I look for where the piece of glass fell to the ground, my eyes seeing nothing but dirt and rocks amongst the stilts that hold the raised porch.

My eyes scan the ground, stopping when the sun glints off of the glass that leans against one of the legs of the porch. I walk over, bending down to gently pick it up, making my first and second fingers into a pincer to grab the glass by the middle, avoiding the sharp edges, when I stop. Carved deep into the wood of the porch leg is M+M. A gasp escapes my mouth as my eyes instantly start to fill with tears at the sight of the physical memory.

When we were little, our parents used to call me and my brother M&M; Melissa and Michael. The memory comes flooding back of us as kids hanging out under the porch after swimming all day, towels wrapped around our shoulders and wet hair sticking to our faces. Michael pulled out a pocket knife he'd gotten from one of the souvenir shops in town, it's handle a turtle shell design, the blade not sharp enough to do any real damage, but pointed enough to hack at the wood of the porch stilt. As I watched him, I got really nervous that we were going to get in serious trouble and I told him not to do it, but he told me to relax, digging the knife deep into the wood. He said no one was going to find it, which made it even more special. Something that would only belong to us as long as the house was standing. When he was done, he blew air onto his carving, making any lingering wood dust fly off before running his thumb over the deep grooves in the wood, admiring his handy work. As my legs give out, making me collapse onto the dirt as I time travel through my memories, old days full of happiness colliding with the present, I can see his blue eyes looking into mine, a huge smile crossing his face as he said, "M&M forever."

At that moment, all of my fear of getting caught faded as I folded into that sacred moment with my brother; one of life's few perfect split seconds, gone as quickly as it came, something I will always remember, but never get to experience again.

Large sobs escape me despite trying to hold them in. I gulp air, crying for the better part of an hour before my body gives up trying to express any more grief. I sniffle, sitting up, dirt on my face and clothes. I reach a hand out, rubbing my own fingers over Michael's carving, thanking his childhood self for leaving this here for me to find; letting me know my family is still with me. I stand, reaching down, plucking the glass from the ground.
"Shit!"

I drop the glass, my finger instinctively flying to my mouth as I suck on my finger tip. I pull my finger from my mouth and see that I did exactly what I was trying to avoid as I watch blood seep through the cut, pooling into a bead that starts to drip slowly down the side of my hand. I reach down again, picking up the glass more carefully before returning upstairs and dropping the bloody piece into the trash.

———————————————   ———————————————

I open the fridge, grabbing another beer, twisting the cap and tossing it with its siblings on the counter. I take a large slug, before setting it down on the counter, my eyes looking over my purchases and what I can use as a makeshift bandage. I end up using scotch tape and a paper towel, returning to the counter for my beer.

When I pick it up, my eyes catch on the flier underneath that now sports a circular wet mark from the bottle's condensation. The picture shows a couple both sporting large packs, workout clothes and giant white smiles, the man's face now split in half by a water ring. I roll my eyes at the people of Aima Island attempting to advertise themselves before reading the giant words that hover over top that say, "MOUNT AIMA; HIKE OUR HOME."

I pick up the flier turning it over to reveal a map of the famous Tapt Trail in Mount Aima State Park; one that I remember local teenagers affectionately referring to as "Tapt that ass". I read the description written below the map that talks about the trail leading to the largest waterfall in the state, named Lyn Falls. The description continues, saying that the word Lyn is Norwegian for lightning. An explorer named Thore Oudenson, supposedly the first to reach the top of the falls, claimed to have seen lightning strike a boulder that sat in the middle of the massive pool of water at the top. The boulder cracked in half and that is where it still remains, water flowing through the middle and around the sides before going over the edge. Below the map is a phone number for making camping reservations and a list of some of the things the Mountain has to offer. Apparently one of those things is an annual Rhubarb festival every May. I set the flier back down, telling myself I'm going to go up the mountain at some point because that's another one of the things Dr. Hartgrove told me to do when I moved here. She told me the outdoors can be extremely healing and I should take advantage of that. I will do just that, but I live here now and in my mind, there's no rush to strap on a camelback and walk up a mountain.

With four beers gone and an emotional breakdown under my belt I get to the task of putting away the rest of my purchases. As I reach down for the first bag, I see that my paper towel bandage is completely red from blood flowing out of the cut on my finger.
"Shit."

I tear off the spent bandage and run my finger under the faucet again, hardly feeling any of the burn as the water flows into the wound, thanks to the beers I've consumed. I make another bandage, this time with a thicker piece of paper towel and wrap my finger again. I make a mental note that this cut may require a dab of super glue to act as a stitch, something I picked up from years of not having health insurance. I pick up the bloody bandage from the counter and toss it into the trash next to everything else. Reaching down, I hook a bag with each hand and walk out of the kitchen to the stairs leading to the top floor.

It takes a while, moving from room to room, placing all of my purchases where they belong. Hand soap and dispensers in bathrooms, 500 thread count sheets in the bedroom, and turkish cotton towels in the hallway closet. After I close the closet door, I open the door next to it, leading into one of my spare bedrooms, now turned into a darkroom. I flip the switch on the wall that turns on a red bulb overhead, everything around me glowing in a deep crimson color. Developing trays on top of metallic countertops, tongs and bottles of chemicals sit next to a squeegee and the pride of my darkroom, a brand new Beseler Printmaker 67 Condenser Enlarger with an attached baseboard. This will allow me to take my negatives and turn them into larger prints for display. I run my hands over everything, letting my fingers touch all the different textures, remembering my years spent learning how to use everything in this room.

I take a deep breath as I feel the alcohol creeping into my bloodstream and the red light starts to give me a headache. I open the door, my eyes adjusting as the natural light bursts into the dark space. I flip off the red light overhead and close the door, walking back out into the hallway. Once all of my purchases from Super Everything are put away, I decide I've earned myself a treat in the form of another beer, lifting the bottle to my lips to add to the other four I've already had. I silently wish that I hadn't offered a beer to the sheriff so that I didn't just empty the six pack, but I decide what's done is done and I toss the empty cardboard carrier featuring a cartoon beaver holding up a foamy beer mug into the trash and pop the cap on the sixth bottle. I obviously realize that I'm doing a terrible job of not drinking, but there have been many days where I have had much more than four beers by this time of day, so in that regard, I guess I'm not doing too bad. Small miracles, right?

Suddenly, the smell of Cilantro hits me, making me remember the tacos I bought right after shopping for groceries. My stomach growls and I feel the odd sensation of actually wanting to eat; something that has become foreign to me over the last year. The thin cardboard box sits waiting on the counter, grease staining one of its corners. I open up the takeout tray, hoping against all odds that the food is still good, but having sat for hours now, the tortillas are soggy and the texture of my first bite turns my stomach. I resist spitting the bite into the trash and swallow hard, bracing my hand on the counter while my eyes slide closed, giving my body a moment to process the grossness that just slid down my throat. Once the feeling has passed, I grab my phone and open up my search app again, once again attempting to avoid cooking, looking for what pizza places are around me. I settle on Nonno Pepperoni Pizzeria, because the mascot is a pepperoni with a big mustache, but also a monocle and top hat. It feels vaguely familiar and looks weird, not making any sense, therefore, it wins my business.

I click the link and my phone thinks for a second before opening the website. Bright colors fill the page with a banner that proudly states the pizza parlor has been in business since 1972, advertising that it is Aima Island's first pizzeria. I scroll through pictures of the restaurant over the years, one picture catching my eye of kids with mullets and teased bangs playing Dig-Dug and Ms. Pacman while laughing and holding pieces of pizza high in the air. I scroll down, the next picture looking like it's from the mid 90's. The arcade machines have changed to things like Die Hard, Ninja Turtles Through Time and Cruising USA, while the clothes have changed to make everyone look like the cast of Saved By The Bell. My brows furrow before I squint my eyes, lowering my face closer to the screen to look at two kids playing MORTAL KOMBAT 3 in the back of the room. I take the two fingers of my left hand and enlarge the picture, a gasp escaping my mouth as I recognize the brother and sister in front of the arcade cabinet as Michael and myself. It all feels like too much, my tears welling up again as I sit back, setting my phone on the couch. I close my eyes, the picture bringing another long lost, distant memory to the forefront of my mind.

"Melissa! Melissa, I'm about to fight Johnny Cage!"
I look around the claw machine that I have been trying to win a Darkwing Duck stuffed animal out of for the past ten minutes, fully realizing that the machine is rigged for you to lose, but wanting the toy so bad, that I keep spending my allotment of quarters trying to get it. I smile at Michael,

who waves me towards him before turning back to the machine before it exclaims loudly,
"FIGHT!"

I press the little red button on the black joystick and watch the claw descend towards the coveted duck superhero I, at this moment, want more than anything. The three metal prongs close in on each other, the claw starting to lift. Darkwing starts to slide out of the claws grip that is notoriously weak as to not give away too many prizes. My quarters spent, I start to walk past the machine to watch Michael play Mortal Kombat 3 when I see one of the metal arms get caught up on the tag that is sewn into Darkwing's tail. I turn back quickly, pressing my face against the glass as I watch Darkwing rise into the air. The claw moves slowly as I cross my fingers on both hands, willing him to not come loose and fall back into the prize pile. A small squeal escapes my mouth as I watch the claw arms fully open over the prize shoot and Darkwing fall through the short tunnel to rest behind the clear door that says PRIZE in bright orange on the front. I squat down, shoving my hand through the hole, grabbing my newest favorite possession. When I pull my hand back through the slot, I scream.

I am not holding Darkwing Duck, I am holding a gray dead hand whose arm extends from the prize slot, its fingers wrapped around mine. My eyes slowly raise up to see a woman's body crammed into the claw machine, her body folded at odd angles, occupying every inch of fillable space, her arm reaching down, bent backwards to be able to hold my hand. She is naked, beads of water covering her gray, dead skin that is pressed flat against the glass walls of the cube as she turns her head to look at me with milky, dead eyes. Her mouth opens slowly, but instead of words, water comes rushing out, a broken main dumping gallons of dirty, rotten water by the second. I watch, frozen in fear as the water fills the machine and the glass cracks from the pressure. As the water starts to leak from every seal and corner, I whimper, my eyes moving up to Michael who is standing next to the machine holding a bottle of wine in each hand. He turns the bottles bottom side up and the red liquid pours out, forming a puddle around his feet. He looks down at me slowly, his skin going gray and his eyes slowly changing, a film covering them like dumping milk into a glass of water. He stares down at me as his mouth opens and he says,

"They are coming for you, Mel. You have to keep your head clear."

I whimper,
"Who is coming for me?"

I scoot back on the floor as my brother is suddenly an adult, not a child, his body broken and destroyed like he just walked away from the wreck a year ago. Still staring down at me, he blinks once slowly and says,

94

"They're on the mountain, Mel."

Tears stream down my face as I ask,
"Who is?"

Before Michael can answer me, a scream mixed with a gargle comes from the claw machine. I turn quickly, watching bubbles fly from the woman's mouth and burst at the surface, just as the glass shatters and a wave of water, wreaking of rot, hits me.

———————————   ———————————

I wake up with a scream that fades into silence in my empty home. It takes my mind several seconds to realize where I am as I look around for my dead brother or the woman crammed into the machine. I quickly stand, running upstairs into the bedroom where my mattress is still puffing up to full size. I reach into a box next to the bed and pull out my well worn Darkwing Duck plush doll, multiple holes stitched up and his hat now completely missing for over a decade. I hold him close, now remembering the core memory of how I got him; the memory that didn't have a dead naked woman stuffed into a claw machine. He smells of age and is incredibly soft. I start to calm down holding this small comfort, my heart rate slowly lowering until my eyes grow wide and my heart beat sky rockets as I realize my clothes are soaking wet.

I spend the next hour scrubbing off my skin under scalding hot water, trying to get rid of the rotten scent I swear I can smell. No matter how much body wash I pour out onto my arms and chest the scent of death lingers, burned into my nose. When I finally get out of the shower, wrapping a towel around myself, I run a hand across the steamed mirror, staring at my reflection, internally trying to convince myself that my clothes were soaked from sweat and not the water that was thrown up by a corpse in a claw machine. I reach down, picking up my brush from where I left it next to the sink, but immediately drop it to the floor. On the tile floor are wet footprints leading out of the bathroom.

I opt to not brush my hair and instead grab my robe, tying it tight and slowly following the trail that has been left going down the hallway. My eyes swing from every corner to each door, making sure no one is lying in wait as I follow the footprints to the edge of the stairs. I hold the railing attached to the wall as I peer down the staircase, trying to see if someone is waiting for me at the bottom. My bare feet touch the carpet, careful to not step in the damp imprints left by whoever is in my home as I creep down the stairs. Five steps up from the bottom, one of the stairs releases a loud creak as I lower my weight onto it, making me cringe and suck air through my teeth as I press my back against the wall. After waiting to see if anyone is going to jump out, but having no one reveal themselves, I take the last five stairs, turning my head from left to right when I reach the bottom. The wet prints lead through the kitchen, into the living room and onto the back porch. I start to follow them, my face suddenly becoming completely confused as I see both of my bottles of wine, opened and sitting in the sink, now empty. I know I didn't drink them, because I would be much drunker than I am, so the question becomes, who is in my house, fucking with me? I lean to the side, trying to peer further into the room when I am startled by a BAM, BAM, BAM.

I whip around, falling over and scooting against the wall when the loud noise is followed by the sing-song ring of my doorbell. I blink my eyes, looking from the silhouette from whoever is on my front porch back to the footprints going across my floor that have now disappeared. I crawl forward looking around the room for the water that was there just moments before, but can find no trace of the footprints anywhere. The doorbell rings again, making my head whip towards the front door. I have no intention of answering it, but then a voice from outside says,
"Nonno Pepperoni's! I have your pizza!"

My eyebrows furrow. I didn't order pizza. Then again, I was just following wet footprints through my home that aren't really there so who am I to say I *did* or *didn't* do anything. I find my voice and choke out,
"Coming!"

As soon as I say it I think that I wasn't loud enough, but the man on my porch makes no more noise, so I assume that he has heard me. I raise myself from the floor on wobbly legs like a calf that has just dropped from its mother, and walk quickly to the front door, checking over my shoulder once to make sure that there is in fact no one in my living room, dead or otherwise. I turn the knob and open the door to an early twenties man standing on my porch with a bright orange, puffy pizza bag and a uniform dawned with the colors of the Italian flag, complete with a hat bearing the famed pepperoni man in a top hat.

The man's eyes go wide and I look down, having totally forgot that I am in nothing but a robe. Cleavage peaks from the top before I grab the sides, pulling the robe completely closed and duck down a foot, making the pizza man's eyes meet mine so he will remember himself. His eyes follow my intense gaze as I stand back up to full height and he clears his throat.
"I um- I have your pizza."

I smile, still holding my robe closed and say,
"I'm sorry, I didn't order any pizza."

He looks confused, pulling out the receipt and checking the address, looking over at the numbers bolted on my house next to the front door to verify. He looks back down at the receipt and says,
"This is definitely the address. It looks like it was ordered by someone named Michael."

CHAPTER SIX

The darkness of the night flows into my home, enveloping me, consuming every particle of light it touches as I double over, my hands on my knees. I take a large breath, deciding that I'm losing my mind. As the darkness slowly slides back out through the door and the light around me comes back into view, my eyes dart back into the room behind me. I completely forget about the pizza driver I've left standing on my porch unaware of why I am having a complete mental breakdown until I hear him ask,

"Um... Is everything alright?"

With my hands on my knees, I lift my head, raising my eyes to look at him before standing up completely, letting out a breath. He has a questioning look painted on his face, but I decide to not explain myself to him. I don't know who is doing this to me and even though I want to ask him to repeat the name he just said, I don't want to hear his fucking little mouth say it again. Instead I just say,
"Let me get my wallet."

Paid and tipped extremely well to take away from how weird he must think I am, the delivery driver pulls out of my driveway and leaves me alone once again. I set the cardboard box on the counter, the whole top of which is covered by the picture of Grandpa Pepperoni in all his glory. I open the pizza box and even though the pizza looks good, being sent a pizza by my dead brother has made me lose my appetite. I stand in my kitchen, my mind going back to the hallucination I had the other day while I was swimming in the lake. I know the woman in the lake was the same one I saw in the claw machine and against my better judgment, I start to question if what happened in the water really was a hallucination.

I take out my phone and open my search engine. I start to type out key words like Aima Island, haunted lake, and ghost, but stop before hitting search and close the app, frustrated with myself for even entertaining the idea that everything going on is anything more than my own trauma response.

I set my phone down on the counter and after looking around, thinking about what I want to do next, I decide I know one sure way to solve this problem. I grab my keys, my buzz still prevalent in the back of my head, nature's way of telling me to not drive a car and me not listening. I go down the garage steps as fast I can without falling and get in the driver's seat, turning the key in the ignition. Cold air hits me in the face as I take a deep breath, trying to steady myself. As I sit in the car seat, the urge to have a cigarette hits me. I haven't had one in five years after Michael and I agreed to quit together and smoked our last farewell cigarette on the back porch of this cabin when I was 22. We laughed as we put them out, knowing it was an empty gesture, but after the vacation ended and I went home, I stuck to it and so did he. Another bond shared between us.

With my head swirling and my out of place nicotine craving, I tell myself that I really shouldn't drive, but I left my better judgment behind three beers ago, so I shift the car into reverse and back up, stopping in the large circular driveway and putting the car in drive, moving past the house onto the main road. The road is dark, no street lights lining the roads this far out in the country. When you leave the city, you discover how dark places actually are. Even with headlights, you can only see about fifteen feet in front of you without your brights on. Add alcohol, nightmares, and trauma on top of that and it makes it really hard to concentrate.

I watch the white lines cruise by, my buzz boring deeper into my brain as the fifth beer I had starts to make me feel more drunk than I did at the house. As I come up on my turn, bright headlights from behind fill the interior of my car, reflecting off the rearview mirror and making me hold a hand up to cast a shadow on my face. The lights grow closer and closer and I yell,
"Shit!"
As it looks like the car behind me is going to ram right into me.

At the last second the driver of the other car pulls hard to the left, flooring the gas and blowing past me. I can't believe my eyes when I see that it is the Chevy. Complete with a bumper sticker showing their support for the 2nd amendment. I look at the license plate, pushing through the cloud of alcohol that surrounds my brain, and try to commit it to memory.
"SACRFCE".

I read the plate wrong first as Scarface, but squint my eyes, and realize that it doesn't read scarface, but sacrifice. My drunker than I'd like to admit face scrunches up and I yell to no one, but myself,
"Christian asshole! I bet you have wet dreams about the South rising again, you piece of fucking shit!"

That last part is punctuated by me hitting the steering wheel with each word, the horn giving four quick honks. After getting it out of my system, I take a deep breath and allow myself to calm down as the Chevy speeds away, brake lights disappearing around the curve into the darkness. With the alcohol in my system, I don't feel scared, I feel pissed. Revenge fantasies fill my head of pulling up next to him, pulling him out of the truck and punching him in the face over and over until it is a bloody mess. As I make my turn I can still see the tail lights of the Chevy in the distance moving further and further away, my inebriated brain telling me that I should follow them. That I should stand up for myself and tell them I will not accept them treating me the way they are. I gas the car, starting to give chase, when I glance in my rearview mirror, back at the road, now behind me, that leads to the liquor store and think to myself that there are more important things than telling an asshole that they are in fact an asshole. I make a U-turn, flicking my hand up, turning on my turn signal and turn left down the dark road. My eyes constantly move between the road and the rearview mirror to make sure Chevy hasn't doubled back, not wanting to deal with this stalker, but even less when it's pitch black out. I decide that I will call Sheriff Smith tomorrow and file a complaint. I'm not going to live like this. I bought the lakehouse to try and find peace in some kind of messed up way that only makes sense to me; not to be harassed by a yokel. Sooner than I realize, I come to the stop sign, the liquor store just minutes away. I look left, then right, seeing that no one is out, but myself. I ease on the gas, making the car pull forward and through the intersection, cautious of any traffic coming out of the darkness. I make it through the intersection, unscathed and pull into the parking lot of Mountain Top Liquor. The sign, lit up in green and yellow neon, features a little cartoon German man in lederhosen and a Bavarian hat, at the top of a mountain, holding up a foamy beer stein. My eyes go down to another sign on the door that says, Yodel-lay-hee-hoo your way to savings.

I can't help myself and say,
"Wow."

Getting out of my car, the air is humid and smells damp; not bad, just wet, like it's saturated with water, even though it hasn't rained. I suddenly feel an ice cold shiver run up my spine. The same kind of feeling you get when you sense someone is staring at you. I turn around, facing the dark parking lot full of empty spaces, looking behind me at the lone light; a single glowing street lamp affixed to a utility pole, standing tall over some overgrown bushes. It emits a low hum; the kind that if you just happened to be walking by, could easily fade into the background of everyday noise that we consider silence, but if you hyper fixated on it, this low sound could bore a hole right through your brain to the place where crazy resides. The bulb flickers, its dirty yellow light going on and off three times before staying on.

It's easy in a place like this with the darkness creeping in at every corner for you to feel like everything exists within a liminal space, your thoughts begging to get away from you, especially if you're a paranoid alcoholic who sees danger everywhere. I turn back to the store, my pace becoming a little quicker as I step up onto the curb and grab the handle to the door, pulling it open and moving quickly inside the shop. As the door opens, an automated bell makes a robotic ding-dong noise as I walk through. The woman behind the counter glances up, then back down, a lit cigarette in her mouth and a book in her hand with printed blood drops on a white cover, making me assume it's some kind of thriller. As the smell of cigarette smoke travels up my nostrils, I think about how her smoking inside can't be legal, but let the thought pass. I am not here to make sure people are following the smoking ban. I am here on a mission to drown my thoughts and not think about my brother ordering our favorite childhood food from beyond the grave.

The whole store is dimly lit and swathed in "rugburn carpet" that looks thirty five years old and feels rock hard, even underneath my shoes. It's the same type you would find in every classroom when you were a kid that would shred your skin instantly, leaving you with what my parents called a "raspberry" if you went down on it. The combination of light and flooring, along with the gray, blue paint on the walls makes everything feel washed out; a drunkard's den and not a place I'm proud to be.

I peruse the shelves, my mouth starting to water as my hands shake and I realize I'm not sure what I'm in the mood for. Walking up one aisle, then down another, I reach out my hand, letting my fingertips brush against the glass bottles, feeling the curves and ridges of each different, molded design, thinking about how good it's going to feel to get absolutely black out drunk.

I end up picking up a handle of spiced rum, gripping it by the neck and heading to the register. The light above me flickers as I put down the bottle and the woman behind the counter sets down her book, leisurely sliding off her perch atop a wooden stool, before slowly coming over to check me out. The yodeler sign hanging in the window casts the whole front of the store in a pale green glow and there's a lingering smell of something old, gone bad a long time ago, leaving a slight sour scent that lingers amongst the stale cigarette smoke. I think about how this store needs better ventilation, then look back at her as she waves the bottle over the scanner that makes a beep sound and looks up at me with an uninterested look.
"Will that be all?"

I look at her green tinted skin that makes her look like a monster that crawled out of the lake while I think to myself how absolutely charming everyone in Mount Aima is. My eyes glance at a shelf affixed to the back wall. On the top is a bottle in the shape of a skull filled with a clear liquid that I assume to be vodka inside. I point at it and say,
"What's that?"

She glances back and says,

"That's Crystal Head Vodka. It was made by that fella in Ghostbusters, or something."

She chuckles, a dry sound that scrapes against worn vocal chords.
"It's $100 and honestly, I don't think anyone will ever buy it. People around here aren't the type to be drinking out of *glass* skulls. Too witchy."

I look at the skull again.
"Well, today is your lucky day. I'll take it."

She gawks at me.
"Really? We have cheaper vodka if you want. I could grab you a bottle of Titos or something."

I figure if the dead are hanging around me, I might as well bring something appropriate for the party. I shake my head, "Nah, I'm feeling wild. Let's go with the skull."

I pause for a second then say,
"Oh and a pack of Camel, No. 9's."

She nods, her demeanor having changed slightly since finding out I was going to spend *real* money in her establishment, her aura having moved slightly from black to gray. Walking to the back wall, she pulls her stool over to step up and retrieve the bottle from the top shelf. When she comes down, she grabs a rag hanging on the back of a chair and wipes dust off the bottle. She rings it up and then looks up at me.

"That'll be $126.15"

I pull out my debit card that dons a custom picture of me, Michael and mom and dad. A ping strikes my heart as I stick it into the reader, waiting for the screen to say *APPROVED*. The light outside flickers again, making me glance over, then freeze in fear, my breath catching in my chest. In the darkness behind the light is a silhouette of someone hiding in the shadows, using the overgrown bushes for cover. I lean forward, trying to see them better. Whoever it is, is massive; wide shoulders that sit on top of piles of muscle. Then my eyes grow large as I watch them stand to full height, which has to be over eight feet tall, cocking their head to the side as we stare at each other.

_______________________   _______________________

Beep Beep Beep. I feel sweat forming on my body, every pore opening all at once to release the stink of fear from inside me. I stay glued to the spot, feeling like I can't move as my mind screams internally that this is not a man, this creature is something released from the depths, this is something old and something dark. A beast, no; a nightmare. Every single part of me knows that I am looking into the eyes of a monster. *Beep Beep Beep.* I stare at the figure that looks back at me as my mind tells me to run.

Run from this thing that will break you in half and consume your insides. Run, Melissa; RUN! *Beep Beep Beep.* A hand on my shoulder makes me jump, turning to the woman behind the counter.

"Maam? You kind of spaced out on me there."

I look back quickly, to the light that no longer flickers, but shines down onto the empty parking spaces below, nothing in the bushes, no monster staring at me, no giant silhouette, no threats to me at all, except maybe my own mind. I make a mental note that my hallucinations are getting out of control and I need to call Dr. Hartgrove tomorrow as I look back at the woman behind the counter.

"Maam are you okay?"

I nervously nod, swallowing hard. I feel my face make a wince as I ask,

"You ever have that feeling where you're not sure if you're awake or still dreaming?"

One of her eyebrows raises up.

"Um, what?"

Out of my periphery I see her hand reaching out slowly for the bag she has already put my bottles into, most likely smelling the alcohol leaking out of my open pores as I continue to nervously sweat, about to revoke my sale. I grab the bag quickly and use my free hand to pull my card from the machine, the swift movement making her jump back. I plaster a smile on my face and say,

"Nevermind, I hope you have a great evening."

Still looking at me skeptically she says,
"Yeah, yeah you too."

I turn to leave and the bell chimes again as I open the door, my eyes searching around to make sure I'm still alone. A gust of wind blows by, making my skin into goose flesh as I get into my car quickly, reaching over and locking the door. I glance up at the window of the store to make sure the clerk isn't watching me before reaching into the black, plastic bag and pulling out the bottle of Crystal Head. Breaking the seal and removing the lid, I turn the bottle up and take a large swig, making air bubbles fly up through the neck of the bottle, bursting at the other end when they hit empty space. I swallow and the burn makes me cough a little, but not enough to stop me from turning the bottle up again in a repetitive motion to take another large gulp. I look into my rearview mirror as the light flickers again. I lower the bottle, staring at the spot, waiting for something to happen, squinting my eyes. A flicker of something makes me sure I just saw movement in the darkness. I turn around in my seat to get a better look, when the largest pair of antlers I've ever seen come pushing out of the night into the flickering light. My eyes follow them down to where they are attached not to an animal, but to the head of a man. My brain screams,
"RUN!"

At this point I don't care if everything I'm experiencing is a hallucination. Even if they are, alcohol is no longer helping and I have to do something, but first, I have to get the fuck out of here *now.* Quickly, I jam the key into the ignition, slamming the car into reverse and pressing down hard on the gas pedal. I turn the steering wheel, making the car whip out of my parking space and shift hard into drive, turning the wheel back straight as I floor it out onto the main road. I drive towards the intersection, taking another swig of vodka that burns harsh as I swallow. I glance into my rearview mirror, half expecting something to be in the road behind me, chasing my car even though I fully realize that is absolutely ridiculous.

I know I did not actually just see a monster in the parking lot of Mountain Top Liquor and if I'm being honest with myself I know it's all in my head. I know I'm the one who ordered pizza and put the name as Michael; I have to be. There is literally no other option. I don't believe in ghosts; especially not ones who order pizza and pour wine down the drain. I know there's no dead woman in the lake and honestly, there's a good chance there's no orange Chevy either, but none of these facts stops me from trying to drive home as fast as I can. I fly through the red light at the intersection and past a stop sign. Another drink burns down my throat as the liquor starts to really hit me. I set the skull in the passenger seat, pressing the stopper back into the neck. I look down at it to make sure it's not going to slide off the seat and grab my pack of cigarettes out of the plastic bag. As I pull the plastic off, I figure now is as good a time as any to start stress smoking again. I rip out the interior paper, while keeping the last three fingers of my right hand on the steering wheel, keeping it steady. I slide out a cigarette and place it in my mouth, tossing the pack into the passenger's seat. I search around with my hands and quick glances to find a lighter and spot one someone has left in my car at some point, sitting in my center console amongst a pile of pennies and receipts from an Ashton sushi restaurant I used to go to once a week called Whack-A-Roll. I grip the lighter and bring it up to the front of my cigarette, spinning the striker wheel. Nothing happens and I flick it again, with the same result. Aggravated, I concentrate both eyes on the lighter and spin the wheel a third time, making the lighter fluid catch and flame appear in front of my eyes. I suck the fire through the front end of my cigarette and make a space on the other end of my mouth, blowing out smoke. I drop the lighter back into the center console and when I look back up, I bring down my foot as hard as I can, slamming on the brakes.

In front of me is a giant humanoid creature with massive antlers jutting out of its forehead, standing in the middle of the road. I pull hard to the right on the wheel and as I do, the images of my family slamming into the guardrail play through my mind as my tires screech, throwing up smoke that flows in front of my headlights. My car hits the grass,

sliding through mud, despite me pressing down as hard as I can on the brakes, and continues going down into the ditch ten feet below the road. A large slam and I come to a stop as my face bounces off of the deployed airbag, the chaos of the crash suddenly silenced. I pull back, blinking and dazed, looking up at the spiderwebbed windshield, trying to realize what just happened. My lips suddenly feel wet and when I reach up a hand to touch my face, it comes back red, the force of my face hitting the airbag, making my nose bleed. I run my forearm across the base of my nose, leaving a long streak of blood on my skin as sharp pain shoots through my face.
"Shit!"

I open the car door, getting out slowly, looking up towards the road which is now empty. The smell of rubber hits my nostrils, mixed with the coppery scent of the blood on my face, taking me back to the day of my family's crash. I climb slowly up the embankment, looking around for any sign that what I just saw was real and my brain didn't just conjure up a monster standing in the middle of the road in Aima Island. The closer I get to the top, I lower myself onto my belly, crawling up the rest of the way, trying to stay as low as I can and out of sight. When I peek out onto the road, I see that whatever was in front of my car, if anything at all, has left no trace ever being there, leading me to lean towards Occam's Razor, that the simplest answer is often the correct one and that my condition is getting worse. I stand, looking left, then right, down the road, seeing nothing in the darkness before turning around to go back down the grassy hill, careful to not slip and hurt myself even more than I have. Back at my car, I take stock of the damage before I curse, leaning in through the open driver's side door to grab the skull shaped bottle and in true "fuck it" fashion, take another swig of vodka, swallow, then down another. As I try to take a step backward, I lose my balance and fall back, turning my body against the side of my car, the liquid in the glass skull I'm holding, sloshing around. I try to right myself, but slide along the side of the car and fall back into the open driver side door, sitting down hard on the seat. I drop the bottle to the ground with a thunk, my head swimming in a lake of liquor. A noise comes from the woods to my right and I jerk my head in the direction of the sound, not gauging the proximity of my door and slam my head into the cold, hard, metal splitting my eyebrow.

"Fuck!"

Blood drips down my face in a solid red line, joining the blood still running from my nose, two streams converging into a river; the flow made faster by the alcohol pumping through my bloodstream. Another noise resembling the snort of a bull makes me jump. I swing my legs inside the car and close the door, locking it. I reach around the backseat, finding a t-shirt that I press against my forehead to try and stop the blood. The cloth smells stale, something taken off after a night at the bar; spilled beer and old cigarette smoke still clinging to every fiber. My head throbs as I lean back in my seat and say,

"Well shit."

The frustration in me suddenly boils to the surface as I hit the side of my car door and yell,
"SHIT!"

Tears form in my eyes as I vocalize my feelings.
"I fucking hate this place."

I wipe away my tears and pull the lever on my seat to make me lean back. I'm going to let myself go to sleep and then I will handle this all in the morning. My eyes start to feel heavy when a loud slam on the hood of my car shakes the whole vehicle, making me sit upright, eyes shooting open just in time to see what looks like a huge hoof, surrounded by hair moving up and over my cracked windshield. Noise comes from the roof of my car as I duck down, scared for my life of whatever this creature is. I slam my eyes closed and repeat,
"It's all in my mind, it's all in my mind, it's all in my mind."

The sound above me stops and I release a shaky breath, continuing to repeat the words over and over, always thankful for the exercise Dr. Hartgrove taught me to pull myself out of my brain's fantastical dark creations. I sigh, starting to ease back into my seat when a loud howl rips through the night air, sounding very similar to the howl that I heard from my porch, breaking me from my mantra; making me cover my ears as more tears form, rolling down my face. The howl stops and my car bounces as whatever is on top of it hops off, landing heavy on the ground beside the car. This can't be in my head. I saw a monster in the road and it is standing next to my car right now.

Still laying down, I lift my head slightly, looking through the window to see what looks like giant deer legs that extend up to the waist, the fur dissipating, fading into bare skin. A whimper escapes my lips and the creature turns, the irises of it's eyes a bright red, the antlers affixed to the front of it's forehead, massive and at least twenty points each. His face looks human as he bares his teeth at me, snarling, nostrils flaring and I see his eyes move slightly focusing on something next to me. Suddenly he lunges forward, his massive tongue shooting out of his mouth, slapping against the edge of the window of the car door and moving up as he lifts his head, licking the metal. I sit, confused, not sure why this creature is licking my car, but before I have time to think about it, a set of headlights casts down the hill, making the creature squint it's eyes and stand to full height before running full speed into the woods. I lay as still as possible, not wanting to sit up. I hear the car stop and someone get out. The pop, slam sound of an older vehicle's door closing breaks the silence. A moment passes before I hear a man's voice call out,
"Hello?...Hello, is anyone there?"

I stay hidden, too scared to speak or even move. A few moments pass before I hear the car's door open and close once again and see the headlights fade as my savior behind the steering wheel, whoever they are, pulls away down the road. I lay in the same position for an hour deciding that I am not going to leave my car until morning, no matter what. There is no way I would ever get out of this vehicle before the sun rises after seeing what I just saw. Slowly I crawl into the back seat, pulling a jacket over my legs before, despite my fear, the alcohol in my body takes over, pulling me down, deeper and deeper into a world of darkness as I fall asleep.

CHAPTER SEVEN

My wake up call comes in the form of a loud tap on my window, making me sit up, the trauma from last night yanking me into the present as I whip my head around to make sure the monster isn't near me. Another tap on the glass makes me turn my head back to the window, seeing Sheriff Smith, the same officer that was at my house, yesterday. As my eyes focus and I realize who is staring at me through my car window, I sit all the way up into the back seat, unlocking the doors and pulling on the interior handle, releasing and opening the door. He takes a step back as I get out of the car, standing up. His eyebrows shoot up as his hand goes up to cover his nostrils at the scent emanating from the interior of my vehicle.

"Whew! Smells like a distillery in there!"

I lean back against the car, rubbing my forehead, not wanting to deal with this at the moment. The familiar feeling of a hangover, an unwelcome friend that always invites themselves over, has established itself in the forefront of my skull while I was passed out and now that I'm standing upright, it has unleashed its full fury. I stumble over what to say, really not wanting the Sheriff in the town I just moved to, to drag me in on a driving while impaired charge.
"Yeah. Hey, Sheriff Smith, I just had an accident last night."

Sheriff Smith looks between my car and me like *yeah, no shit* before leaning his head to the side, looking at the front of my car fully slammed into the bottom of the ditch. His eyes move back to me and he says,
"That wouldn't have anything to do with that skull of liquor underneath your car, would it."

I close my eyes, my lips folding into my mouth and disappearing. With everything else going on, this is seriously the last thing I need right now. I open my eyes and see the sheriff's eyebrows raised up, a questioning look still on his face. I rub my forehead again.
"No, I um…There was something in the road and I swerved. I drove off the side of the road and crashed. I had just come from Mountain Top Liquor so I decided to have a drink and wait with my car until morning."

He gives me a skeptical look, writing down what I've said in his notebook before he flips it closed, sticking it back in the front pocket of his uniform.
"Uh huh. Got your license?"

I walk around the car to the passengers side and open the front door, reaching in to retrieve my purse from the floorboard, pulling it out by the strap. As I do, it snags on my seat belt buckle, making the bag turn and dump all of its contents onto the floor. Sheriff Smith watches me as I let out a heavy sigh, throwing my purse down onto the seat before I crouch down, digging through the mess to find my wallet, opening it and retrieving my ID, walking back over to him and handing it over. The sheriff glances over it, turning it over to look at the back for a reason only known to himself. He turns it back to the front, lowering it and looks up at me over his sunglasses.
"From Ashton, huh? How long did you live there?"

I shake my head, not wanting to participate in this forced human interaction.
"Um…always; I mean my whole life until now."

He simply makes a "Hm" noise, turning his vision back down to my ID. Then looking up, outstretching his hand and giving me back my license.
"A lot of gays up there, I've heard."

His words shock me and it takes a second for me to register what he's just said.

"What?"

He raises an eyebrow.
"We've all heard about what goes on in Ashton."

My mouth hangs open, flabbergasted, but before I can respond he says,
"Anyways, what was in the road?"

A noise comes from the trees, making me whip my head to the right, towards the woods, looking where that thing, if there was a thing, would have run off. I realize I didn't answer his question and I turn my head back to look at Sheriff Smith.
"Sorry, what?"

Still holding out my ID, he shakes it once to get my attention and I take it back as he asks again.
"You said something was in the road that caused you to have an accident. What was in the road?"

My brain dives into an internal debate about what I'm going to tell the Sheriff and how much. I decide I'm going to tell him it was a possum, but as he stares at me, the words that come out of my mouth are not what I anticipated.
"Well, um…it was big and kind of looked like…"

His pen hovers over his notepad.
"Looked like what?"

I sigh.

"Like; like a man. But had antlers…"

The Sheriff chuckles, shaking his head back and forth. He puts away his pen and pad, pushing up on the front of his hat, moving it up on his forehead so he can wipe at the sweat gathering there. I can tell my face is full of annoyance as I try to explain.

"Look, I know it sounds crazy, but it was a man with antlers *and* deer legs. After I crashed he came down and snarl-"

The Sheriff puts up a quieting hand and says in a low, but audible voice,

"Ms. Monos, Aima Island is a good town. It's a good town full of good people; lots of them may be worn out and tired, but they *are* good. Now what I want you to understand is that I don't need some drunk out of Ashton moving down here and causing trouble. Trouble that includes you going around spouting stories of a sighting of the Mount Aima Antler Man."

My face sinks into a state of confusion as I try to explain, "Who? Wait, Sheriff, I don't want to make trouble, I jus-"

"Save it."

He licks his bottom lip before it disappears under the top one as he mulls over his thoughts and I stand in front of him, silent.

"You're going to have to get that car out of here. Do you have a towing service you can call?"

I shake my head.

Smith rubs his chin and says,
"There is Aima Island Paint and Body. They could probably tow it for you. Want me to give them a call?"

I nod, forcing a smile.
"That would be great."

The sheriff walks back to his cruiser, taking out his phone and looking through his contacts before lifting it to his ear. He looks back at me a couple times during his conversation before hanging up his phone and sliding it back into his pocket. Walking back over to me he says,
"Looks like Jim can be out here pretty soon actually. You got lucky. Usually by this time he's out scraping accidents off the freeway."

I feel a disgusted look cross my face but quickly wipe it away for one of gratitude.
"Well thank you for calling him."

As he turns away he says,
"Yup, if you want to leave your keys in the driver's seat, I can go ahead and give you a ride."

He starts to walk back to his cruiser, but turns when he doesn't hear me walking after him.
"You coming?"

I look from him, to the keys, my eyes moving to the car.
"Are you sure it's a good idea to go home? I don't want someone to try and steal it.

A laugh breaks free from him; one of those barrel laughs that you know without a shadow of a doubt that the person letting it loose is laughing *at* you and not *with* you.
"Home?! Maam, you need to go to a hospital. I'm just trying to save you the cost of an ambulance and I don't know if you've seen your car lately? I hate to break it to you, but there ain't no one in six counties that's going to want to steal that thing."

He chuckles again, speaking to himself.
"Someone stealing a broken down foreign compact; hilarious."

As his laughter calms, he sees that my face has remained stoic, not joining in on the joke.
"Okay, okay. I can't force you to go to the hospital and if you want to wait with your vehicle, Jim is going to be here pretty soon and you can ride with him back to the shop to get a rental."

I nod slowly, thinking about my options, but knowing I truly don't want to place myself inside the Sheriff's squad car.

"I think I'm going to wait."

He looks at me like I've personally insulted his hospitality before wiping his hand across his face.

"Suit yourself, but I think it would be real foolish to not have a doctor look at your nose."

He turns to walk away, but hesitates, turning his head halfway back towards me.

"Oh, and ma'am, I will be checking your story with Betsy over at Mountain Top and don't let me see you out here drinking again."

He winks, making a finger gun and a clicking noise as he points it at me.

"Until next time, Melissa Monos."

I don't even attempt to continue my lie and tell him I wasn't drinking and driving; instead, considering myself lucky to not be in handcuffs in the back of his squad car waiting to be processed at the local jail. My eyes move to the side as I think about what Betsy will have to say about me asking her weird questions before running out into the parking lot with two bottles of liquor and speeding away. His door closes and I watch as the lights on top turn off, the cruiser pulling away from the grass and onto the road, the sound of his engine slowly fading into the distance, leaving me by myself with the forest and my car. Noises from birds come from the woods and as I look around, completely alone on the side of the road, I wonder if I made a mistake by not going with the Sheriff. Despite the fear that still lingers in my stomach from the night before; a burning acidic puddle of alcohol sloshing around in the pit of my guts, I try again to peer in between the trees to see any trace of the creature that stomped on my car the night before. Any kind of evidence that will reassure me that I haven't completely lost it. It must have left tracks somewhere before it jumped on my car.

Remembering the stomp on the roof makes me turn to examine the damage done to my car by the deer man or whatever he was. My roof is bowed in towards the middle and I ask myself if this is conclusive evidence that there was a giant monster on top of my car the night before. As I take in the massive amount of damage, I can't help but think how ridiculous it is how much my car has gotten fucked up in a matter of days.

I sigh, telling myself there's nothing I can do about it now except wait for Jim from Aima Island Paint and Body to come tow my car, the internal thought punctuated with the thought that I seriously need to figure out a plan for stopping this destructive cycle of drinking. I narrowly escaped getting hauled off to the station just now and I need to be careful. Leaning against my driver side door, time crawls by painfully as I keep glancing at my phone as an hour passes, my frustration growing. I open the driver's

side door, sitting in the seat and retrieving my pack of cigarettes, opening the box to reveal nineteen mechanically rolled, filtered, coffin nails left in the pack. As I slide one out, placing it between my lips and lighting it, I ask myself outloud what people around here consider "soon". I pull out my phone again from my back pocket and open up my contacts. I scroll down, stopping at the L's, my finger hovering over my therapist's number before I click the button on the side of my phone, turning it off and ditching the idea of calling her. As the screen turns off, turning it into a black mirror, I catch sight at the state of my face and can't help but say,
"Oh shit."

I set down my phone and pull down the sun visor, sliding the plastic door to the side to reveal the mirror contained within. My nose isn't crooked, but there are bright purple crescents that have formed under each one of my eyes, meaning one thing; my nose is either fractured or broken. I touch the cut on my forehead from slamming my head into the door and wince as pain radiates through my head. I lean back, looking up at the ceiling of the car as I take another drag of my cigarette and blow the smoke upwards, making it spread against the car's ceiling before flowing out of the open door.

Another torturous hour crawls by before my exasperation heightens and I give up, deciding to walk home. I pop my trunk grabbing my old Jansport bookbag, still bearing some hand drawn graffiti from when I was in highschool like the

Super S, made by drawing three lines, then three more underneath, finally connecting all of the lines and adding a point to the top and bottom, amongst other things like an anarchy symbol and a sword stabbed into a skull. Jansport bookbags hold a specific smell that you only know if you've owned one and it makes me stop for a second, my brain trying desperately to take me back to a time of cafeteria pizza and worrying about who "liked" me enough to ask me to prom, when I and my family walked amongst the living, but this time, I wave it off, not interested in bringing up another memory as I say to no one but myself, "We're all dead."

I unzip the bag and put both bottles of booze into it, zipping it back up and starting to walk. The clink of glass quickly becomes annoying and I decide to remove the skull bottle, holding it, while leaving the handle of rum in my bag. This of course leads to the thought of taking a swig of the Crystal Head Vodka, which doesn't last long before thought turns into reality, because despite literally just having told myself I need to stop drinking and walking away from a drunk driving accident, today already sucks, so why the fuck not? I raise the bottle and toast to no one.
"Wise men once said, "Why the fuck are you here if youre not going to drink?"

I drink, making the walk more enjoyable, but my thirst grows for water instead of liquor. Despite craving a cool drink that doesn't light my throat on fire, I keep slugging back shots, now past the point of no return. I keep telling myself that it's not that far to my house as I light cigarette after cigarette, making my lungs burn to match my throat; another barrier I am willingly putting up to make the walk harder, but despite making my way home, the road seems to grow longer and longer, the forest stretching out, making the distance triplicate in size. A car or two passes by, paying me no mind thankfully, instead of slowing and offering me southern salutations as a primer to ask if I need any help, but then I hear a louder noise; one I've come to recognize. It stands out like a sore thumb in a world that has become full of hybrids and silent electric vehicles. I turn slowly, my reaction speed dulled by the vodka, as the Chevy comes blasting down the road. With me in his sights, the driver edges closer and closer to the side of the road, making me nervously try to step back away from the white lined edge.

I step onto dead pine needles, taking two steps further back to show I am giving him a wide berth, but I watch in horror as the tires of the truck hit the side of the road, kicking up dirt and coming directly for me. I leap out of the way into the trees as the car flies by, barely missing me and steering back onto the road, the tailpipes spewing black diesel exhaust as they drive away.

As I lay in prickly leaves of a Holly tree, the small needles that tip the edges of every leaf, poking into my skin, I curse at myself for not telling the sheriff about this asshole and slowly pick myself up from the ground and leave the treeline, looking both ways before fully coming out. I look down at my arms and legs covered in scratches. I reach down, pulling a thorn out of my thigh, the pain searing, then disappearing under the weight of the vodka as a droplet of blood wells up and then slowly runs down my skin, making me regret wearing shorts when I left the house the night before. It takes me a minute before I start down the road again, my anger rising as my heart hammers in my chest. I seethe, wanting to drag the driver out of that truck and shove my fingers into their eye sockets. I know deep in my mind that I could never do such a thing, but liquid anger is even more potent than liquid courage and can lead to people doing drastic things they never thought themselves capable of. Things that usually end people up in jail with a lengthy sentence.

I finally start to walk again, thinking about what a mistake it was to come to Aima Island. Regret of buying this house and moving here fills me, making me wish I had just stayed in Ashton amongst the street performers and holistic healers, slowly drinking myself to death. This is not at all what I imagined my experience to be like. To be honest, I'm not sure what I thought would come with this house that has the bones of my family metaphysically tied to it forever. Doctor Hartgrove thought coming here could help me heal; while I, if I'm being honest, was leaning more towards this place helping me die. Whatever I thought, in my mind Aima Island wasn't full of dead bodies in a lake and an antlered monster chasing me around in the middle of the night. I know none of it is real, but then again, if experiencing something; if seeing it, hearing it, and even feeling it is all it takes to be part of your reality, then these ghosts and the beast roaming the woods are some of the realest things I have ever witnessed.

I finally turn, walking up my gravel driveway, my forehead sweating and making me feel itchy as gnats try their best to chew on my flesh. I instinctively slap the side of my neck as a mosquito joins them, feasting on my blood, trying to drink its fill and leave me with a mountainous lump that will itch to no end, possibly filled with malaria. My hand comes back with a blackish red smear on it and I wipe my palm on my pants as I unlock the deadbolt, entering through the front door. The cool air hits my sweat, making the 74 degree room feel much colder. I set down my bag on the counter, unzipping it and taking out the bottle inside, setting both of them on the kitchen counter. I start to walk away, but then pause, my eyes drifting back to the skull bottle. I pick it up, removing the lid, leaving it on the counter as I take the bottle with me. I take a swig and walk to the living room, taking a heavy seat on the couch and pulling out my phone. As I start to scroll through the ether of mindless bullshit that we have been convinced is fun to participate in, but really is just companies that have figured out how to make us create content for them for free so they can pump our brains full of advertisements, red light hits me in the eyes, making me blink and look up. On the far wall above me is a small stained glass window featuring red glass with a deer's head in the middle. Between the antlers is a five pointed star hovering in the air. I know from living through the satanic panic that swept the country that despite what most of America and *especially* the people of the South may believe, the five pointed star is actually a symbol of protection instead of a dedication to Satan. I don't remember this house having stained glass, but that doesn't mean it didn't. My memory is not the most trustworthy after the accident and the subsequent months of throwing my brain into a metaphorical olympic sized swimming pool full of hooch. Flashbacks from the night before come to me as I stare at the stained glass antlers. That *thing* in the road, the weight of the car shifting under it's massive frame. Was it really there? Did my car almost flip when it went down the embankment? Maybe the roof slammed into the side of a tree. I shake my head, unsure of anything in my life at this moment when suddenly my nostrils twitch as the scent of rancid grease assaults my senses. I lift my hand to my nose instinctively and scream out as pain shoots through my face. I walk into the downstairs bathroom and take in the pitiful state of my face in the glass of the mirror. The bruising has set in and it is obvious that my nose is broken. I consider going to the hospital like the Sheriff suggested, but I am once again drunk and am not going to stroll into a hospital drunk and asking for help. I pull out my phone and search *how to fix a broken nose.* I click the first article that populates and sigh a breath of relief.

If the bridge of your nose is not crooked, the only thing needed is rest and an ice pack. Give yourself proper time to heal and-

I close the article. As far as I'm concerned I don't have to do anything at this point except not swerve away from

imaginary deer men and crash a car again. I walk back into the kitchen, wobbling as the Sheriff's words come back to me and I repeat them mockingly.
"I don't need some Ashton drunk causing trouble."

I scoff.
"Fucking Prick."

I make it to the counter without falling or puking and *that* is a win. I grab the pizza box that has my brother's name written on the top in Sharpie, sliding it towards me. I open it and just like the box in front of me, my brain, a rolodex placed inside my skull, opens, bringing back another memory.

Sitting sadly in the box before me is a pizza that has different toppings on every slice. Michael and I used to order this *exact* pizza to the disdain of every restaurant we ever ordered it from. We called it pizza roulette, where we would close our eyes, spin the box and pick a random slice. The rules, made by my brother of course, were simple. Pick a slice, eat it; no matter what toppings are on your slice. There were only a couple of times where my decision proved *very* fatal. One time in particular was the first and only time I have had anchovies. Having them laying in between chunks of pineapple and blue cheese made the slice especially rank. Michael laughed his ass off as he told me to eat my piece of "Hawaiian Fish Surprise".

I stare down at the coagulated cheese and old grease soaked into the cardboard of the box before closing it, taking the box outside. I lift the lid to the trash can and toss the whole thing into the garbage with a thud, Nonno Pepperoni looking at me with disappointment as I close the lid.

I climb the steps in the garage, coming back in the house and head directly for my bottle to take another drink. I swig down a large gulp, then head back to the bathroom to pee. It feels like I'm on the toilet forever before I stand, ready to flush. When I turn to wash my hands, a scream escapes my throat as I stare at a woman, the *same* woman that was trapped inside the claw machine in my dream. She stands near me, her image reflected in the mirror. My eyes move past her to see Michael, standing dead and gray in the hallway. I whip my body around, ready to see these dead people standing directly behind me, but am met with nothing but empty air. I turn back to the mirror, my red cheeked face the only one gazing back at me.

Tears form in my eyes as I feel at my wits end, my body filled with stress and fear; a taut wire ready to snap at any moment. I thought I could handle my issues on my own, but I have had more than enough of seeing dead people. I feel absolutely fed up. I walk quickly into the kitchen, grabbing my phone off the counter, opening my lock screen and repeating what I did earlier, tapping the phone icon. I scroll down to "Lindsay Therapist", my thumb hovering over the button, knowing I should call her, but debating on if I should tell her that I'm having some sort of psychotic break. I can't help but think that even more than telling her that, I just want to talk to someone who isn't a part of "the good people of Aima Island"; who isn't part of this awful place. Someone who isn't woven into the fabric of Mount Aima. I still can't fully convince myself to call her and I turn my phone off again, setting it back down on the table. Walking out to the deck, I stare out at the lake wondering to myself how much of a mistake I've made moving here. Either I'm losing my mind or there is something seriously fucked up going on. No sooner has the thought crossed my mind that I see something bob up from under the water to float on the surface. I am about to close my eyes and tell myself that whatever is floating in the water is all in my head when I notice something different. It is not the woman who keeps showing up in my dreams and waking life. I squint my eyes and see that it's not Michael either. I lean over the railing for a better look, staring down at a child, floating face down on the surface of the water.

What comes next is a blur. It no longer matters if this is real or not. There is a child floating in the lake and I can't stand by and not react. I don't know how I get down to the water, but before I realize it, my bare feet are slapping against the old wood of the dock. I come to a sliding stop, feeling the skin on the bottom of my feet burn as I brace them to stop my movement. I stare down, the small body floating in front of me, water lapping at their cheeks. I can see now it is a boy in an orange and white striped shirt with blue jeans, and even though I can see them, inches from me, I still hesitate for a split second, trying to decide if what I am seeing is real, unable to trust my own mind. I decide it doesn't matter and I can't take the chance, imagining myself having to explain to the Sheriff that I left the boy floating in the lake because I have brain issues and thought he wasn't real.

Without another thought, I crouch down, reaching out my hand to grab his shirt and pull him up. As I stretch my arm, making my fingers linger right above the soaking wet fabric, the stench of death wafts up, pushing its way into my nostrils and down my throat. My stomach decides this is a good time to evacuate all of the liquor sloshing around inside of me and I pull my hand back, closing my eyes. I lean back, separating myself from the tainted air and take a deep breath, swallowing hard in an attempt to tamp down my body's reaction to throw up the poison inside me. I count to three, then reach out slowly again and almost fall into the water as the boy's body gives one violent shake.

My mouth fills with stomach acid mixed with vodka, a vicious mixture that somehow tastes worse than it feels. I still refuse to throw up as I force myself to swallow it back down. My eyes go wide as I scoot back as fast as I can on the palms of my hands as I watch gray, dead fingers grab onto the wood of the dock.

The boy pulls himself up, his waterlogged body slopping onto the dock as a puddle forms around his decrepit frame. He stretches out his hands one at a time, his dead, rotted fingers gripping between the boards, pulling himself closer and closer to me, leaving a trail of brown water in his wake. His white eyes move up, staring at me as water leaks out of his mouth. I am frozen in fear and do nothing but watch as his right hand grabs my shoe. My mouth hangs open as I stare down, a scream edging its way up my throat, but only a small pathetic, shrill screech comes squeaking. I hear bones crack as he twists his head to look up at me and says, "You must help us Melissa."

I finally find the smallest voice lingering inside myself and whisper shakily,
"Wh-What?"

Suddenly the water starts to bubble violently before being ruptured by heads breaking through the surface. It pours off of their dead features as they float in place, staring at me from their watery grave, perhaps more than that; perhaps not their graves, but their fluid prison from where they are all trying to escape. I try to move back but the hand on my foot holds firm, with more strength than I would have thought possible from a half rotted child. All of the faces in front of me are different ages and genders, having only one thing in common; their gray, dead skin. Suddenly they all open their mouths in unison and say,

"Help us."

The boy in front of me reaches out further, his cold dead fingers wrapping around my ankle. His mouth opens too wide as he yells,

"THEY'RE AT TIIE DOOR!!"

My full voice finally returns, bubbling over like a hot pot left on the stove, my voice overflowing out of my mouth in a scream as I sit up on my couch, drenched in sweat; the phantom feeling of a wet, small hand on my ankle.

CHAPTER EIGHT

I sit on my couch breathing hard as my lungs fight to pull enough oxygen into my body to make me calm down and convince my heart to not explode out of my chest. As my brain slowly registers that I am safe, it simultaneously brings back details from my dream. I turn halfway around, looking towards the deck and jump up from where I'm sitting, running over to the door and looking out at the water that glistens in the sun, calm and not full of dead gray bodies. A bird flies by, the world outside of the cage that is my mind, completely at peace. I can't help but think of the image of that dead little boy laying wet on the dock and say quietly to myself,

"fuck."

A loud knock makes me jump and turn around, bracing my back against the glass sliding door. As I stare at the front door all I can think of is the dead boy yelling,
"They're at the door."

I walk forward slowly as another knock comes harder this time, making my door shake on its hinges. I walk quickly through the front hall, coming to stand close to the door and lean close to the window next to the door, peering through the glass and seeing that it is the sheriff. Sighing, I unlock the deadbolt and slowly open the door. His head lifts at my emergence and he takes a step back giving me room to come out while he lifts a single hand and says,
"Well, that didn't take too long."

He looks me over, his eyes moving from the ground up to my face as he cocks one eyebrow.
"Maam, are you alright?"

I take a deep breath and reply,
"Yeah. Yeah, just a bad dream.

He nods slowly twice before licking his lips and continuing to talk.
"Uh-huh. Well Ms. Monos, I'm here because Jim came and got your car; said you were nowhere in sight. He went ahead and took the vehicle to the shop, but said I might want to come check on you."

I scoff, not believing what I've just been told.

"I waited for two hours and then walked home because he didn't show up!"

The sheriff rubs the back of his neck, clearly uncomfortable.
"Well now, there's no need to take a tone, Ms. Monos. I can't speak to that, but Jim told me he towed your car twenty minutes after I spoke to him."

My eyebrows furrow as I consider what I've just been told. That can't possibly be true, can it? Did I imagine it had been two hours when it hadn't? The sheriff sees me obviously struggling to comprehend what's happening and says,
"Well, I just came by to make sure you were okay and to tell you Jim said he's going to need a week with your car, but that she will be as good as new when he's done with her."

I nod.
"Oh…okay, that's fine.

He sticks out his thumb, motioning behind him and when my eyes follow, I see a car sitting in my driveway.
"I went ahead and got my deputy to follow me over here to bring you a rental."

The deputy climbs out of the driver's side door, lifting a hand in the air. I plaster on a fake smile and return the gesture. I look back at the Sheriff and say,

"Well thank you. You really didn't have to-"
He raises his hand and says,
"It's no problem. Serve and protect. This is the serve part."

As he turns to leave, I remember what I've been meaning to
tell him and I say,
"Wait!"

He turns around with a look of confusion and I take a step
forward.
"There has been someone in a truck harassing me."

The niceties he gave me just moments before fade as he
pinches the bridge of his nose, obviously annoyed with me.
"Harassing you?"

I nod.
"They have been following me whenever I am driving and
today they tried to hit me with their car."

He raises an eyebrow and says,
"That's a very serious accusation. The driver didn't happen
to have antlers, did he?"

I am shocked into silence that he would take this
opportunity to make fun of me as a small smile turns up at
the corner of his mouth.
"Are you making fun of me?"

He holds up his hands in mock surrender.

"No, no. I'm sorry. What can you tell me about the vehicle?"

I think hard for a second.
"Well, it's a classic Chevy."

I watch as the color drains from his face. He slowly asks me,
"And a license plate? Did you happen to see it?"

I try to think back to when I saw it. What did it say? SCARFACE? No, no it was…
"Sacrifice. It was spelled S-A-C-R-F-C-E."

All his humor is gone as he chews the inside of his cheek.
"I see."

He pulls out a small pad of paper and unclips a pen from his pocket, writing down the information.
"Classic Chevy, Sacrifice. Got it"

His reaction makes me hopeful and I press further.
"It's a small town; do you know who the truck belongs to?"

He shakes his head back and forth,
"No, I'm afraid I'm lost on that one."

He snaps the pad closed and says,
"Well, I can definitely look into that for you and go talk to whoever is driving this truck."

I hold onto my door frame leaning forward.
"Well, I'm sure someone would know if the driver was-"

Now his face grows angry as he speaks through gritted teeth.
"I told you, I don't know who drives an orange truck. I'll put it through the system and see what comes back, but until then, I expect to not have to respond to anything else that involves you."

I say nothing as his face shifts back into the one of the friendly town Sheriff and he says,
"Alright now! Make sure to pick that car up when it's ready!"

He turns, and I watch him walk back to his car. Suddenly a barrier in my brain breaks. He said *orange* truck. I never told him the Chevy was orange. I look up quickly and the Sheriff is standing next to his car. He raises his right hand, his thumb stuck out and turned to the side. He reaches over to the left side of his neck and drags his thumb across his throat in a gesture to tell me I'm going to die. I slam my eyes shut and say over and over to myself,
"It's all in my head. It's all in my head."

I slowly open my eyes as the Sheriff's cruiser kicks up gravel, backing out, turning around and leaving. I sigh as I watch him turn out onto the road, walking back inside, straight to my phone that still sits on the side table next to the couch. I pick it up, unlock the screen and press the phone icon, clicking on Lindsay Therapist and raise the phone to my ear.

CHAPTER NINE

"So you saw a dead body and then it spoke to you?"

I nod as I speak into the phone.
"Yes."

Doctor Lindsay sits in silence for a moment, the sound of a pen, the same blue one she always uses, I'm sure, scratching on paper coming through the phone's receiver. I hear a loud tap as she puts a period on her sentence.
"Melissa, I'm becoming overly concerned about these delusions. More than ever, if I'm being honest. You said that you've seen multiple dead bodies in the lake, one of which was a child. You've seen your deceased brother that

spoke to you in part of a dream, but you also saw him and this woman who was inside of a game machine in your dream, reflected in the bathroom mirror during your waking life. I'm worried that your delusions are trying to break free from your brain. They want to engrain themselves in your everyday waking life; they want to become part of it. Essentially, your subconscious is fighting to make itself integrate with your consciousness. Of course, the problem with that happening is you could face a shift in your personal reality to one where you are a danger to yourself and others. On top of all of that, you think there is someone who drives an orange truck that is after you and a local Sheriff that is threatening you, which based on the other delusions and hallucinations you've been having, we can't say without a shadow of a doubt that those are true either. All of that, plus the antlered man that made you crash your car."

She pauses for a second then asks the question I knew was coming.
"How much have you been drinking?"

My eyes cast down to the coffee table sitting in the middle of my living room..
"Some."

"More, less, or the same as before?"

Doctor Lindsay has worried about my drinking ever since I showed up to one of our first sessions, drunk. I tripped over

her coffee table and fell, knocking into a lamp and breaking it. In a slurred voice, I had told her to add it to my bill, but she never did. A good therapist, she was more worried about my well being than a broken lamp which is one of the reasons I have decided to continue to use her services, even though she is in Ashton, which is two hours away from Aima Island. I readjust myself on the couch.
"The same."

"Were you drinking when you saw this creature?"

I nod, realizing she can't see me, then say,
"Yes."

She gives a small sigh.
"I'm not here to judge you, Melissa and I hope you know that's not a place where I am trying to take this conversation. I'm here to help you."

For someone that isn't here to judge me, I feel very judged as I say,
"Yeah."

She takes the hint, not leaving space in our exchange and gets to the meat of it all.
"Well, the good news is that I can tell you why this creature and other imagery is manifesting itself in your life."

I look up quickly, my eyes wide. This is not at all what I expected her to say.

"You said this humanoid creature has the legs of a deer with hooves and large antlers protruding out of its forehead."

I nod, pressing the phone tight against my ear, eager for more information. After a moment, she continues,

"I think the message is clear. The deer is a symbol of transformation. This is shown naturally by the deer shedding and regrowing its horns each year. You are in a state of transformation, having changed your environment and *hopefully* your habits. Melissa, your mind has been in panic mode ever since the accident. You are caught in a never ending pattern of never feeling safe, never allowing yourself to feel comforted. I believe the many visits from your childhood to Aima Island have exposed you to stories of this cryptid; this, Mount Aima Antler Man, most likely just in passing, lodging them into your subconscious. That combined with your trauma could very well be why your mind has decided to create a seemingly physical manifestation of your internal panic. The orange truck is also a symbol of this, as orange is a color that can be associated with danger. This also goes hand in hand with why you're seeing people that are seemingly deceased. This isn't the first time this has happened as you reported to me that you experienced this while still recovering in the hospital. The point is all of these things are linked to each other and the last thing we can learn is that when you are presented with hard situations, the symbol of the deer teaches us to respond with grace and self control, something that I think we both know you are in desperate need of at the moment."

I sit back disappointed in this answer. It makes sense I suppose but, how would my mind know what to make this cryptid look like. Maybe like she said, it's little pieces of something I learned as a child and forgot. Her voice brings me back to the present as she asks,
"Didn't you tell me that your father used to tell you stories of mythological figures when you were a child?"

I hear her set her pad down on the table, then her glasses, setting them next to the pad. I can see the whole scene of her, dressed smart, in her office on the sixth floor. At the mention of my father and the stories he used to tell me, I choke on my sadness a little as I tell her.
"Yes, he was always interested in world mythology. He liked to tell me some of the stories before bed."

"I think your father encouraged a massive imagination that now is reaching out for the familiar to try and make you feel safe, but is having the opposite effect. This creature you're seeing sounds very much like a creature of myth. When we are put through something so devastating, our minds try to anchor themselves to something. When our brains attempt to block out a traumatic experience, it leaves a gap. Over time your brain will try to fill this gap in. This isn't always a positive step and can actually hinder you in your progress. I told you this could happen when you bought that house and moved to Mount Aima."

I look around at the house that surrounds me.
"You told me to shock my system."

Another sigh starts her reply,
"I wasn't suggesting buying a home in the town your whole family tragically died in and upending your entire life."

I take a second, thinking about how reckless I have been.
"So what do I do?"

I hear her chair squeak, meaning she is shifting positions; most likely looking over her notes splayed out on her desk.
"If you were sober? Well, I'd love to put you on Olanzapine. That would however be irresponsible of me, knowing your current level of alcohol consumption."

She pauses, allowing the silence to say what she doesn't. When I don't venture to speak, she does.
"If you're not willing to stop drinking, you're going to have to face your trauma. You're going to have to stand up for yourself against your internal obstacles and make the world mold to the way you wish it to be. You do have the ability to change your circumstances, Melissa. But my ultimate advice is the same as it has always been. Put away the booze and put in actual work on yourself. Are you pursuing your photography?"

I nod, my eyes glancing over to my camera sitting on the coffee table, knowing there are no more than a few shots cast onto the film resting inside.

"Yes. I've been taking some black and whites."

"Good; that's good."

The silence finally creeps in, a slow rolling fog that comes in thick, filling in every crack and corner of the hole in the conversation. This would happen every time we had a session, the two of us arriving at a stalemate every time; me not willing to ditch my addiction and her at a loss of how to help me further, without me taking the first step. I fill the empty space this time and tell her, instead of the other way around.
"Hours up."

I hear her inhale softly, then sigh, most likely checking the clock that hangs in her office behind the patient couch, to confirm that the hour is actually up. She wraps up our session by telling me to think about what we talked about and to call her when I decide I would like to schedule a video call appointment and I thank her, knowing *if* I do that, it's not going to be for quite some time. I can't have her see the state of my face.

As I hang up the phone, relief hits me. Despite everything that has happened, or that I'm imagining has happened since moving to Aima, talking to Dr. Hartgrove feels like part of an old life now, like standing on my own grave; everything from the past a rotting and decaying corpse left behind as my old self dies. An intrusive thought creeps through the lobes of my brain like a slimy worm, making me touch the thick scar on my neck as my mind creates images of the whole town of Ashton filled with wriggling maggots. Waves of them falling out of doorways and bursting from windows. Their white, pill bodies wriggling out of cracks in sidewalks and falling onto the heads of passersby from the trees and windows that sit high overhead. I shake the thought away and do my best to clear my mind.

I walk into the kitchen, taking my bottle of rum, the glass sliding against the counter and filling the silence of my home with noise. I pour three fingers into my mason jar, telling myself I really need to get some glassware. In an effort to relax, I turn on a 90's playlist that blares through the portable speaker on my kitchen counter. I know it's ridiculous to reach out for advice, then instantly go against said advice, but just because someone offers advice, doesn't mean you don't need to consider it and make your own decision. I have to think about what Lindsay said and I need time to think.

The talk of mythological figures with Lindsay has left thoughts of my father lingering in my mind as Third Eye Blind comes on in my mix and I belt the words as the sun sets, making it look as if a god has sliced through the sky with a giant scythe, spilling blood across the top of the world.

I unsurprisingly end up on the back porch once again, completely drunk, listening to the sounds of Aima Island, or rather the lack of sounds as the stars come out, dotting the dark sky. This time, on my way out of the sliding glass door, I found the lightswitch that turns on the two lines of string lights that start at each corner of the roof and come to a point at the center of the porch, forming a triangle of edison bulbs overhead.

The soft light coats me as I lay back in one of the lounge chairs, staring out at the branches of the trees that surround the house, reaching out into the night like hands with obscenely long fingers, waiting to grab whatever they can. I hear a now familiar sound of movement in the woods and sit up, straining through my drunkenness to hear, feeling the slick chill of eyes on me. A loud crack carries through the air sounding like something just broke an entire tree over it's knee. The echo fades out over the lake as my paranoid thoughts flood through my brain, a broken dam with nothing but shit on the other side.

At first, I see the Antler Man standing in the road, then the scene changes to my home; his red irised eyes looking through my window, watching me as I sleep. I am yanked forward back to my place on my porch as a crashing sound comes from underneath me. I run to the edge, looking over, ready to stare one of my hallucinations in the face, but am instead met with a black and gray creature, rummaging through my garbage. The raccoon looks up at me, it's eyes

flaring in the light from the porch as it chitters, holding a piece of pizza in its little hands.
I instinctively yell out,
"Hey!"

The raccoon practically falls off of the trash bin, hitting the pavement and doing a "Scooby Doo" run before it gets its legs under itself, turning and running into the woods, the pizza slice hanging out of its mouth..

I laugh at the ridiculous display of little furry arms and legs flailing, the piece of pizza almost as large as its whole body. I should have known better than to put an entire pizza in the trash and this is what I get. I shrug, thinking that at least it didn't all go to waste, as I turn walking past my chair to pick up my pack of cigarettes, moving over to the rail, only drunkenly stumbling a little. I light my cancer stick and blow a plume of smoke into the night air, the cloud hovering above my head, catching the light before dispersing into the night. The nicotine instantly floods my senses, mixing with the alcohol pumping through my veins in nothing less than a sweet symphony playing my senses.

I take another drag and cough on it hard when the ear piercing howl that I now recognize, rips through the night's silence. It makes me jump, but I manage to hold onto my mason jar, not dropping it and making more broken glass on the porch. I waste no time, no longer having any desire to investigate the source of the noise, quickly walking inside, closing and locking the sliding glass door behind me, having had enough of the nocturnal creatures of Aima Island, whether they are real or not.

I turn off the porch lights, not trying to make the lights on the porch act as a beacon for anything lurking in the woods. I totter over to the kitchen counter, examining my bottles of liquor. I decide to switch from rum to vodka, picking up the skull shaped bottle, moving towards the stairs, stopping to pick up my laptop, tucking it under my arm. At the top of the stairs, I look down onto the living room, my hand hovering above the copper plated light switch on the wall. Instead of turning off the lights, I internally decide to leave them on, convincing myself it's for no reason and not because I am terrified of corpses and cryptids walking out of the darkness. I lower my hand, walking down the hallway, lifting the latch and pushing open the heavy wooden farmhouse door at the end to go into my, until now, unused bedroom. I close the door, locking it from the inside like it would make any difference from stopping anything larger than a house cat from getting inside. I look down at the little metal handle and think about how many precautions we have in the modern world, but also how much of it isn't worth anything more than giving us a false sense of security and nothing more. Despite this thought, the lock *does* make me feel slightly better and I set my bottle down on the floor, next to the bed, crawling on top and taking a cross-legged sitting position. I lean my back against a pillow propped against the wall and open my laptop, making the screen illuminate and come to life.

I move the mouse to the internet icon, clicking it to open up a new browser before sliding the mouse to the top right hand corner of the screen, clicking a plus sign and opening a new tab. The search engine opens, suggesting articles and links based upon what it has recorded I am interested in or search for; the appropriate things anyways. Search engines apparently avoid giving you tips on suicide methods. I click the bar and type in *"creatures of mythology"*. Articles and images populate of beasts of all sizes. Lion heads, snake tails, human torsos, and horse bodies cover my screen. It is not the monster I've seen, but Doctor Lindsay was right when she said that the things from these ancient stories are close. I clear the search and type in *"Monster in Aima Island"*. Results populate and the first links to an article about a record size buck being shot back in 1999. The second is a paid advertisement for a monster truck rally and then the third link down catches my attention. It is for a website called cryptidcatcher.com, the description underneath the website name, giving a preview of the page the link will take you to, saying,

"Is the Mount Aima Antler Man real?"

I click the link and it takes me to a poorly built website that looks like it hasn't been updated in quite some time. The layout is complete chaos, looking more like a paranoid monster hunters journal than an actual website. There are sketches of different creatures with names next to them. Things like The Point Pleasant Mothman, Chupacabra, Bigfoot, The Jersey Devil, and even Bat-Boy, made famous by The Weekly World News, but later believed by some to

actually exist. I scroll down, looking through the pictures, some hand drawn and some grainy photos, then I spot it. A crudely hand drawn picture of a man's face with red eyes and large horns jutting from his forehead. I look at the name next to the picture and read aloud,
"Mount Aima Antler Man."

I click the name that is a blue link and the page opens, showing more sketches and amateur drawings next to a long article. I start to read, scrolling through accounts from different people, all claiming to have seen a giant man with antlers walking the woods of Aima Island. Some are outlandish; claiming things like the antler man gave them a prophecy of who was going to be the next president, or that they watched him climb into a 1950's science fiction style flying saucer to fly out of the woods and up into the sky, and even one story about seeing the Antler Man with Elvis, but as I get further into the article, things get less preposterous and more disturbing. Scanned newspaper headlines replace sketches. Headlines like:

ANTLER MAN CLAIMS SURGE IN AIMA ISLAND
WOMAN GOES MISSING DURING CAMPING TRIP
FAMILY DISAPPEARS WITHOUT A TRACE
HONEYMOON TURNS TO DISASTER
And finally
BOY GOES MISSING AT MT. AIMA

Images fill my mind of the little boy, dead, floating in the lake making me take pause. I close my eyes and take a deep breath, steadying myself before opening them and continuing to read the headlines that progress on and on, each one making anxiety seep into my body like a leak in a roof, slowly filling a bucket, drop by drop.

The articles all hold a similar theme. They are filled with claims that people come to Aima Island, but they never return, their disappearance blamed on bears, hiking trails, and the lake. One thing connects them all. None of their bodies have ever been found. After the article, there is a haphazard story written by the person who runs the website, claiming they have an account from a witness, noted as a Cryptidhunter.com exclusive. Presented in interview style, the man is asked to tell his story and goes on to talk about being in Mt. Aima State Park on a camping trip with his son when he came across a cave full of people dressed in robes with head dresses made from deers heads and antlers. The interviewer suggests that this could be the famed group called the Cult of the Antler, the name of which is highlighted in blue, showing that the cult's name is yet another hyperlink to it's own page. The man continues, saying he isn't sure about who they were, but that he didn't hesitate and stick around to find out.

After reading through the rest of the story, the man talking about running with his kid, leaving all of their gear behind, vowing to the interviewer that he will never return to Mount Aima. I scroll back up to the Cult of the Antler link and click it, a new page opening up. The article claims that there is a cult in Aima Island, founded hundreds of years ago, that participates in human sacrifice, specifically the sacrifice of people that travel here. The claims state that they are offering up these people to the Antler Man, who is named Krotus. This makes me sit up, peaking my interest in this name, since it has not been mentioned until now. Once again the name Krotus is a blue hyperlink and I feel myself falling down the rabbit hole as I click it. Another tab opens, this one a description of Krotus from antiquity.

It states that Krotus is the son of the god Pan, a fact that immediately grabs my attention like hands reaching out from my screen, holding my face forward. A skilled archer, he spent his time surrounded by the muses. Although interesting, I see nothing that would lead one to believe that a god's child from Greece would have traveled to the East Coast of America to terrorize a sleepy mountain town.

Then at the end of the article, towards the bottom of the page, the tone changes completely, growing darker with an urban legend saying that when the town of Aima Island was formed, the ground turned out to be infertile, the people who had settled the land, believing they had been cursed by the native people living on the mountain. There was starvation and disease that spread through the settlement like wildfire, the smell of burning bodies filling the air, the settlers trying to stop the disease from spreading. In their darkest hour, the people turned to a woman named Helen who had immigrated from Athens and joined the settlement. She told them an ancient method to make their land yield crops; one handed down through her family for generations. A sacrifice would be made to Pan, the god of the wild.

I look at the picture of Pan, set off to the side. He is very close in appearance to the creature I have seen, but instead of having the legs and antlers of a deer, Pan has the animalistic features of a goat, the fur stopping at his waist just like Krotus. The other major difference is where Krotus' antlers are massive and protruding from the front of his forehead, Pan's horns are tiny, placed on top of his head, amongst curly hair. My eyes drift back to the article and I continue to read.

Helen told the settlers of the Island that according to her grandmother, who was at this point long deceased, the larger the sacrifice, the greater the results. The townspeople decided that a human sacrifice would please the god most, despite Helen's warning that a sacrifice of flesh would turn the god feral, creating an insatiable desire in him for the taste of mortal blood. In the end they decided to not only carry on with the human sacrifice, but to sacrifice Helen herself after a man by the name of John Carver accused her of being a witch. When the decision was made, Helen pointed a finger at Carver and told him he had just cursed the entire town for the rest of time.

Helen was not offered a trial, instead being immediately tied to a stake on the shore of the lake, kindling piled at her feet while Carver stood in front of her with a lit torch in hand. He pulled a knife from his belt, walking closer to her.

He told her she would never point an accusatory finger at anyone again and cut the finger she pointed at him from her hand, letting it drop onto the pyre at her feet.

Right before she died, as blood dripped from her severed finger, sizzling as the flames carried the scent onto the air in the smoke, she called out to Krotus, telling him to come forward in place of his father, not wanting Pan to bless their land. The legend says the settlers watched as he stepped from the woods to consume her life force, making the deity taste blood for the first time and causing him to become addicted to it just as Helen said he would. Krotus, who had rested for hundreds and hundreds of years, placed amongst the stars as a constellation, demanded more and more blood every year, to which, according to the article, the town has readily provided. Despite feeding the god, the town never received their blessing and this is explained as why there are no farms or natural growing crops in all of Aima Island or Mount Aima, only trees and natural vegetation growing. Over the next two hundred years as people lost belief in the old gods, the stories fading into myth and legend, Krotus became known as The Mount Aima Antler Man, being known less for his divinity and instead, joining the ranks of other cryptids. This name of course is hyperlinked in blue, leading back to the page where I started.

I close the laptop and lean my head back. I think about how I have stumbled upon the truth of Mount Aima. I am not hallucinating and I have seen the result of Helen's curse.

162

Suddenly, I sit up, shaking the thoughts from my head and say to myself,

"What the fuck is wrong me?"

CHAPTER TEN

The next morning, I can't completely shake the thoughts from what I read the night before, but repeatedly tell myself that some piece of shit geocities site is not the answer to my problems. Getting rid of alcohol and getting on medication is, just like Dr. Hartgrove told me. I watch the tiny waves of the lake lap at the shore as I pour my coffee, the steam rising from my mason jar, who is honestly my closest companion at this point. I grab a dish towel, wrapping it around the glass that is not meant to insulate hot beverages and walk through the front door, headed out to the rental car that was left here for me yesterday. It is a four door Toyota, the logo making me think of a man with horns, before I push the thought away. I carry my camera, the strap swinging back and forth by my thigh. I set it on my passenger seat next to my bookbag as I get in the car. After talking to Lindsay yesterday, I felt the guilt of having only taken a few photos in this landscape and brought my camera out this morning to take more, determined to have a peaceful, sober morning. The car smells musty as I turn the key and air flows out of the vents. I roll down the driver side window and reach into the front pocket of my bag, pulling out my cigarettes, lighting one, not caring about the sticker on the dashboard that says NO SMOKING. I put the car into drive and make a small, tight turn through the lawn, back onto the gravel, heading out onto the main road.

Aima Island feels sleepy this morning as not many cars are out. I know the spot I want to go to to take photos and make it there without any trucks hunting me down or anything jumping out at me from the woods. As I pull up alongside the launch dock, I put the car in park and get out, taking in the view of the bridge crossing over the water, the sunlight dancing off of the small waves made by tiny gusts of wind. I brace my elbows on the hood of the car, looking through the viewfinder and finding the perfect shot. My shutter closes and a feeling passes through me. I'm not sure what it is, but it is definitely not depression. It's something closer to contentment. What I'm doing right now is the existence I imagined in Aima when I was packing all of my things to come here.

After taking a couple more shots, I grab my bag out of the car and my jar of coffee, still warm, but not too hot to hold with my bare hands at this point and I walk away from the dock, heading through the woods. After walking for ten minutes, the debris of human life; grocery bags, beer bottles, cigarette butts, and even discarded clothes fades away, being replaced with pine cones, broken tree limbs and logs with mushrooms sprouting from the bark. I press on, going deeper, conquering my newfound fear of monsters in the woods. My ears perk at every sound, but I am doing it. I am showing that I am strong and am not a coward. Sweat slicks my body as it starts to nag at me for a drink of booze, and I lift my mason jar, sipping more coffee to fill my body with a less harmful substance. After a few more minutes, I see the trees open, sand creeping up from the water in front of me. A rumble comes from above, making my eyes lift to the bridge that is now directly over me, cars passing by overhead. I snap pictures of the massive legs of the bridge, fog passing by as the water of the lake warms under the morning sun. Graffiti covers some parts of the cement, more bored teenagers looking to impress each other, when not shooting stop signs with a .22. I snap shot after shot, my mason jar sitting in the sand. When I return to it, the coffee inside is a disgusting lukewarm temperature, absolutely undrinkable. Some people will tell you that you can't just add ice to coffee that has gone cold, a crime against the grind gods, but I do it anyway, pulling out my insulated water bottle, removing a handful of cubes and dumping them into the jar, swishing it around, then taking a sip, my alcohol replacement consumable once again. A couple more shots and I put my camera in my bag, putting my arms through the straps and start to head back to the car.

——————————— ———————————

I'm half way back when the sound of a snapping twig comes from behind me. I whip around, my eyes searching every inch of the forested expanse to see who or *what* has followed me here. I brace myself, my legs ready to run. I see an antler come from behind a tree, dread filling me as the points reveal themselves slowly, the antler growing bigger and bigger. Another antler reveals itself alongside the first and I know this is the end. I made the stupid decision to come out here after what I saw in the road and this is what you get for making stupid decisions. You get fucking torn apart and gutted by an ancient creature a witch beckoned out of the forest. I feel myself about to cry out, not as brave as I felt I was when I walked into these woods when a head protrudes from the forest and a sigh of relief escapes me. The antler is attached to a deer's head, not some mythological son of the god of the wild. I chuckle, but stop as the deer steps out fully, his eyes trained on me. We stare at each other, neither making a move when it cocks its head to the side, examining me. I can't be sure, but as I watch its black marble eyes move around, I can swear that I just saw it bare its teeth at me. I squint looking closer at the slick substance covering its maw. The blood increases, thick streams of it dripping from the buck's mouth as it casts a full growl at me. I close my eyes, repeating my mantra and when I open them, the deer looks normal. It lowers its head, ripping a fresh grown leaf from a stalk, before chewing it and turning to leave. Another sigh of relief flows from my lips as I turn and pick up my pace, making it back to the car in just a couple minutes. When I get back to the parking lot, I turn to look back and see the deer standing stationary in the woods, watching me.

_______________   _______________

I stop at a Biscuit Barn, a cartoon cowboy on the side of the building sporting biscuit boots, a biscuit belt buckle and even a ten gallon hat made of fresh biscuit. I order a country ham buckaroo biscuit along with another coffee, this one coming in an actual coffee cup. I am informed by the tinny voice coming through the speaker that if I pay seventy five cents extra, my meal can come with an order of wrangler wedges and I relent, knowing that having an appetite is something I need to take advantage of. As I drive back towards the cabin, I sink my teeth into my breakfast sandwich, the warm, buttery biscuit, blending perfectly with the salty, fried ham. I reach into the white, paper bag, grabbing a wrangler wedge and pull it out, lifting it to my mouth. The warm slice of potato is dusted in garlic, salt, and dill, and I involuntarily make a noise of satisfaction. I finish the rest of the cardboard carton and take my last bite of biscuit as I pull into my gravel drive and down into the garage, brushing biscuit crumbs off myself as I get out of the car.

After I set down my things, I decide I don't want this high to end, this being literally the first good time I have had since moving here. I take my Biscuit Barn coffee and head towards the back porch, sliding open the glass door and taking the stairs that lead from the side of the porch down to the backyard. I try to enjoy the scenery around me, breathing in the crisp air as I take a walk down to the lake with my coffee, that for the first time in a long time doesn't have a shot of liquor poured into it. My camera hangs around my neck, swinging from side to side as I get closer to the lake. I look around and as inspiration strikes, I set my coffee down on the first board of the dock and walk down next to it, snapping a photo of the lake. I take a few more pictures, the time passing easily, nothing but the sounds of nature and the click of my shutter surrounding me.

Fog rolls off the mountain that looms high in the distance, reflecting off the water like mirrored glass. I close my eyes, embracing the peace and taking a breath of fresh morning air, forgetting about everything that plagues me for just a minute. I feel empty, but now it's in the best way. Empty of cares, empty of alcohol, empty of fear. A shadow starts to cast itself over my morning, my dark thoughts creeping in from the corners of my mind like spilled paint rolling across a kitchen floor. I try my best to not let them interrupt what I am doing; to not put an oar in and disturb what I know to be healthy growth. Despite my effort, they eventually win out over my moment of peace as I think about the man and his son, fleeing the mountain to escape the townspeople that murder tourists and offer their blood to an ancient Greek god. I push it away, taking another deep breath, finally feeling my body relax. I walk back by the dock, picking up my cup, surprisingly still steaming in the morning air and step across the few feet of sand to stand next to the dock at the edge of the water, letting the water lightly lap at the toes of my rubber boots.

Tap, tap, tap.
I open my eyes at the foreign sound that docsn't belong in this moment of peace.
Tap, tap, tap.

I look down and gasp at the gray, waterlogged hand sticking out from the water, the first, black nailed finger tapping the end of my rubber boot. My eyes follow the hand, down the arm to the head laying on top of the shoulder, a body washed ashore. The eye lids snap open, showing her white eyes that focus when her head turns to look at me, the bones in her neck making a cracking sound as they shift and grind together. She opens her mouth, water dripping out and down her chin. From behind brown teeth, a black tongue moves as she says,

"Why won't you help us?"

My body starts to shake, the fear that is this place once again filling my entire being. My foolishness that I could just start new, finding my home on this cursed island, fading away. I open my mouth, but am unable to form words as nothing but whimpers escape my lips. Her face grows angry and she grits her teeth.

"Why won't you help us?!"

I scoot back, not able to breath, all the air in the world around me being sucked into a vacuum. I cannot speak to this rotted corpse; this specter in front of me. She reaches out her other arm, bringing it down and gripping the ground to pull herself further from the water. As she does, my eyes dart down to her right hand where her first finger is missing. I cannot even process that the woman; the corpse in front of me is Helen as I watch her inch closer and closer before she braces herself, her legs popping as she shakily stands and reaches out her arms. Her naked body is covered in algae and full of bloat as she stumbles forward, making me turn away from her and slam my eyes shut.

"It's all in my mind, it's all in my mind, it's all in my-"

A heavy hand on my shoulder makes me scream, whipping around and dropping my coffee to the ground, the cup hitting the grass with a thunk, making the lid pop off and

coffee slosh out onto my boot. A man jumps back, putting his hands up in surrender and says,
"Woah! Woah!"

I look at him, blinking as his face comes into focus. He is handsome, his five o clock shadow and flannel blending well with the forest around him. My confusion as to who this man is and why he is here suddenly gets slammed to the least of my worries. I turn around quickly, expecting to see Helen standing behind me, but am met with nothing but empty air. I look across the lake, staring at the water, devoid of any bodies, gently touching the shore. A peaceful scene, lacking any of the terrors I've seen since I moved here. I turn back and reexamine him. He looks like he is made of this place. His combed hair and jawline making him look like a physical manifestation of the Brawny paper towel man. He lowers his hands slowly, taking a step forward.
"Are you alright? You were just standing here, staring down at the ground and shaking."

I lift my left hand, rubbing my brow ridge in a circular motion.
"I-I'm fine. I just caught a chill."

He reaches out a hand,
"Can I get you anything?"
Not wanting human interaction and definitely not wanting to be touched, I take a step back, shaking my head.
"Thanks, no. I just need to go back to my house."

He says nothing as I walk past him and back towards the cabin. As my hand touches the railing, right before climbing the stairs onto the porch, the realization hits me that I am the only house on this part of the lake. My cabin sits on a 15 acre piece of land and someone would have to *want* to come here. There's no way they would just stumble onto my land.

I glance back and see the man still standing by my dock, staring at me, watching me go home. Thinking about how there isn't a reason he should be here, makes my pace quicken as I climb the stairs. As soon as I get inside, I lock the door and slowly walk over to the windows facing the lake to see if he's still there. To my relief or possibly my horror, there is no one standing by the lake and all that is left of this morning is my abandoned coffee cup, a little dot on the grass, sitting in the sun. I tentatively open the glass door, walking slowly out onto the porch and lean over the rail to look around as much as possible, but do not see any sign of him anywhere. I am becoming really worried that my mind is deteriorating as I sigh, a single tear rolling down my cheek as I feel I am on the brink of a mental breakdown. My eyes drift back out to the water and I shiver as I think of the dead woman; of Helen, reaching out to touch me.

Walking back inside, I separate myself from the lake, retrieving my laptop from my bedroom, where I left it the night before and bring it into the living room. Trying to find a last sliver of evidence to prove to myself that I am not crazy, I open my search browser and search:
Bodies found in Aima Island Lake

Results populate and I click the first article with the headline:
 LAKE SEARCHED FOR MISSING PERSON

I click the article and read that four years prior, an effort was headed up by the Aima Island Sheriff's department to search the lake for a couple named Don and Hannah Burton that had gone missing in the area after camping at the base of Mount Aima. It seems the sheriff department ran a week-long search, turning up nothing to show the couple had ever even been there, all of their equipment and even their vehicle having disappeared before the missing persons report was even filed. I read further down and the article says this search brings back feelings from three years prior of naturalist and author Misty Martin, who spent time on Mount Aima, studying the local bear population. She also disappeared and a search was led, turning up no results.

I sit for a minute, thinking about how the lake was searched for Don and Hannah and then three years prior to that, Misty went missing. I open a new browser window and search for missing persons in Aima Island with a date three years before Misty went missing. An article comes up of a man named Albert Longston who went missing while writing his newest novel. He was staying in an Aima Island rental home located high on the mountain. The article says there was a blackout during a winter storm and by the time the sheriff made it up the mountain to make sure everyone was alright, his rental was empty and he was never heard from again. I search again, this time for three years prior to Albert. Another hit comes up. This time a whole family of five that were driving through the mountains. Their car was found empty and abandoned on the side of the road, no sign of what happened to them, not even one footprint left in the dirt. Three years before that, another couple and three years before that, another woman. I lose the trail a few times, finding that the further I go back, the longer the spacing between missing persons. In the nineties the pattern falls into a four year period, the eighties, five years. I trace all the way back to the fifties, where the pattern of missing people takes a whole eight years, making the pattern something that would not hold up as evidence for most people. I start to try and search the forties when I hit a wall, the articles suddenly stopping. The Aima Island Crier was started in 1949 and I cannot find digital records of the newspaper that existed before.

One thing is for sure, the disappearances do form a pattern and the celerity has quickened. For the past twenty one years, people have gone missing every three years without failure, except for now. Albert Longston went missing four years ago and then nothing. For the pattern to continue, there would have had to have been a death last year. I feel the blood drain from my face as I search the Crier articles from last year and I see it.

FAMILY KILLED IN CAR ACCIDENT. ONE SURVIVOR.

I stare at the picture below the article of my family's mangled car, the guard rail still sticking through the side. The next picture shows me on a stretcher, being prepared to leave the scene. I have never seen this picture of myself, bruised and broken, and it makes me feel as though I am not looking at myself, but someone else; some other unfortunate woman who had her life ripped out from under her in one quick swoop. Standing here, alive, it makes me want to reach through the fluidity of time and pull her out of that pain. As tears well up in my eyes, I decide I can't take it any longer and close the browser, shutting my laptop harder than I mean to. After a series of deep breaths, I feel my heart rate slow as calm or the closest thing to it creeps into my body. As I sit in my chair staring at my closed computer, I can't help but think that this gives credence to the Cryptid Hunter website. Could the people of Aima Island really be sacrificing humans to the god, Krotus? I shake my head, realizing I am forcing myself to admit to the fact that either I am having a complete mental breakdown stemming from trauma and post traumatic stress syndrome or Greek gods are real and one of their children is terrorizing the Aima Island area, killing people every three years. Neither option is preferable.

176

I start to feel the air leave the room, my suffocation becoming a constant theme in Mount Aima; in this space that overlooks a lake packed with the ghosts of dead people. I stand, walking over to the counter and pick up the bottle of rum sitting alone on the marble top. I twist off the cap that falls, hitting the counter first, then rolls onto the floor. I put the bottle to my lips and turn it up; but before the liquor touches my mouth, I stop. I turn the bottle down, looking at it in my hand. Whatever I am part of is bigger than getting drunk. My family's accident might be part of something much larger than my addiction. *I* might be part of something much larger. I look out the window above the kitchen sink and take a deep inhale through my nostrils. One that I hope infuses me with strength, before I close my eyes and turn my hand, dumping the whole bottle of rum down the sink.

I throw the bottle into the trash bin and return to my laptop, opening it, watching the screen come to life. Once I type in my password, I pull down my browser history and return to Cryptidhunter.com. I scroll to the bottom of the page where I find a link labeled *Contact*. With the age of this website, I know it's a long shot, but I click the blue hyperlink and watch a new window pop up on my screen, ready to compose an email to *info@Cryptidhunter.com*. Another sigh, not fully believing I am about to do this, but I steady myself and I start to type.

Hello,

My name is Melissa Monos. I live on Aima Island and am wanting to inquire about information regarding the Mount Aima Antler Man.

I think for a second about what to say then continue,

I am a new resident and am interested in local folklore of the area. Anything you could offer would be of great help.
Regards,
-M.

I stare at the screen, my finger hesitating, hovering over the mouse button. I close my eyes and click down, sending the message off into the void of internet space. I watch a box pop up in the bottom left hand corner of my screen asking if I want to unsend the message. I move the mouse, making the pointer hover over the "yes" button, but steel my resolve, moving the mouse off the button and watching the box disappear after three seconds. Deciding there's nothing left to do but wait, I start to clean my kitchen, first by turning on the hot water in the sink, washing away the pungent aroma of rum. I turn off the tap, drying my hands. The thought occurs to me that the skull bottle of Crystal Head is still sitting next to my bed upstairs. I turn to head to the stairs, wanting to retrieve the bottle and set it to the same fate as the rum when I hear a noise come from my laptop. It's only been a few minutes, but I see that I already have a new email. I open my browser and see it is in fact a reply from Cryptidhunter.com. I sit quickly, opening the email and reading the absolute chaos within.

Holy shit!! You're THE Melissa Monos?! Like from the car accident last year? If it's truly you and this isn't some member of the cult messing with me, which now that I think of it, I wouldn't be able to tell or not, except maybe if I saw your ID.

Yes! Yes, that's it. If you're the real Melissa Monos, then attach a copy of your ID to your next email. You can blur out whatever information you want. I just want to see your name and face. I guess if you have killed Melissa and have her ID in your possession, then I'm just going to have to take the risk.

Anyways, you need to be careful and not trust anyone. Aima Island is dangerous and everyone there is a killer. Seriously, Melissa, if you are in fact Melissa; DONT. TRUST. ANYONE.

Message me back with your ID and we can go from there.
-D.

I stare at the message, suddenly wishing I hadn't dumped all of my rum down the drain. Of course he recognized my damn name. I internally scold myself for being stupid while I stand, walking over to the sink to get a glass of water. I open the cabinet, but it's empty. I look around the sink, but my trustworthy mason jar is nowhere in sight, then I remember, it's sitting in the cupholder of the rental car down in the garage. I walk down the wooden steps and open the car door, reaching inside and retrieving the glass. As I stand back up, my eyes drift out of the open garage door and see that during my research, the entire day got away from me. The sun is lowering behind the Mountain, making the sky light up in pinks and oranges as it fades into the blue hour; the time when the sun is exactly at the right height to make everything take on a blue hue. Despite being scared out of my mind, now that I know the woman in the lake is Helen, I feel drawn to investigate. I return inside, mustering my courage and grabbing a flashlight, clicking it on to test it and once I see that it is good, head out the glass door and towards the deck stairs to cross the grass towards the water.

As I walk, I feel the lack of liquid courage in my system, swinging the light from side to side, trying to cover as much space as I can. Whether the dead people I'm seeing are real or not, I'd rather not have them come out of the darkness and make me piss myself. As I approach the dock, my light lands on the spot where Helen and I stood earlier, marked by my Biscuit Barn cup, making me take pause. A crack comes from my left from deep inside the woods and I jump back, flashing the light over the dense forest of trees.

As my heart pounds, I turn back and scream as my brother, Michael is standing right in front of me.

<hr>

I fall back on my ass hard, dropping the flashlight to the ground, making it roll a few feet behind me, turning to the side and shining to the right. I whip my head around to find it, crawling across the grass quickly, grabbing it and turning the light forward to see; no one. There is nothing in front of me except my coffee cup from earlier laying in the grass. I crawl forward again as quickly as I can, bracing the flashlight against my chest, pointing it forward as I stand. I take a step to move towards the hose and run directly into the corpse of my brother. The impact makes the flashlight break free from my hand once again, but this time it gets jammed between our two bodies, making it turn up and illuminate his face from underneath like we are camping and he is about to tell me a spooky story. I stare into his milky eyes, as I feel frozen in place, unable to move, unable to scream. He blinks once slowly, his eyelids spreading a thin film of moisture across his dead eyes, before turning his head down towards me. I whimper as the smell of his rot reaches my nostrils and I attempt to take a step back. His hands shoot out, gripping my biceps, holding me in place. His mouth opens and his voice, the same as a year ago, but with a rasp that was never there in life says, "You have to get us out of the lake, Melissa."

He coughs directly into my face, little specks of dirt and rancid lakewater spotting my skin, and it makes me slam my eyes shut and whimper again until he gives me one hard shake and yells,
"LISTEN TO ME!"

I open my eyes and he has disappeared once again, the flashlight laying on the ground, at my feet. I look around to see where he is, but my eyes land on no one. I don't give him time to return, breaking into a full run towards the house. When I get to the stairs, my foot slips on the first step and I slam my knee into the second, crying out in pain, blood speckling my skin.

Another unknown noise comes from the woods as I pick myself up quickly, despite the pain and run up the stairs onto the deck, through the open sliding door and into the house. Lacking any alcohol, I wash out my mason jar, filling it with tap water and chugging down every drop before filling it again and sipping it slower. As I catch my breath my eyes drift over to the laptop on the table. I sit down, setting my mason jar next to my computer and activate the screen, opening a new search bar. I type:
Aima Island ghosts and click search.

Results instantly populate and the fourth one down is a link to a website titled Aimaghostwalk.com. I click the link and the site materializes on my screen. My hopes sink as I read the banner at the top of the website that says,
AIMA GHOST WALK WILL NO LONGER BE AVAILABLE AFTER 10.29.21
Thank you for ten wonderful, spooky years.

Despite the feeling I won't get much help here, I scroll down anyways and see a woman in a cheesy Indiana Jones style outfit with a caption underneath that says,
"Aima Amy" leading a tour around the lake."

As I look further down, there are more pictures of Amy around town and at special events that appear to have been organized by the ghost walk. Towards the bottom there is a link that has a cartoon ghost standing on each side of the words, dressed the same as Amy. The link reads,
"Grandpappy's Ghost Stories"

Realizing this site is a waste of time, I place my finger on the mouse to move it up to the backwards arrow to go back to the search engine and look at other results, but something nags at me and I scroll back down clicking the link. The page changes and a picture of a man in a straw hat and overalls sits cocked at an angle at the top of the page. I scroll down past silly stories of goblins living on Mount Aima and even one about a Were-duck feasting on cattle back in the winter of 1957. I roll my eyes about to move on when I see a link for:

Helen, the Mount Aima Witch

A shiver carries through me, the vision of Helen standing naked on the grass, arms outstretched towards me flashing through my mind, as I click on the link. The story is pretty much what I've read already with one major detail that wasn't in the cryptidhunter.com legend. After Helen was sacrificed to Krotus, the people of Aima Island threw her body into the lake. Grandpappy claims that since that day, Helen haunted the lake. Under the story there is a drawing of what Helen looks like and when my eyes land on it, my stomach turns, threatening to make me throw up all the water I just drank. Looking back at me from my computer screen is the *exact* likeness of the woman from the lake who has spoken to me. She's been in my dreams, in my house, she has even touched me. I sit back, my lips parting as I say to no one but myself,
"It's all real."

I click the back arrow and scroll to the bottom of the page for contact info, hoping I can have as much luck as I did on Cryptid Hunter. There is an email, but the tours having ceased years ago doesn't make me place much faith in it still being checked. Under a header titled "event details" I see there is an address listed and I highlight it, copying and pasting into a new search bar on a separate tab.

When I search the address, I see that it is less than ten minutes away and, needing a break from my haunted property, decide to go see it.

184

My headlights light up a faded sign, the cartoon Aima Amy ghost waving from the corner. I get out, looking around to make sure I'm alone before walking up to the door. I cup my hands on either side of my face, peering through the glass to see if I see anyone on the other side. A voice comes from behind me and I almost piss myself.
"Help you?"

I whip around and see exactly who I'm looking for.
"Aima Amy?"

She chuckles,
"Not anymore. Names Linda."

I take two steps forward, holding out my hand, but lowering it when I see hers are occupied with two bags from a Chinese take-away restaurant.
"My name is Melissa. I just moved here and I was wondering if I could ask you a couple questions about the ghost tour. Well, really about the lake."

She considers my request, her eyes roaming over me before she nods.
"Come inside."

I follow her through the front door, my eyes taking in old signs and pamphlets for the ghost tour as we walk through the office area to a back room. We walk up a staircase to another door that she unlocks, opening up to an apartment located over the business. She sets down the bags on the kitchen counter and says,
"I got food from Jade Dragon. I'll make you a plate."

Food twice in one day feels like far too much, but I don't disagree, trying to use this opportunity to find out more information. She opens clam shell containers, loading beef and broccoli and vegetable fried rice onto my plate. She takes out small, single serving soup bowls and ladles hot and sour soup into each. We sit at the kitchen table and I manage to take a few bites of soup before Linda speaks first.
"So forgive me for the cliche, but you look like you've seen a ghost."

I look up slowly.
"It's why I'm here, actually."

I set my spoon down, clearing my throat.
"I've been seeing things out by the lake. I thought I was just losing my mind, but then I saw your website and your…grandfather's stories."

She chuckles again.
"Yeah, those are stories I collected. Grandpappy is just a character like Amy."

She looks up at me as she picks up a piece of beef with her chopsticks.

"What have you seen?"

She sticks the meat in her mouth, chewing and chokes as I say,

"I saw Helen."

I spend the next hour telling Linda about everything I've seen since coming here. She watches me intently, nodding and not treating me like an absolute psychopath. When I finish, she sets down her chopsticks and wipes her mouth with a napkin.

"I heard about Helen the first time when I was a kid. I would walk out by the water and try to see her, but I never did. I told my friends, my mom, hell; I told everyone I could that I believed she was out there, but no one believed me.

She sighs,

"Anyways, as I grew up, I did as much research as I could, finding the stories of the area *and* admittedly creating some of my own."

I raise an eyebrow.

"Were-duck?"

She laughs,
"No, believe it or not that is actually a real local legend."

She takes a drink from her styrofoam cup.
"It wasn't until after the Aima Ghost Walk was closed down that I finally saw her.

My eyes go huge.
"You saw Helen?"

She nods,
"Sure did. I was out at the water and I saw her walk out, gray and dead, a sharp contrast to the blue sky and summer day by the lake. "

Her face grows serious again as she asks,
"What do you think they want?"

I take a deep breath,
"I don't know. Helen seems to just be haunting me, but my brother seems to be trying to reach out. He told me that I have to get them out of the lake."

I tell her about the Cryptid Hunter website and the theories on the cult that sacrifices people to Krotus. I expect her to laugh, but she just nods in response.
"To be honest with you, I know about all the disappearances. Most of us do, just not everyone believes

they are anything more than people getting lost in the woods or attacked by bears."

This shocks me and I lean forward.

"Well, have you told someone? Why isn't anyone investigating it?"

She shakes her head.

"The sheriff and the cops over in Stadton, don't want to hear it, trust me."

She looks around her apartment and her eyes fall on a cardboard cutout of Aima Amy propped up against the wall, by the front door.

"I miss doing the ghost walk, but honestly people aren't really interested in something that's not just a fun tourist attraction, but actually run by someone that truly believes it, trying to prove there's a pile of bodies in the lake. I never made a ton of money from it and my sister always said I should shut it down and get a "real" job. The only reason I'm still in the building is the fact that people aren't exactly breaking doors down to open new businesses in Aima."

She lifts her styrofoam cup, filled with Pepsi and says,
"A lot of weird things happen here. I'll tell you that. You keep pushing this, be careful that nothing pushes back."

I nod solemnly while I watch her reach over to the center of the table and pick up a fortune cookie. She cracks it open and pulls the slip of paper from the inside, straightening it out and reading the words aloud.

"You've just stepped to the edge of the looking glass."

Our eyes meet as she raises her eyebrows and pops the cookie into her mouth.

WHO
AM
I

CHAPTER ELEVEN

That night when I go to my room, I use the lock on my door again; a habit I'm becoming quite used to. When I walk over to my bed, I look down, seeing the bottle of Crystal Head Vodka sitting on the floor. I stick out my foot, showing more willpower than I have in a year and slide the bottle under my bed, so I don't have to look at it. I undress, letting my clothes lay wherever they fall, before climbing into bed and propping my phone up on the nightstand. I turn on Charmed, one of my comfort shows to help me fall asleep and for the first time in a long time, attempt to rest, completely sober. Even though the show is the perfect amount of cheesy, the monsters of the week do not bring me comfort, making me think of the monster lurking in the woods, stomping on my car; looking through my window. I turn off the show and instead, I just turn on a noise machine app I have installed that offers rain sounds with a night light. I was never afraid of the dark, not even as a child, but ever since being on this island, I am finding new fears; ones that are coming out of the darkness.

I wake up in the middle of the night with a dry mouth, making me cough. I lay in bed, not wanting to move, swallowing saliva a few times, hoping the problem will solve itself. After a few minutes, my throat still thirsting for more than spittle, I force myself to get up and walk downstairs to get myself a glass of water. I turn on the light over the kitchen sink, walking over and turning on the tap to fill my glass. When I pick up the jar off the table where I left it before going to bed, a piece of paper is stuck to the bottom, naturally glued to the glass by condensation. I pull the paper off and look down at what it is. The words HIKE OUR HOME stare back at me with a water ring cutting through the center of the happy faces on the front of the pamphlet. I sit down, opening up the pamphlet to look at the map in the middle. I see that one of the trails named the Fovos Trail leads to a series of caves. It is advised by the pamphlet to admire, but not enter the caves. My mind thinks about the man's story on Cryptid Hunter who claimed to have seen the Cult of the Antler meeting taking place inside one of the caves on the mountain. I realize the water is still running and I stand, getting my glass. I take it over to the sink, filling it up and drink while I stare at my bruised, gaunt reflection in the window, the black backdrop of the night surrounding the house turning the glass into a mirror. I decide I'll hike the mountain and have a look for myself as I set the glass down on the counter and say, "Fuck it."

In the morning, I come back downstairs, grabbing my Jansport bag and setting it on the table. I unzip it and throw in some things I might need like a hoodie, my camera, and a change of shorts and underwear. I was always brought up to know that if you're going somewhere you're unfamiliar with, you *always* bring a spare pair of underwear.

I walk down, into the garage, each step echoing on the wooden stairs. I toss my bag into the passenger seat, press the button to open the garage door and as it rumbles overhead, I turn on my rental car, putting it in reverse. As I pull out of my driveway, driving onto the main road, my stomach growls and I realize two things. Eating food and not being drunk has started a cycle I am not used to of actually being hungry and, more importantly, I haven't had a drink in 24 hours. I decide that since I am still a walking rack of ribs, I can afford to grab some more greasy and gluttonous take-away before going snooping around the mountain. I am not the best person to go exploring caves in search of a 300 year old cult, but if it means I stop seeing dead people coming out of the lake, I will gladly volunteer myself. More than that I need to know if this group of people destroyed my family. I need to know that it wasn't a cruel twist of fate and there are people to blame. Someone to focus my rage on.

I drive in silence, the world and my mind clear and in focus when they're not being soaked in alcohol. I think about all the things I read yesterday and D from Cryptid Hunter, someone who not only believed me, but was excited at the prospect of talking to me. I haven't decided if I actually will respond, unsure of where continuing a conversation with someone who runs a cryptid website could lead, but it made me feel better about myself to know someone out there thought what I was experiencing was real. That and talking to Linda; someone else who claims to have seen Helen. In the past, I would have absolutely been skeptical about her claim if I hadn't seen the walking corpse myself; the same one that matched the drawing on the ghost walk website, exactly. I have never believed in coincidence, so I don't even consider it to be a possibility as my stomach rumbles again and I look at the fast food buildings passing by.

200

I must have lost myself in my thoughts because a screech followed by a blaring horn brings me out of my stupor as I look into my rearview mirror, seeing that I just ran a red light. I look around, trying to figure out where I am and then I see it. Parked in front of a Poseidon's Treasure fast food restaurant is an orange Chevy, but not just any orange Chevy. It is *the* orange Chevy and leaned up against it is the Brawny paper towel man from the lake yesterday, this time in a white t-shirt and a hat that matches the color of his truck. I grip the wheel hard, no longer able to contain my emotions.

"MOTHERFUCKER!"

I slam on the breaks, more horns blaring as I make a sharp U-turn, turning around fast, cutting off traffic, turning and gunning the gas, rage burning from my core, a pot boiling over, anger filling every crack and crevice inside of me. My tires screech as I turn into the parking lot and slam to a stop directly behind his truck. I hammer my car into park and get out as he looks over, startled at what is taking place. His eyes grow large and his hands shoot up in surrender as I point a finger at him and say,

"You stay the fuck away from me."

With his hands up just like they were yesterday morning, he says,

"Hold on now."

I slap one of his hands out of the way, swinging it up, knocking the bright orange trucker cap from the top of his head to the ground and speak through gritted teeth.
"Hold on, nothing. You have been following me, fucking with me, and then youre hanging around outside of my fucking house? I'm fucking done with that."

His eyes glancc over to the restaurant, then back at me as he bends over and picks up his hat and says in a low voice,
"Now just hold on, I'm trying to help you. You have to get out of town."

My eyes grow wide, a sick smile spreading across my face.
"Help me?! You are out of your mind! You stay the fuck away from me or I will have you arrested!"

Now he holds up his right hand trying to get me to quiet down.
"Okay, okay just lower your voice."

At this request, my mind decides to do the exact opposite. My rage burns hotter; a fire freshly stoked, consuming everything it can. My warning turns into a threat as I tell him,
"I don't know what the fuck is going on in this weird ass town, but if any of you come near me again, I'll fucking kill you!"

At this, two men walk out of the restaurant and one of them says,

202

"What's going on, Billy?"

He holds a hand up to them as he uses his other to place his hat back on his head, forcing a smile,
"Oh, nothing fellas, it's all good!"

He leans in closer to me and says,
"Trust me Melissa, I'm on your side. You've been marked."

I lift both hands and push him back.
"Fuck. You."

I turn, walking back to my car, past the two men who watch me as I pass. I stop before getting inside as I see people staring at me through the windows of the fast food restaurant. I turn, giving them all the finger, one mother gasping and reaching over quickly to cover her child's eyes, before I get back in my car and speed away with a loud screech as my tires burn out on the pavement. I turn out of Poseidon's Treasure, slamming my foot down on the gas, flying down the freeway, going faster than I should, feeling good about telling Chevy; Billy, off. I'm tired of all of this shit. I know I'm not crazy and I know I'm not imagining things because something is going on in this town and Billy is part of it.

The fact that he was at my house makes me feel unclean, wanting to climb into my shower and let scalding water flow over me. It feels invasive and I tell myself I'm going to have a security system installed. My thoughts break as movement in my rearview mirror catches my eye. I lean forward, peering into the mirror as I see the orange Chevy move out from behind an eighteen wheeler into my lane, speeding up and pulling closer to my car.

"Shit."

I consider that my anger may have compromised my safety as I didn't really think about the consequences of pissing this redneck off. My rental makes a revving noise that fills the inside of the car as I press down harder on the gas pedal, trying to distance myself from him. I look into the rearview mirror and see him switch lanes, following suit and speeding up to catch up with me. As I watch his truck creep closer and closer, gaining car lengths as he pulls alongside me, my stomach starts to heave from the fear filling me. We fly by cars, driving well past the speed limit when suddenly dirt kicks up from my right, making me turn my head to see the Sheriff's cruiser speed out onto the road, lights flashing and sirens blaring. Cursing again, I release the gas pedal, watching my speedometer fall as I put on my turn signal, easing over to the shoulder and coming to a stop, but when I look in my mirror, the cruiser is already stopped far behind me. The sheriff has pulled up behind Billy and his orange Chevy, already approaching him. I watch for a moment as they talk to each other through Billy's open window. I see the sheriff look up from his conversation towards my car. He stands up fully, turning towards me before he lifts a hand, waving at me to move forward; telling me to leave. I sit for a second confused. I would think he would want a statement, to hear my side of the story and give me a chance to explain what's going on, but I am honestly not entirely sure how these things truly work, and when he waves me on again, I shift my car into drive and pull back onto the freeway, merging back into traffic. As I watch their cars fade into nothing but dots in the distance, I can't shake the feeling that something feels off. I know the sheriff should have at least asked me what was going on and why I was driving over 100 in a 55 mile per hour zone.

———————————   ———————————

My stomach growls again, not relenting, so I drive another mile up the road until I see a roadside store called Mountain Grocery. Adrenaline flows through me, but I am glad the Sheriff has caught this man who has been harassing me the whole time I've been here. I pull into the gravel lot, stopping in front of a log laid on the ground to mark a parking space. As I get out of the car, my attention is grabbed by a mini merry-go-round placed to the side of the building. Each horse of alternating color have their mouths open; an attempt to make them look as though they are whinnying, but to me it looks like they are screaming, wanting to escape from the place they are being held against their will. To me, they look just like me, wanting nothing more than escape. I lean into my car, unzipping my backpack and grabbing my camera. Little puffs of dust move around my feet as I stroll across the lot, bending forward and snapping a photo of one of the horses, it's knees chipped and gray instead of white. I feel like I'm being watched, the hairs on the back of my neck standing on end as I stand back up to full height and turn to look at the door into the store. I think I see someone move away from the glass, but I can't be sure since there is a screen door blocking my view. I walk back over to my rental car, setting my camera down on top of my bag, turning to walk up the wooden steps of this store that looks more like a rundown hunting cabin than a grocery. I open the screen door first, grabbing the handle on the main door, then stop, reading a neon green flier that is taped to the glass of the entryway. It is from last year's Halloween, advertising a costume contest with prize money for the best Mount Aima Antler Man costume. Below the advertisement is a scanned, black and white photo of a group of children holding up their hands on either side of their heads; tongues out and eyes crossed. I guess I shouldn't be surprised. Many towns embrace their local legends, people donning red tinted goggles, horns and wings, claws and teeth to resemble the cryptid rumored to haunt their community; but because of what I've witnessed, it feels grotesque, making my stomach turn.

I press down on the latch and push the door forward, feeling cool air rush out from inside, carrying the stale scent of a window unit. As I enter the humble space, a small ding announces my arrival into this musty shop. My eyes land on the coolers holding a rainbow variety of beer cans and my throat instantly feels dry, my body craving booze. The withdrawals have already started creeping in, making me shake with longing, although I am trying my best to hide it. I push the feeling away, pulling my eyes away from the coolers as a man leans his head around the corner of a shelf to look at me. He stares at me for a moment, before moving back behind the shelf from where I hear him say,

"Let me know if I can help you."

I thank him, and when I do, I cringe slightly; my voice sounding too loud in this small space. I walk straight to the opposite side of the coolers, as far away from the alcohol as I can, where I find there's not much selection, this store catering more to the things that men dressed in all camouflage would enjoy. I glance back to the other rows of chilled boxes, my brain telling me to pick up a twelve pack wrapped in camo cardboard with orange writing, my mouth watering at the thought of the first sip. I internally war with myself, continuing to push the desire down as I remember one of the brands in the case running an LGBTQ campaign and getting "canceled" by redneck culture for it. They claimed that the beer company was trying to groom children to be gay even though children shouldn't have anything to do with alcohol in the first place. It would be laughable if it wasn't so completely stupid.

The thought breaks my brain's cycle of trying to convince me to break my newfound sobriety and I shake my head, reminding myself what I'm here for. I open a different door, grabbing two big bottles of water. I move to the aisle, picking up two extra spicy jerky sticks, knowing they're going to hurt my stomach later, but keeping them in my hands anyway. My supply run is finished with a cliff bar, a bag of Cheetos and a peach Redbull as I carry everything up to the front.

At the sound of me setting down the products on the counter, the man's head pops back around the corner like a dog that has just heard kibble fall into it's bowl. We make eye contact and I offer a polite smile; one that is not returned, his mouth staying in a straight line as he disappears again, a few more sounds of shifting product coming from behind the shelf.
"Be right there."

He stands, his joints obviously sore as he relies heavily on his left leg, his right knee visibly giving him trouble. He starts with a limp, but eventually straightens up, walking without any trouble as his body adjusts. He comes around the back of the counter, looks at me, his eyebrows moving up then down as he takes in the state of my face and my injuries from the car accident, then turns his eyes down at the things I'm buying as if he needs to approve of my purchase before it takes place. He doesn't have a barcode scanner, but instead, starts typing the cost of each item into an antique register. I find it utterly amazing that people who have had stores like this for such a long time have been able to memorize all the prices of the products on their shelves. He suddenly stops typing, looking back up at me and says,
"$15.65"

I nod, reaching into my purse, pulling out my wallet and paying in cash, sure that this establishment doesn't take card. He hands me back my $4.35 and bags my items, holding the bag up over the counter for me to take. I reach out, wrapping my fingers around the handle and say, "Thanks."

As I turn to head for the door, the man says, "I know who you are."

I freeze, turning back around slowly. "You do?"

He nods. "You just moved into that house on the lake. The Sacrficer's place."

His words make blood rush into my ears as my heart feels like it's going to beat out of my chest. My mind flashes the license plate of the orange Chevy; Billy's license plate, in my mind. SACRFCE; sacrifice. I force a smile. "Sorry, what did you say?"

His eyes turn up slightly as his brow furrows like he is literally trying to remember what he just said. "The high priced place. I heard about how much it sold for. Quite the pretty penny."

I want to get out of here now. I suddenly realize how hot it is inside the store. The sweat on the old man's forehead making me queasy as a fly lands on his face.
"Well, you can't put a price on privacy."

His mouth stays a flat line as he says,
"I'll have to take your word for it."

I turn to leave and don't look back as I hear him say,
"Be careful out there…all by yourself and all."

A breeze blows in off the freeway, the fresh air hitting me hard, making the sweat on my brow cake instantly. I gulp in breaths as I walk as quickly as I can, without breaking into a run, to my car. Once inside, I lock the doors before putting the key into the ignition and kicking up dirt as I peel out of the parking lot. I glance back in my mirror and see that the old man is standing on the porch, watching me drive away. I glance between him and the road in front of me as I say to myself,
"What the fuck is wrong with these people?"

I head back the way I came on the opposite side of the freeway, wanting to see what is happening with Billy and

Sheriff Smith. I come up on where they were pulled over, slowing slightly to get a good look, but no one is there. No orange Chevy, no cruiser, nothing.

"Hm."

I guess it didn't take long for the Sheriff to tell him to leave me alone. It is a fact that lots of "tough guys" crumble when they're put up against any type of authority figure.

I keep driving and don't even realize where I am on the road until I see it. The white cross an overzealous Christian decided was appropriate to place on the death spot of my family. They have hung a wreath of fake flowers next to the guardrail, where my family's lives ended and mine was destroyed. The events of today compiled on top of everything that has happened since I've come here make my brain go black and my vision red as I yank the wheel to the side, hitting the shoulder hard, stopping in front of the guard rail where my life was changed forever. I get out of my car, walking pointedly towards that ugly white cross, a bandaid on a wound I am trying to heal despite the universe doing its best to make the wound a permanent festering line of rot on my flesh.

I grip each arm of the tribute and pull up hard, straining as hard as I can with no fluctuation. The cross is rooted firmly and does not budge, but I try again, screaming out in effort as I try to release it from the dirt. A third try makes me fall over, sweating and breathing hard, but not ready to give up. I stand, walking back over to my rental car and climb into the driver's seat. I turn the key and glare forward as the engine turns over.

"Ok, motherfucker."

I press on the gas and the car creeps towards this religious eyesore. I hear a crunch as the front bumper pushes up against the cross and know I'm going to owe Jim at Mount Aima Paint & Body an explanation along with some cash when I bring the car back. I feel the marker give resistance and I press on the gas again, hearing a creak before feeling the pressure give way. I put the car in reverse and back up, getting out of the car and assessing the damage. The driver's side headlight is busted and the hood is scratched; something I'll just have to worry about later. I turn my head to look at my present enemy standing crooked in front of me. Cars continue to rush by as I let out another scream and run at the monument, kicking it hard with the bottom of my shoe. We both fall over at the same time, as pain radiates through my right foot. I take a minute, laying on the ground next to a discarded Sundrop can someone couldn't stand to have exist inside their vehicle long enough to throw it away when they got to their destination. Eventually with a foot that's still sore, I sit up, then manage to stand, walking over and picking up the cross by the arms, turning and throwing it down into the embankment. I pick up the wreath of fake flowers and throw it like a frisbee into the woods. The job done, I go back to the car, my foot aching with each step as I speed back onto the road.

I continue down the freeway, feeling my pulse in the arch of my foot as I take the exit for Mount Aima State Park. It takes me another thirty five minutes of driving through mountain roads and following brown, wooden, directional signs before I pull past another sign that says,
STATE PARK 12 MILES AHEAD.
I spot a drugstore on the side of the road, right after the sign and I pull in. I'm tired of people looking at my face like I'm some kind of trauma victim, so I go inside, buying concealer. Thankfully the store has self-checkout machines installed and this side quest does not involve more interaction with the "good people" of Aima Island.

Back in the car, I apply the concealer with my fingers, making the bruises on my face much less visible, using a napkin to blot and smooth the makeup and clean off my fingers. I pull out of the parking lot and drive for another twenty minutes, mountain forests passing by on either side and birds flying overhead, before I pull up to a wooden security booth, painted a deep brown, with a woman standing behind the glass. A sign hanging under her reads;
PARK ADMISSION AND AUDIO TOUR:$20
PARK HOURS: M-F 9AM-9PM
SATURDAY:10AM-7PM
SUNDAY:CLOSED

I look at the clock on my dashboard and see that it is 2PM. Since it is Saturday, that gives me five hours to find…whatever it is that I think I'm going to find. I roll down my window and the woman slides one of the panes of glass to the side, leaning out of hers. My quick makeup job must have worked because she hardly gives my face a second glance before telling me,

"Twenty to get into the park, please don't feed wildlife and refer to the included pamphlet I will give you for any questions on park etiquette and rules."

I smile and hand her a twenty dollar bill.

"Great, thanks."

She reaches into a drawer and hands me a usb flash drive with my receipt.

"Plug that into your car and it will give you the audio tour."

I look down and see the spot she is talking about, next to the auxiliary power outlet. I plug in the usb and look back at her.

"Thanks, have a great day.

Without any emotion in her face she replies,

"Yup, you too."

As she moves to close the glass, a poster hanging on the wall, inside the booth catches my attention.

"Excuse me?"

She sighs, sliding the glass back open.

"Yes?"

214

I point my finger at the wall behind her and ask,
"What's that all about?"

She turns and looks at the poster that has the M.A.P. logo at the top in a circle, the letters arched over a simple graphic of a leaf. Under the logo for Mount Aima Parks and Recreation are bold letters that say,

**HAVE YOU SEEN THE
MOUNT AIMA ANTLER MAN?**

She turns and looks back at me.
"Couple years ago, some guy showed up wanting to make a documentary about the Antler Man. I guess Parks and Rec. thought it was going to be a big deal; something that could bring in money, so they had a bunch of different posters printed, promoting the Antler Man, trying to get people to come see for themselves."

I nod,
"And did anyone find him?"

A laugh sputters from her lips, followed by a cackle.
"No; no ma'am I don't think they did. As far as I know, the movie lost funding and was never completed."

I nod and pull through the gate as she closes the glass window. I drive past pine trees and a statue of a black bear standing on it's hind legs welcoming visitors into the park. Immediately, my car starts to climb a winding road as a man's voice, backed by the soft sound of a bluegrass banjo comes over the speakers of my rental.

"Welcome to Mount Aima, where the wild things roam."

The roads are full of sharp turns and I make sure to pay close attention as I wind through one curve after another; a black snake of pavement laid across the mountain landscape for people like myself to travel easily to the top and have a day of mountain views, instead of actually having to put in effort to reach the top of a mountain. Each sharp turn comes with me tapping the brakes and internally being glad I'm not drunk.

"Mount Aima was originally inhabited by the Ye Iswa tribe before being colonized in 1779. Many people-"

"Wow, that's all we're going to say about that, huh?"

"-have made Mount Aima a destination for hundreds of years for its scenic views and beautiful wildlife. Settlers who first arrived consisted mainly of Irish, Swedish, and Greek peoples, later being inhabited further by English settlers in the early 1800's."

"The mountain, whose original name has been lost to the test of time, was said to get it's name from local folk legend; Aima being the Greek word for blood. Much like the witch trials of Salem in 1692, Mount Aima was not free of its own trials that took place on Aima Island soon after

the land was settled. Local legend says a woman by the name of Helen was accused of consorting with pagan gods, which led the settlers to blame her for the trouble they were having with growing crops to sustain their settlement. After a lengthy trial, the people of Aima Island found Helen guilty, her punishment being death. It is said that as she died, she called out to the gods she consorted with to curse the mountain and the town below, but in our modern time, we thankfully know this is nothing but local legend."

I think about how I have seen Helen for myself. How I have felt her icy fingers on my skin and watched her vomit water in my dreams. I saw her footprints in my house and have heard her voice. Nothing but local legend; right.

"Through the 1800's the town flourished, and would eventually become a destination town for the differing landscapes of the lake and mountain. On your right is your first stop. Park your vehicle and take a look over the guardrail at the beautiful expanse of land below; Our lovely town of Aima Island.

I turn off the radio and pull into a parking spot. There are a few people walking around, but the area is mostly empty. I look at the radio, thinking about the differences in the story of Helen from cryptid hunter and M.A.P.

Cryptid Hunter said there was no trial and that after John Carver accused her, the settlers instantly tied Helen to the stake. Cryptid also said that Helen was calling upon her gods to help with crops, not that she was the reason for the failing agriculture.

I get out of the car and walk to the edge where there is an established lookout point, a viewfinder that can be used if you insert a quarter, next to a sign warning to not climb onto the guard rail because of the risk of injury or death. As I look out at the "island", which is not actually an island at all, only being surrounded by the lake on three sides, not all four. I have to admit that the view truly is beautiful and I take a moment to take it in and ask my family silently in my mind to help me with whatever is happening to me.

A buck catches my eye, running sideways along the steep drop beyond the railing. It stops, turning its head to stare at me, it's horns making me have a flash back to the night on the road, coming home from Mountain Top Liquor and I start breathing fast as a panic attack tries to creep its way into my brain, its eyes making me feel like it is a lookout for Krotus himself. Suddenly the buck runs full force towards me, climbing up the steep incline with incredible speed, making me back up quickly as it rams its head into the guard rail, its horns slamming through the openings. Its skull makes a loud ringing sound from the metal rail and I hear a sickening snap. The buck falls to the ground, lifeless; it's body falling back down the mountain, into some brush. I look around quickly, but no one else has seen what I just have. I correct myself in my mind. What I *think* I just have. I walk slowly to the guard rail, peering over, trying to reassure myself that what just happened is real. There is no sign of the deer's body now and as far as I'm concerned, this can be added to the long list of crazy bullshit my mind has concocted. On the other hand, I have talked to a woman who claims to have seen the same ghost I have and I am standing on the side of a mountain because I have decided to try and find a cult that someone on the internet is claiming meets in a cave, so I can't really rule anything out at this point.

I turn away quickly, getting back in my car and leaving the parking lot to continue further up the mountain. The deer has left me rattled and I press the radio dial to turn it back on, trying to focus on the man's voice as he continues,

"Well, well. Welcome back! Wasn't that view amazing? On a clear day, you can see ten miles out from that lookout. A truly natural wonder."

I turn around another curve and the audio tour follows along,

"Make sure to watch your turns. Sometimes the mountain roads can be a little tricky to handle. Make sure to follow the speed limit of 20 miles per hour and take your time. Here on the mountain, we like to do things at a slower pace."

Another turn and my tires squeal as I hit my brakes, seeing I was going 45, my nerves feeling shot after I watched a deer commit suicide trying to get to me.

"Now if you look up to your left, you will see an amazing set of caves bored right into the side of the mountain. It has been debated for some time if these caves are natural or carved out by human hands. In the early days of Mount Aima, some of the settlers took refuge in these very caves until they were able to construct homes of their own from local timber, growing on the sides of the mountain."

I look up through my driver's side window at the caves that the man's account on Cryptidhunter.com claimed he saw the Cult of the Antler meeting in.

"Now don't get any crazy ideas. The caves are off limits for the safety of our guests. Many years ago, tours were offered, but it was found to be too dangerous to continue to do so. A good rule of thumb is that if the trail is roped off, that means don't go there."

I click off the radio. That trail is *exactly* where I want to go. Two more turns and I pull into the second parking lot, which only has one other car in it with a coexist sticker below a "save the trees" and "my other car is a bike" stickers. A kayak sits on top of the small four door and I wonder how much effort the owner puts into making other people know how much they love the outdoors. I look around and don't see the dendrophile that owns the car in sight, so I act quickly, throwing my stuff from Mountain Grocery into my bookbag and walking towards the cave trail that has a thick rope, painted orange for emphasis,

draped across the entrance. If the orange rope wasn't enough to show people that they shouldn't be there, a wooden sign hangs from the center and says,
NO ENTRY

I walk directly towards the trail and when I reach the orange rope, I take one more look behind me. When I see no one, I duck under and quickly walk up the trail as fast as possible, moving out of view.

———————————   ———————————

Having not been used for years, the old trail hasn't been maintained, now overgrown, and I trip multiple times on roots sticking out of the ground before I find my rhythm, looking down and avoiding the natural arches sticking out of the dirt, waiting to grab you by the foot. Even if it wasn't overgrown, the cave trail is not for amateurs and I am out of shape from pickling myself with booze for a year and not eating well or at all. Not to mention, I just messed up my foot before coming here and every step I take reminds me of that fact, shooting pain all the way from the bottom of my foot, up my right calf. I fall multiple times, sustaining cuts and sore spots that I know are going to end up as bruises, purple and yellow, spotting my legs like bad fruit. At this point, I'm just adding them to the collection, the ones on my face starting to turn a sickly yellow, hidden under a thick layer of concealer. There are large stones that

I strain to pull myself over, and there is even a part of the trail that is so steep that you need to hold onto a rope affixed between two four inch pieces of wood, one at the bottom of the incline and the other at the top, to avoid falling. This rope however is no longer there, having rotted in the center and broken, so I have to crawl up on my hands and knees, taking a few failed attempts before I reach the top.

I am drenched in sweat by the time I finally reach a part of the trail that is flat and my adrenaline kicks in, making me walk faster to reach my destination. I come out of the thick trees, ready to explore the caves and see; nothing. Well, that's not true, I see a mountain wall, but there are no caves. I look behind me at the trail I walked up on and wonder where I took a wrong turn. I walk back to the trail, retracing my steps. Halfway down, I see a place that looks like it might have been a part of the trail at some point and I follow it. I walk for another forty five minutes and start to look at the forest floor, seeing nothing but leaves and pine needles. I once again try to retrace my steps to the original trail, but an hour later, I still haven't found it and fear starts to creep in as my right foot throbs. I decide to try and make myself relax by taking a break. I find a good tree to sit against and open my bag, reaching in for a snack and a drink. After eating one of the jerky sticks, I reach back in and my hand touches metal. I wrap my fingers around my peach Redbull, but something is off about the shape. I grip the object, pulling it from my bag to see what it is. When the object hits the sunlight, I immediately start to sweat.

I turn my silver flask back and forth in my hand, my mind quickly diving into a debate with itself on what I should do with it and more importantly, with the contents inside. I know what I *should* do and unscrew the cap, turning the flask sideways to pour it out. My hand starts to tip, but then the scent of the rum lingering inside catches my nostrils and I stop, my mouth watering as I tell myself in my mind, *"Pour it out. Just pour it out, Melissa."*

I war with myself as the minutes pass by, the sounds of the forest surrounding me; but in the end, addiction is a bitch and I ruin the beginning of my sobriety with one of the most satisfying shots of liquor I've ever tasted. As the alcohol enters my body, I lean back against the trunk of the tree, letting it hold me up. I drink greedily at the flask now, a woman who has stumbled upon an oasis in the desert. As my buzz crawls through my brain, I hear birds overhead, carrying on with each other. A rustle comes from beside me, but now, I can't even be bothered by it and just continue to drink. I say silently to my family, the ones I wanted to solve this mystery of Mount Aima for, that I'm sorry and I start to cry drunken tears that stream down my cheeks. Suddenly my grief turns to anger and I yell out to no one,

"YOU KNOW, YOU SHOULD BE THE ONE APOLOGIZING TO ME! NOT THE OTHER WAY AROUND! YOU'RE FUCKING HAUNTING ME BECAUSE YOU LEFT ME! DO YOU HEAR ME!? YOU.LEFT.ME!

I break into sobs and the tears burst forth from my eyes again. I hear a loud crack come from behind me, somewhere distant in the woods and I instantly go silent. I lean to the side, twisting my body to look behind the tree. I squint, seeing nothing but woods as my head feels like it's swimming. I start to turn back around when I see a dark figure move behind the tree line in front of me.
"No, no, no, no."

I close my flask, twisting the cap on hard, tossing it into my bookbag that I zip and throw over my shoulder. I stand, running and trip over another root sticking out of the ground, making me fall hard. The alcohol slows my reaction and I don't put my hands out in front of me to stop my fall, instead slamming my face into the dirt. Pain rockets out from my nose, spreading across my face and down into my neck. I lift myself up as I hear a rustle behind me and stand, shakily, the pain in my foot and face present, but the alcohol dulling it as I run deeper into the woods. Branches scrape at my skin as they fly by, my mind not able to process any real direction to head in, just knowing I have to get away. Another loud crack to the rear of me sends birds flying out of the trees and I turn to look behind me. I see nothing, turning back to see where I'm headed and run face first into a tree, throwing me into a world of absolute darkness.

CHAPTER TWELVE

A cough bursts from my mouth, making dirt spread away from my lips. I sit up, my head pounding. I open my eyes and fall into fear as I see that everything is still black. My mind fills with worry that I have caused myself permanent damage in my drunken stupidity until I look up and see that I am not blind; the sky is full of stars.

"Fuck."

Something falls from my neck and I look at my camera, running my finger over the spiderwebbed lens, cursing quietly. I stand up slowly, brushing my hands off on my jeans, the skin of my palms burning from hitting the ground. A sharp pain shoots through my skull and I lift my hand, gingerly touching the dried blood that rests on my forehead. It takes me a moment to put together what I'm doing out here, but when my hand slides down over my scar, my mind focuses. I bend over to grab my bookbag and my whole body hurts, making me realize I have done more damage to myself than I first thought. Wincing, I pick up my bag from the ground, pine needles falling off of the fabric as I sling it over my shoulders. I immediately start in on an internal guilt trip, telling myself how incredibly stupid I was to get drunk out here. Nothing but a pathetic addict. I tell myself how disappointed my family is in me and that it's time to just go back to Ashton. I can't even control myself for a couple of days. I'm not going to "Nancy Drew" this cult mystery and save the day for the ghosts in the lake.

A howl carries across the mountain from deep in the woods, pulling me out of my self deprecating session fueled by my recent potation and I start to get very nervous, realizing I still have absolutely no idea where I am or how to get back to the car and now it's dark as well. I think about how stupid it was to try and take a trail that has been closed down for who knows how long. After a moment of scolding myself again, I start to walk, because I'm definitely not going to get anywhere by staying put. I walk for an hour, aided only by the moonlight as every noise around me makes me jump.

I stop, leaning against a tree and realize I have water in my bag. I set it down to unzip it and when I reach inside, my hand touches the cold metal of my flask. Anger burns through me as I pull it out, the liquor that remains inside of it offering a sloshing noise; an invitation to come back and keep fucking my life up. I turn, throwing it as hard as I can into the darkness and hear it make a thud sound as it hits the forest floor. I open a water and turn it up, downing the contents. When I pull the water away from my mouth, I gasp air, catching my breath, but immediately go silent when I hear a voice in the distance. I zip my bag and move towards the sound slowly, trying my best not to step on leaves and sticks. One voice turns into two and then three, the closer I get. I know better than to reveal myself to random people by calling out, so I stay silent, hidden in darkness behind the trees. I peer through and see that there are three robed figures huddled together. One of them is holding a torch that casts an orange glow around them, while another stands, smoking a cigarette.

"The time is growing near and we do not know how he will react if we do not deliver."

"You want to know how he will react? I'll give you one guess."

The smoker blows out a cloud of smoke and says,
"All of us will be dead if we don't give him what he wants."

He flicks his cigarette into the woods and I have to stop myself from making a noise as it hits me in the chest and

falls to the ground. They turn, heading into a cave, their voices fading. I whisper to myself,
"No way. The Cult of the Antler is real."

A chant starts up, coming from the mouth of the cave as I creep closer. I can hear the people inside, but have no idea what they're saying because the chant is in another language. I decide I have to get a look, maybe see if I recognize any of the weird people from around town. I have to know what they're doing.

I get close enough that the light from the inside of the cave gives my skin a light glow, my fingers sliding against the rough rock as I peek around the edge of the cave entrance. My eyes grow wide as I see a room full of figures, all dressed in blood red robes except for one who wears black. I cannot make out any of their faces as they are covered by masks fashioned from deer skulls; the one in black wearing a massive headdress, larger than the rest, placed overtop the hood of his robe. It is the skull of a deer with ten point antlers sticking up into the air, affixed on top of what looks to be a human skull. Their chant stops and I try to listen to the words that come next.
"The time has come. We are on the edge of giving our lord the blood that was stolen from him. Our time of withering is almost complete, for when he feeds upon the one that

was lost, he shall breathe life back into us all. We must slaughter the pig so we all may be fed."

The rest of the cult repeats,
"Slaughter the pig."

Suddenly the one in black yells,
"WE MUST MAKE HER SUBMIT AND SACRIFICE HERSELF!"

My veins instantly fill with ice, the sense that I have made a grave mistake by coming here filling me. I start to slide back from the entrance to the cave, hoping I can find my way back to my car and get off this mountain, but stop as I hear the leader say,
"The blood moon approaches. In three days time our sacrifice will be made and things set right."

Suddenly I'm pulled backwards off of the rocks surface by fingers grabbing my backpack hard. I fall to the ground and look up into the dark circle of a hood where a face should be, but only a skull protrudes from darkness.

———————————   ———————————

I open my mouth, a scream begging to escape like a convict halfway over a prison wall. A hand shoots out from the robe, covering my mouth and muffling the sound that tries

230

to squeeze between the fingers wrapped hard over my mouth. Another hand grabs my arm, pulling me up and pushing me to the side of the cave entrance. The robed figure holds me against the rock wall, the gaping eye sockets of the faceless skull whip to the side as confused sounds come from the cave, questioning the noise that I just made. The hole turns back to me, the hand on my arm loosening. It reaches up, grasping the hood and pulls it back. Anger replaces my fear, flowing through my body instantly, filling every vein, pumping directly into my heart. The skull turns back to me and a hand lifts, removing it from the cult member's face. I am not faced with a monster, some cryptid, or mythological creature. I am looking into the face of Billy.

———————————   ———————————

I grit my teeth, about to tell Billy the stalker to get the fuck off of me, when he holds a finger up to his mouth and shakes his head "no". He motions to the woods even further away from the cave and he pulls me away as the voices from inside the cave come closer. He pulls me past trees and I trip, trying to keep up. The further into the woods we get, the more I realize Billy is taking me away from everyone else to murder me and I start to resist, pulling away from him. Finally he pulls me into another cave entrance and lets go and I spit,

"Don't you fucking touch me, you freak."

He holds up both his hands and says,
"I'm not trying to hurt you Melissa, I'm trying to save you."

My ears burn as my anger radiates from the inside out.
"Save me?! Save me?! You tried to run me over! You have followed me, no; stalked me. If this is you trying to save someone, then I don't want to see what it's like when you hate someone."

A noise comes from outside and he reaches out for me, but I yank my arm away from his grasp. His eyes flick to the entrance of the cave where a light has just shown, someone searching the area. He looks at me and says,
"Please lower your voice. If they find us, they will not hesitate."

I whisper back viciously,
"Hesitate to do wh-"

Billy spins me around and wraps one arm around me, holding his other hand over my mouth as he pulls both of us against the cave wall. I try to wriggle out of his grasp, but stop when a light shines directly into the mouth of the cave. I hold my breath, not wanting to be found by this group of psychopaths. As I watch the light turn away and fade, I release my breath, at the same time feeling Billy loosen his hold on me. I'm still pissed at him so I raise an elbow, throwing it back into his stomach, making him try to hold in the noise from having his intestines rearagend. I spin on him and whisper angrily,

"Why the fuck does your little beastiality club want to kill me?!"

He straightens up, regaining his breath and whispers,

"You were marked. Your whole family was; a year ago. You surviving threw everything out of whack. I couldn't believe it when your lawyer let your name slip when he called about the house. That's why I set the price so high. I didn't expect you to actually agree and after you did, I had to try a more drastic strategy. I was trying to keep you away from all of this and I admit it may not have been the best tactic, but I thought I could scare you into leaving Aima Island. I thought I could save you."

I motion back towards the cave.

"I bought *your* house?! That's *your* house?! And what do you mean I'm marked? What the fuck are you talking about?! Are you and the Spirit Halloween crew for real or are you just fucking with me and dressing up to come have a circle jerk in a cave?"

His eyes go towards the ground. And my jaw drops.

"Is that *really* what you guys are doing?"

He looks up,

"NO!...No, that's not what we're doing, but I just want to say, it would be fine if we were."

There is something very wrong about "Chevy Billy" taking this opportunity to explain to me that he is not homophobic. He takes a step towards me.

"The house has been in my family since before I was born. We never lived there, just used it as a rental. I told everyone I was tired of keeping up with it and was going to sell it. The truth is I was going to use the money to run; to get away from the cult once and for all.

My face is confused as I try to take in all the information I'm hearing.

"Wait, you're telling me you want to kill me because I bought your house?"

He inhales slowly,

"No. People are picked at random, marked to be given to… well you know. You and your family's names were given and when you survived…"

Billy's features are lit by the moon and I can see his face is pained as he has trouble telling me what comes next. I take two steps back, holding up my hands in a defensive position.

"Billy, stay back. If you're trying to tell me that your little Mickey Mouse Club wants to sacrifice me to Krotus, then you need to do the right thing and turn yourself in."

He shakes his head back and forth.

"It's complicated."

"Complicated?! How the fuck is you killing people for ritual sacrifice complicated?!"

For the first time in the conversation, I see anger pass through him. I can already tell it is not natural to him. This is something learned, not gifted to him by nature.
"You think we're the only ones doing things like this?!"

He takes another step towards me.
"Do you know how many small towns in America alone are governed by pagan gods? Hell, it goes even higher than that. You think New York was ignorant to the fact that the Statue of Liberty is a representation of The Light Bringer or that it's just by chance that a building in Portland has a thirty five foot statue of a goddess holding a trident?! The government tried to revive George Washington as a god and when that didn't work, they tried again with Lincoln! That's why they both have statues depicting them as Kings of the gods! Plus, you know, not to mention the building that oversees the nation's security is the exact shape that fits a protective, five point star. They probably "accidentally" made their building have five sides, five floors below ground and five above. It definitely couldn't be so that they could triplicate the number to ensure its magical capability. Why do you think there is a full scale Parthenon in Nashville? You think it's just for decoration? I hate to break it to you, but things like this happen everywhere, every day. The only reason I didn't take the money and run was because I am trying to save you from it, so maybe you should fucking listen to me.""

A yell comes from outside of the cave, the cult communicating with each other that their search has turned up empty. I turn my head towards the sound and when I turn back, Billy is right in front of me.

"I couldn't save your family, Melissa, but I can still save you."

I look up at him, fear crawling through me as I try to maintain a brave face.

"What the fuck does that mean!?"

He looks up, past me, then to the side. He reaches down pulling a knife from his waist and I take a step back, holding my hands up in front of me. I watch him turn the blade in his hand so that the handle is facing me. I can see in the moonlight drifting into the cave that the handle is made of carved antler and I know instinctively that it is deer.

"Take this. Hide here until you don't hear anyone."

I decide I have to ask him; I have to know.

"Have you seen the ghosts in the lake?"

He looks towards the cave entrance, then back to me.

"I've been forced to be part of something terrible my whole life. I am always haunted by ghosts."

I feel like Billy is talking about metaphorical ghosts, instead of physical manifestations, but before I can elaborate he says,

"When I leave, walk back towards the cave. You'll see glow sticks on the ground that lead to a path. Follow the path down until you come out at the visitor center. From there, walk down the hill to whichever parking lot your car is in and get the fuck out of here. When you get back to the house, go down into the basement. I assume you haven't been down there because you haven't asked about the safe."

I open my mouth to ask what he's talking about, but he holds up a hand, glancing to the side again, feeling like he is running out of time.

"In the basement of the house, there's a gun safe. The combination is 0,3,7,9. I'll come to the house tomorrow and tell you everything."

Before I can respond, he shoves me slightly to the side and moves past me, leaving the cave and trudging through the woods. I take a couple steps, my back against the cave wall; edging closer to the opening, but staying out of sight. I slide down to sit on the cave floor, trying to calm my breathing, not wanting to be found by the people Billy just admitted to me, sacrifice humans to a pagan god. I hear a voice carry through the silent woods. One that I feel like I recognize.

"Sacrificer, where have you been?"

Billy's voice comes next.

"Just having a smoke."

"You know how important this time is for us. Don't fuck it up, Billy. You were already getting too close to that bitch in town; trying to finish her off yourself."

They are talking about me. I am the bitch. But if he was trying to kill me, why didn't he take the opportunity to do it two minutes ago? I hear Billy say,
"Yes, I know."

"Come on then. Everyone else is waiting to do the ritual. They're all in the lower cave."

I wonder how many "everyone else" includes as the footsteps fade and I wait five minutes before I stand slowly, creeping out of my cave, nothing lighting my way but the moon. I try to retrace our path towards the cave the cult was meeting in to find where Billy told me I would find the glow sticks lighting the way out of here. When I get close, I jump as I hear the familiar voice scream out from inside the cave,
"KROTUS, WE BEG YOU FOR YOUR FORGIVENESS. WE DEDICATE OURSELVES TO BRING YOU THE BLOOD YOU CRAVE BY THE BLOOD MOON. PLEASE AID US IN BEING YOUR LOYAL SERVANTS!"

I look to the side and see a green glow coming from under a leaf and I walk towards it as silently as I can. When I reach it, my eyes land on another, laying close by. I walk to that one, then the third, then the fourth and before I know it, my shoes are hitting the pavement of the road that leads all the way from the bottom of the mountain to the top. Now, far from the cave, I break into a run, my shoes making loud sounds as they slam down. I fall as I come to a sliding stop at my car, dumping my bag off my back and reaching in, grasping my keys. I unlock my car and pull myself inside, shoving the key into the ignition. I crank the car and am sure the cult hears it all the way up to the cave, but I don't stop to think about it. I slam the car into reverse and pull out of my spot, making the tires squeal as I shift back into drive and peel out of the parking lot, down the mountain. When I reach the bottom, I see the gate arm down, with the security guard having left to go home hours ago. I don't stop, instead pressing down harder on the gas, picking up speed before slamming through the wooden barrier, making it snap and flip over the top of my car as I turn left hard and drive into the darkness.

My headlights cut through the darkness as I head back to Aima Island, my heart slamming in my chest the whole way. I go through a checklist in my mind as I grip the steering wheel with sweaty hands. There is a cult, I am living in a house that was owned by one of its members and they are out to kill me; completing the sacrifice to a Greek god made over a year ago when the deaths of my family were orchestrated to take place on our vacation.

A flash out of the corner of my eye comes into view as a deer runs across the road towards my car. I slam on the brakes, but not soon enough as the car hits the deer, making it slide over the hood and come to rest against the windshield. I stare at the body, its head lulled to the side, fur pressed against the glass as I breathe hard. I reach over, fingers wrapping around the door latch and pulling slowly, making the door pop open. I unbuckle my seat belt and reach a leg out when a scream comes from my lips as the body on the hood of the car moves. I slam the door closed, pressing the button to make all the doors lock again as the deer starts moving his legs and bucking his head. He gains footing and presses down hard, leaving a crack in the windshield as he jumps off, running towards the woods on the opposite side of the road. Suddenly lights coat the pavement coming from the other direction as an 18 wheeler honks, trying to make the deer run out of the way. I look over, horrified, as the buck stops in the middle of the pavement, turning its head to look at me right before the truck slams full force into the animal, making blood spray onto the passenger side of my car. I feel my stomach turn as chunks slide down the glass of my windows. The truck doesn't take the time to stop, the driver most likely on a time crunch; leaving the road left in bloody silence as the deers mangled body lays in the grass. It takes a moment for my brain to realize what just happened and when it does I speak to no one except myself in my rental car sitting in the middle of a dark road, covered in blood.

"What the fuck?!"

240

My eyes flick up to the rearview mirror as I see headlights approaching behind me. I react, putting the car back into drive and speeding away, not stopping until I'm home. I stand, in the garage, the smell of copper filling the space as I stare at the carnage that is the side of my rental. I internally debate with myself if I should take the time to clean it now or wait until morning, but when a piece of furry flesh slides down the window and drops onto the cement floor with a slap, the latter wins out and I climb the garage stairs into the house.

CHAPTER THIRTEEN

My mind races as I run around, making sure all of the windows and doors are locked, constantly shifting my curtains to the side, peeking through the glass to make sure no one is in front of my house. Over and over again I try to talk myself down. If I am going to get through this, I have to root myself in reality, despite my brain trying to pull away from me. The trauma of my life has made me extremely good at dissociating, but I can't. I can't pull away from the fact that Billy just admitted to me, in a cave on the side of Mount Aima, that he is involved in a cult that performs human sacrifice to an ancient Greek god.

Despite knowing this, I don't know what to do. Of course my first inclination was to call the police, but what if they are involved? Who can I trust in this small town? Am I really going to let Billy come to my home tomorrow to, as he put it, "tell me everything"? The same man that tried to hit me with a truck, has been stalking me, and is in a cult? The thought of what Billy told me brings back another thing he told me in the cave. My eyes shift slowly to the basement door and I walk to it, turning the handle and opening it. A stairwell, just like the one in the garage, leads down into darkness. I spot the light switch on the wall to my left and flick it up, the lights flickering, then turning on fully, illuminating the space. I walk down the steps, each footfall on the unfinished wood making a thud with an adjoining squeak. As soon as the wall to my right ends, I see the empty room below, very much resembling the garage. In the corner, just as Billy said it would be is the gun safe. I walk over to it and find the keypad, entering the code he told me. 0,3,7,9. A loud thunk and a light that turns green lets me know the door has unlocked. I reach forward and pull open the door and gasp.

Inside the safe are a modern shotgun, next to another that looks much older, four handguns, an assault rifle, and; I freeze. I feel my eyebrows furrow as I bend over and look at a shelf inside the safe. I say outloud to myself,

"Is that a fucking grenade?"

I close the safe, turning my body to lean against the wall for support. I slide down, sitting on the cold floor while I try to gather my thoughts. Why would Billy leave all of this here and why would he tell me how to access it? Could he really be trying to help me? I consider the possibilities for a few more minutes, but can't decide on anything except the fact that I need to use these weapons to my advantage. I pull out my phone, opening my search engine and give myself a crash course on how to load and use the weapons inside the safe. I'm halfway through the training video I found on handgun use and maintenance, having identified the pistols as Beretta 92 FS nine millimeters, when I hear a knock from above.

I stop the video, sliding my phone into my back pocket and reopening the safe door. I grab the shotgun, a Mossberg, according to the photo identifier app on my search engine. I check to see that it's loaded. Billy wanted these guns to be ready apparently because I see that the gun has a full five shells inside. I close the safe, hearing it lock and run upstairs, stopping outside of the basement door. I look around, not sure what to do, my nerves screaming that I am in danger; that the cult is here and they want blood.

I stop moving, standing in the middle of the living room, not sure what to do next when another loud knock comes from my front door, sending me spinning around to look at the source of the sound. I stand silent, a spring clenched,

ready to release. The knock comes again and I pull up the shotgun, aiming it at the door. A moment passes and then I hear the Sheriff talk loudly through the heavy wood.
"Ms. Monos? Are you home?"

I walk towards the door, unlocking the deadbolt with a thunk and open the door slowly, keeping my hand holding the shotgun hidden behind the thick piece of wood. I fully realize the Sheriff also has a gun and that he probably knows how to use it a lot better than I do, but if he or anyone else tries to come into my home right now, I'm going to do my best to put a round of shot into each one of them. As the door opens, the thought passes my mind that there were a lot more than five people in that cave and that it was incredibly stupid of me to only bring up one gun. It's too late now and the thought is pushed away as my eyes meet the Sheriff's. He looks at me for a moment in what feels like an examination then finally says,
"Ms. Monos, how are you this evening, maam?"

I do my best to not act terrified and smile.
"Good Sheriff, how are you?"

He cocks his head to the side slightly,
"Well, you know, just wrapping some things up before heading home. I'm sorry to come by so late, but I wanted to tell you that I talked to Billy Walker today and got some things settled."

My eyes glance past him, trying to see if I can make out any other figures in the darkness.
"What kind of things?"

He sighs,
"Well, I told him that he has been making you very uncomfortable and that it would be best for everyone if he kept his distance."

I know I need to play this off. I need to act like Billy isn't the one who gave me a code to his gun safe and is coming to my house tomorrow. I raise eyes back to his as I gawk,
"Making me feel uncomfortable? I'd say that's an understatement. He tried to run me over!"

The Sheriff rubs his forehead.
"Ms. Monos, I'm just trying to do what's best by everyone. I've got a whole town to worry about. Tourists, campers, a whole lot of people."

I don't know why I do it, but before I can stop myself I say,
"Like all the people who have gone missing?"

He stops, his demeanor going flat. He responds in a low tone.
"Now what would someone like yourself know about something like that?"

I bluff slightly trying to get more information to figure out who I can trust.

"A whole lot actually. I also know that when I confronted Billy, he tried to convince me to leave town. Why do you think he would say that, Sheriff?"

He quickly snaps back into his "law-man" persona and says,
"People say crazy things when they're mad, Ms. Monos and there's some people around here who have just absolutely convinced themselves that outsiders are just no good. I couldn't tell you more of what he meant than I could the local drunks that tell each other they're going to fuck each others mothers."

I am no foreigner to the word or the act, but hearing it come from his mouth feels dirty and wrong. A moment of silence lingers and he says,
"Whelp, I'm going to go ahead and get out of here. You let me know if you need anything else."

I grip the gun tighter behind the door as I ask,
"Who owned this place before me?"

His face goes dark.
"Well, I don't rightly know that information."

My eyebrows pop up then back down as I give him a look of disbelief.
"No? Seems like something that would have been listed on the deed you looked at when I moved in."

I give a shitty fake smile.
"You know, public record and all."

He takes one step forward, closing the distance between us and stares directly into my face.
"I'd suggest you realize your place and do it quickly."

I lift the gun slightly, sweat coating the palms of my hands as I swallow hard. After a moment of silence his face turns back to the friendly Sheriff as I watch his eyes trail down to my waist.
"That's a nice knife you have there. Pretty unique handle. Where did you get it?"

I look down, Billy's knife sitting in its sheath, attached to my belt that runs through the loops of my jeans. I try to think of something to answer him with, but all that comes out is,
"I don't remember."

He nods and smiles at me.
"Well, have a good night.

He turns to walk away and I start to close the door, but stop when I see him slow and turn his head back towards me.
"Oh and Ms. Monos? Be careful out here. All by yourself and all."

My eyes grow wide at the recollection of the words of the man at the store and I slam the door, locking the deadbolt and placing my back to it, peeking out of the curtain next to the door and watching the Sheriff leave.

I am coated in sweat, wreaking of fear as I drop the gun, sliding my back down to sit on the floor. Tears threaten to burst from my eyes as I rack my brain to form a plan. Nothing comes and I really wish I hadn't gotten drunk in the woods earlier. It feels like a setback, like I would be able to defeat this much easier if that hadn't slowed me down. I tell myself that actually, truly regretting getting drunk is probably a step in the right direction. My phone lets out a ping and I pull it from my back pocket to look at the alert. I have a new email marked as urgent from *info@Cryptidhunter.com* with the subject line:
ARE YOU DEAD?

I open up the email and read;
Melissa,
If that is your real name. I haven't heard back from you and I know first hand how dangerous the people of Mount Aima can be. Please respond to this email so that I

    A. Know you're real

        and

    B. Know you're alive.

This will be very unfortunate if the cult has killed you and has your phone unlocked and are reading my message right this second...
OK, bye
-D.

I don't know if I want to email "D." back. On the one hand it is comforting to have someone that believes me, but on the other hand, he seems pretty on edge and I don't know if forming a connection with someone like that will be positive. I wrestle with the thought and then sigh, deciding that having someone in my corner is better than not. As far as I'm concerned, everyone in Aima Island besides myself and *maybe* Linda is involved in this and I need contact with someone on the outside. I open a blank email and type;

D.,

I am in fact THE Melissa Monos, but I must admit I am not interested in talking about my family's accident. However I do have information regarding The Cult of the Antler. I went to Mount Aima and found the cave they meet in. I was apprehended by one of their members, named Billy Walker, but he did not hurt me. He told me that he would explain everything tomorrow and after he does, I am planning to alert authorities and expose this group that thinks they are interacting with some ancient Greek deity. I will keep you updated.
-Melissa Monos

I take a picture of my ID and attach it to the email before pressing send and lean the back of my head against the door, sighing.
"This whole place is fucked."

My phone pings and I pick it up seeing I have another email from D. with the subject line reading,

ARE YOU COMPLETELY INSANE?

I am not a fan of his wording, another man referring to a woman as insane, and decide against reading the email at the moment. Instead I stand, pick up my gun, and head upstairs to carry out my now nightly routine of locking my bedroom door and trying to get some sleep. The difference this time is there is a shotgun leaning against the bedside table.

I lay in bed, eyes wide and staring at the ceiling. Of all the new fear I've accumulated, I have also started to become afraid of falling into the world of dreams and finding my dead brother there; or something worse. I am afraid if I close my eyes, Helen will be there, waiting to throw up water and grab me with her dead gray fingers. Another hour of laying in bed and I pull out my phone, trying to scroll news articles until I finally get tired. Without anything grabbing my interest I flip back to my home screen and see the red "1" on my email. I sigh and open D's email.

Melissa,
A MEMBER OF THE CULT IS COMING TO YOUR HOUSE?! Do not involve yourself with these people! You

may not want to talk about your family, but your family is at the center of this whole thing!

I hate to be the one to tell you this, but they were sacrificed, Melissa. Your family's car accident wasn't an accident at all. They were set up. And Billy Walker?! You should DEFINITELY not be involving yourself with him. He is the Sacrificer! That means that HE IS THE ONE IN CHARGE OF KILLING PEOPLE. You need to get out of there now! I told you, I've dealt with these people before! They don't THINK they are interacting with Krotus, Melissa. They ARE interacting with him. The lake is the key. It lays directly on a ley line. Blood is offered to Krotus, but the soul is trapped through the lake. You need to leave now!

Why are you even in Aima Island anyways?

-D.

So there it is. Someone else confirming my fears to be true. The things D has just said to me leave me trying to figure out my feelings. Billy Walker is at least partly responsible for the deaths of my family members and who knows how many others. If I am to believe what I am being told, then The Cult of the Antler not only organized the car crash, but did it in an effort to sacrifice us to Krotus. I feel fearful, but that soon turns into rage; rage that must be directed somewhere.

I exit out of the email app, opening a new search window. I type in ley lines to see what it is D is talking about. Results populate instantly talking about Earth grids and prominent locations. It turns out that ley lines are straight lines that can be drawn between sacred sites and places that have a tendency to emit a lot of energy. The Great Pyramid is on one, Stonehenge, Machu Picchu, and upon finding another website where you can view if you are on a Ley Line, I find that what D has told me is true. One runs directly through the lake. My eyes feel heavy as everything has drained every ounce of energy from my body. I close the search engine and turn on a sound machine, rolling over, eager to get tomorrow over with and get out of town. I know now that emailing D was a mistake. I'm not going to listen to some kid who has a poorly maintained website in the corner of the internet tell me what's what. Just because the lake is sitting on some imaginary line, doesn't mean anything. A howl comes from outside and I press my eyelids together tight, not being able to decide if my waking life or the land I find when I'm asleep is scarier. I moved here because of what happened to me and my family, because I was at my ultimate low; but the only thing I've found in Aima Island is that things can always get worse.

CHAPTER FOURTEEN

Just as I suspected, my dreams are filled with images of my family, the car crash, and specifically Michael, reaching out for me from the smoking wreck as I stand in the middle of the road, crying; asking me why I won't help him. It continues on a loop for hours, my parents twisting their bloody, bruised faces towards me and joining in with my brother, asking why I refuse to help them. Every time I reach out, their fingers turn to char, the darkness spreading up their arms before covering their whole bodies. They break apart, falling to the ground, nothing but piles of dust that blow away in the breeze, leaving me staring at nothing but charred and twisted metal. When the dream resets for what feels like the tenth time, the car hitting the guard rail and sailing into the air, I lift my head, yelling into the nothingness around me,

"STOP THIS! WHAT DO YOU WANT?!"

The world around me freezes, my family's car suspended in mid air, whoever is in control pressing pause. Everything has not only stopped, but all sound has ceased, leaving the dream world in endless silence, which allows me to hear bare feet on the hot pavement as footsteps approach. I look around and see Helen walking towards me. I feel fear, not sure I'll ever be able to get used to seeing the bloated gray corpses of the dead approaching me, but the difference is now I know it is because of her decayed appearance and not because I think she's going to harm me. I stand my ground as she comes closer, water dripping from her body and steaming off the summer asphalt. She stops in front of me, her neck popping as she looks up. She opens her mouth, water dribbling out, falling off her chin onto her bare. gray breasts and down her stomach. Her milky eyes move up and down, examining me before lifting and staring into mine. A gargled raspy voice escapes her lips.

"Hello, Melissa."

I say nothing in response, continuing to stare at her. She leans her head to the side, like her neck is growing tired from holding up her head. I hear joints pop as she lifts it back up, her movements clunky like I'm watching her through a strobe light.

"Your family needs your help."

She turns her head, looking behind her.
"We all do."

I finally speak, my voice shaky.
"Who?"

She turns back to face me, her neck bones readjusting, moving visibly under her skin as she does.
"Everyone who has been killed for Krotus."

My eyes drift past her as I see faces start to form from the ether that makes up the boundary of my dream, the features of men, women, and children coming out of the mist. My eyes drift back to Helen who stands still, staring at me.
"How many are there?"

She turns fully now, her back facing me with protruding spine under taught, stretched skin.
"Many."

They continue to come forward, a crowd of death walking towards us as she tells me,
"When the town; the town that I sought to help, signed me to my fate, I did not know that bringing down a curse upon them would have these results. I did not mean to cause so many people's lives to be forfeited and to have them join me in the lake, haunting this place for the rest of time. I did not realize that the lake was a magical nexus. One that would be used to trap all of us."

My mouth has gone dry, but I try to swallow whatever saliva my tongue can find to moisten my throat.

"And how am I supposed to help?"

She turns around quickly, now directly in front of me in an instant, her rank breath traveling up my nostrils as our eyes stare into each other's. She reaches out her hands and clenches them down on my shoulders.

"You are not the first to see us; the ones in the lake, but you are the first who has escaped the grasp of the cult. The fates brought you back to us to stop all of this. You have to stop the cult, Melissa. You have to stop the one that wears the antlers on a human skull!"

I wake up in bed, sitting up, covered in sweat. I move around quickly, trying to make sure I'm alone when a loud crack makes me scream as I realize it's raining outside, lightning flash followed by the bellowing sound of thunder as the storm rolls off the mountain. Gray clouds block the sun, casting the whole island in a shade that looks like the skin from the people of the lake. As rain beats at every window, I make a cup of coffee, pouring it into my mason jar. I think about how this is usually when I would have my first taste of alcohol for the day and my body pulls at me, craving it, despite how badly things went yesterday when I gave in. I down my coffee quickly and make another, eager for any kind of substance to be flowing through me, to ease the craving. Caffeine is definitely not alcohol, but it will have to do.

After I finish my second cup, I pack my clothes, ready to leave this town behind me after I talk to BIlly. I feel bad for my brother, my parents, and everyone else stuck in that lake, but I am not a ghost hunter. I am not some dime store detective who is going to save the day and fight a cult to lay people to rest. I will alert the authorities and leave this to people much more capable than myself. I stop packing, looking out the window at the woods in front of my house. I sigh and whisper to all of them,
"I'm sorry, I am just not the one."

———————————   ———————————

I drop my duffle bag by the front door, deciding to leave everything else I've bought for this house behind. After Billy says whatever he has to tell me, I'm going to offer to sell him back his house at a fraction of the cost. He can sell it to some other unfortunate person and do whatever he wants with the money. I am fucking done with this. I sit on the couch and glance at the clock on the stove. An hour has passed and still no word. I stand, walking out onto the back porch to look down at the dock where I saw him face to face just days prior. The rain makes the lake into a symphony of nature, the sound peaceful, but I know what lurks underneath. I look up and down at the shore line for any clue to BIlly's whereabouts, but see nothing. I sigh, leaning on the rail, letting the rain soak my hair as I breathe in the scent of the storm. Suddenly, my eyes catch movement in the water. It starts to churn and gurgle, something big stirring beneath it's surface. This time however, I know better than to investigate and I stand up, turning and head inside, leaving whatever wants to haunt the lake to do it by itself. As soon as I close the glass sliding door and turn around, my heart leaps as I see Helen standing in my kitchen. I slam my eyes shut and reopen them, relieved to see no one standing before me.

Another two hours pass, feeling more like four and I decide to not wait any longer. I grab my bag, taking it down the garage steps and throwing it into my trunk. I will get to Ashton and send money for this car or pay for it to be towed back.

I walk outside of the garage door and crouch down to look at the carving made by my brother one last time. I run my fingers along the grooves; something etched into the fabric of time when the world was a better place for myself. A lone tear drags itself down my cheek as I say,
"Sorry, Michael."

I stand up, trying to convince myself that Michael would want me to get to safety, not potentially risk my life fighting some cult. D was right about one thing; I have to get out of here. I get inside my car and as I drive up the driveway, the rain starts to make clear dots in the dried blood left on my car from the carnage of the deer being pulverized by the truck the night before. I glance at my rearview mirror looking back at the home that used to be such a focal point of joy, but turned out to be rotten inside; a corpse of its own, laying still, looking beautiful; but truly nothing more than a dead body, covered up with mortuary makeup.

I stop at the end of the driveway, looking back once more as I internally war with myself on what the right thing to do is, then after a moment's thought, I turn on my signal, listening to the clicks it makes as I turn the steering wheel and pull out onto the road.

As I drive towards my first turn out of Aima Island, passing the endless woods and the row of mailboxes, a leaf drifts down, floating through the air and landing on my windshield. It sticks to the glass, water soaked, the light from the sun hidden behind clouds, illuminating its orange color, highlighting the veins that sprout from its stem. I take my focus off the road for one second to appreciate its beauty, then slam on the brakes as I see another deer standing in the middle of the road. The smell of burnt rubber floats through the air as the deer turns it's head, examining my car and me inside of it. I stare back, my heart pounding.

Suddenly the deer whips its head to the side, focused on something new. I turn my head slowly to the side just in time to see Krotus, The Mount Aima Antler Man barrel out of the woods and slam his head into the side of my car so hard it flips over.

CHAPTER FIFTEEN

A scream flies from my lips as I sit up, panting. I look around quickly, not knowing where I am, as my brain works to catch up and register that my car being flipped by Krotus was just a dream. Movement makes me look down, seeing that I am sitting in the small wooden row boat that always stays attached to the dock outside of my home.

The sound of someone clearing their throat makes my eyes shoot up. I stare, speechless at my dead brother sitting at the other end of the boat. He lifts his head slowly, making eye contact. We stare at each other in silence until he finally says,
"You can't leave, Mel."

I whip my head from right to left, expecting the dead; expecting Helen to come surging from the lake, hands outstretched to pull me down with her. Michael speaks again, making me turn back to him.

"They're not coming. I told them to let me talk to you alone. I told them I could make you see what you need to do."

I finally find my voice, looking back at the house, then to him.

"What am I supposed to do, Michael? I'm trying to deal with my own problems. I am trying to work through my own shit; through Mom and Dad…and *you* dying. I'm trying to stop drinking myself to death every day and on top of that, a lake full of dead people want me to stop a cult that meets in a cave in the mountains and sacrifices people?"

I shake my head,

"I'm afraid I'm just not cut out for that."

A millipede crawls across Michael's face and he reaches up with gray, waterlogged fingers, plucking it off and flicking it into the lake.

"You have to be cut out for it. You have to find a way."

Frustration fills me.

"Why? Why do *I* have to be the one?"

Sadness fills his face as he stares at me.

"Because they marked you, M. They marked all of us, but you're the only one they've marked for death who survived."

I close my eyes for a split second, but open them quickly as I feel hands on my shoulders. Michael looks at me directly in the face, his eyes milky white; the eyes of the dead.
"They will always hunt you, Melissa. They will not stop until their god sinks his teeth into your flesh and quenches his thirst with your blood."

He releases me at the same time that I pull away and my back hits the side of the boat hard. I reach out my hands for him, but it is too late, our fingers brushing against each other as I fall backwards, my back hitting the water and I open my eyes for the second time.

___________________   ___________________

I look around the inside of my house, having fallen asleep sitting on my couch, waiting for Billy. My duffle bag lays by the front door, urging me to pick it up and leave. I stand, walking over to the sliding glass door and look out. A gray figure in the boat, still tied to the dock catches my eye and I rub the sleep from them, looking again, this time at an empty boat that floats in the miniature waves made on the lake by the passing wind coming down from the mountain. I take a deep breath, Michael's words of always being hunted lingering in my mind like the stale taste of beer when you wake up from a three day binge.

"Fine."

I turn, walking through the kitchen and grabbing my keys off the counter. I look at my duffle before I turn, leaving it where it is as I walk down the stairs to the basement. I type in the code to the safe and when I hear the thunk sound, I open the door, reaching down and taking one of the 9mm pistols, sticking it into my purse. I close the safe, walking back up the stairs to walk down an identical set into the garage. I toss my purse onto the passenger seat and crank up my rental car, that is still covered in deer's blood. I hold my phone up, pressing and holding the button on the side that will activate the digital assistant. When it makes a noise for me to speak, I tell it,

"Take me to the sheriff's office."

———————————   ———————————

The station is only ten minutes away, the drive holding gray, cloudy skies and the same old pine trees, casting shadows across my car as I drive down the road. A couple times at stop signs, I try to press my right thumb through the palm of my left hand, a tactic I learned when I first started having trauma based hallucinations. The thought behind the exercise is that if you believe you can press your finger through your palm and it works, you are in a dream.

If it doesn't work, you are in the waking world of reality. When I press my thumb down and it holds against the flesh of my palm, refusing to move through, I decide I am in the real world and press down on the gas, continuing on my way. I pull into a gas station that has a QWIK CAR WASH and pay ten dollars, pulling through and letting the suds and flaps whip away the deer's blood coating the car. I pull out, park and get out to inspect the machine's work before deciding to go through again, just to make sure the sheriff doesn't have a reason to ask me about my car being covered in blood.

I pull in past Sheriff Smith's lone cruiser parked crooked in a parking spot next to a blue Jetta. I park and walk inside where I am met by a desk with a woman in her twenties, filing her fake nails, visually bored with her circumstance. Her heavily shadowed eyelids flick up as she looks at me. I see her face make a small movement, almost undetectable, but I swear I see her eyes narrow when she looks into my face, recognition covering hers, even though we've never met. Her accent is as thick as molasses as she asks me, "Can I help you?"

I keep my purse close, knowing there is a gun inside that is not registered to me and I take a breath.
"Yes, I was hoping to talk to Sheriff Smith."

She, continuing to inspect and file her nails, tells me without looking up,

266

"The sheriff isn't available at the moment, but I would be happy to take a message and have him get back to you."
I look around the empty room, wondering what could possibly be "keeping the sheriff busy." I lean forward, placing my hands on her desk. The movement and interjection into her personal space, makes her file come to a stop, her eyes lifting up to look into mine.
"Well-"

I turn my head slightly showing her that this is the point where she tells me her name.
"Charlene."

"-Well, Charlene. Really, Billy Walker is the one I want to talk to. You look like you've lived in Aima for a while. Maybe you can point me in the right direction."

She picks up on the dig of me insinuating that she's small town and opens her mouth to give me a quippy reply, but before she can, Sheriff Smith's voice comes from the back of the room , making me look up.
"Why do you want to talk to Billy Walker?"

I stand up fully, my brain rushing to form a lie.
"He-uh, he wanted to talk to me; to apologize I think. You talking to him must have worked."

Sheriff Smith stares at me then says,

"Hmm. Well, unfortunately Billy Walker left town yesterday. Something about a job a few towns over. Won't be back for a while as I understand."

The air in the room suddenly feels thin as alarms go off in my brain, his response wreaking of a lie, but I smile and say,
"Oh, how odd. He told me yesterday he wanted to talk to me today."

I shrug,
"Must have slipped his mind."

I turn to leave when the Sheriff's voice makes me stop in my tracks,
"I talked to Jim this morning. Said your car's ready. Might want to stop by and take care of that."

I slowly turn around, a fake smile plastered on my face from ear to ear.
"Well, thank you, Sheriff."

He nods his head at me and I turn again, walking through the doors to the freedom of the outside world. Once I'm back in my rental car, my hand instinctively moves to the controls on the driver side door, pressing the button with a picture of a closed padlock. An audible click carries through the silent car, making me, once again, feel a false sense of security; having closed myself in a metal cage to feel protected from the outside world; a metal cage that is half, very breakable, glass. I slowly inhale, filling my lungs, before letting the spent air carry back into the empty space around me. I stare through the windshield before my anger boils over and I hit my fist on the dashboard. Billy used me. He got me to wait so the cult would keep their eyes on me instead of him. He left me here and ran. A job a few towns over. Yeah, right.

I slide the key into the ignition, turning and cranking the car up. I look in the rearview mirror and see the sheriff standing outside of the front door watching me as I back up and pull away.

———————————   ———————————

Down the road I pull over, taking a few more breaths before I ask my phone where Mount Aima Paint & Body is located. It thinks for a minute before pulling up the address and directions, a map generated with a blue line leading from the dot, which is me, to the destination. I glance into the side mirror, making sure no one is coming towards me on the road and shift the car back into drive, pulling from the side back onto the asphalt.

When I get to the shop, I see my car sitting in the garage as I pull into a free spot. A small bell rings when I enter the waiting room that smells like oil and bad coffee. Not a moment later and the door leading from the waiting room

to the garage opens, a man stepping in with a patch on his shirt that reads, "Jim." He finishes wiping his hands on a rag that is so dirty, there's no way anyone could convince me that it's cleaning anything. He tosses the once orange rag onto the desk in front of me and asks,
"Help you?"

I start to reach in my purse while explaining why I'm there. "The Honda in the garage is mine. Sheriff Smith said it was ready for me to pick up?"

I don't have enough effort to make my smile not come across as completely fake and ingenuine. My hand moves past Billy's pistol in my purse and my fingers grip my wallet, removing it from my bag.
"How much do I owe you?"

The smile falls from his face and I think I see a flicker of anger in his eyes, before it vanishes, his face turning back to normal.
"Total comes to seven thousand, three hundred, and twenty dollars."

This is an amount that would normally make me gawk and demand to see a list of what was done to the vehicle, but I just hand over my card. He takes it, running it through his now ancient credit card reader. As the machine "thinks", sending signals back and forth to verify and charge my card, I realize the smell of oil mixed with body order has filled and permeated every inch of the room. The smell is thick and each breath makes me feel more sick to my stomach. I feel my mouth start to water in the way that only happens before you throw up. I turn, ready to run outside when Jim says,

"All done. There you go."

I turn back, looking down at his hand gripping my card, dirt and who knows what else caked under his nails. I take the card slowly and drop it into my purse as he walks back out to the garage. I quickly step outside, gulping breaths of fresh air, trying to calm myself. I hear my car crank up in the garage and moments later, see it pulling around the side of the building with Jim behind the wheel. My eyes move from my car to one parked half way behind the side of the brick building. It is covered in a tarp, but I can see that the color of the tailgate peeking out from underneath is a burnt orange. Ice flows through my veins as my eyes drift down and I see the license plate. S-A-C-R-F-C-E. The realization that someone has done something to Billy and stashed his car here dawns on me. I'm broken from my trance by Jim who is already standing outside of my car, the engine running,

"She's all yours."

I hand him the keys to the rental and watch his eyes glance over to the car, sitting in a parking space.

"Woah. What happened to my rental?!"

I get in my car, quickly shifting into drive and pulling away as I roll down the window and call out,

"Send me the bill!"

Once I hit the main road, I roll down all of the windows, trying my best to get Jim's overwhelming stink out of the vehicle. The fresh air rushes into the car and I gulp it thankfully. As I come to a stop at the red light, I try to decide what to do next. One person whose willing to help me is on the internet and can't physically do anything to help. One is a member of the cult and has now vanished, his car stashed at the local body shop. And the last is an ex ghost hunter that says she has also seen Helen, but-

Terror rushes into me as I realize that if the cult knows I talked to Billy, they probably know I talked to Linda. I pull out my phone, pulling up her number and sending the call through, the sound of the phone ringing, coming through my car speakers. The phone continues to ring and ring until the automated voice comes through, telling me the person I am trying to reach is unavailable. I click off the phone. "Shit."

The light turns green and I press down on the gas pedal, easing forward, determined to drive to the tour shop and make sure Linda is alive and okay, but movement from my right makes me slam on my breaks as a buck runs out into the road and stops, turning his head to stare at me inside of my car. The deer's movement makes me afraid I'm stuck in another false reality, actually at home asleep in my bed, but I know I'm not. This is real.

Another blur of movement makes me break my stare and turn my head back to the right as a dozen deer come running out of the woods and over the road, heading towards the other side. More movement comes from the trees and a sea of brown fur comes bursting from the pines. Hundreds of bucks, does, and fawns' hooves hit the pavement as they all cross under the guard of the giant buck in front of me. Just like the cult, they are watched over by the one with the biggest antlers. I stare with my mouth open as they keep coming from the woods in a torrent of brown. When the rush finally stops, one last deer limps across the road, covered in blood and missing a patch of fur. The realization dawns on me that it is the same patch of fur that fell off my car onto the garage floor. My lips part and I whisper to myself.

"He is the deer. They are all Krotus."

As the injured animal crosses the road, the buck turns his body to match his head, the whole of him now directed towards me. He raises his head slightly before lowering it and pressing off the ground, running full speed towards my car. Fear fills me, making my insides feel rotten. I shove my thumb into my palm, trying to make myself wake from this nightmare, but nothing happens. I jam harder as he comes closer to impact. I yell,

"IT'S ALL IN MY HEAD!"

I look down at my thumb pressed against my palm and something in me shifts. I am sick and tired of the world, the cult; and Krotus fucking with me. My instinct kicks in, this

time to fight instead of run. I slam my foot down on the gas, making my tires spin and scream and the rubber burns on the pavement. I fly forward and slam into his body, making him flip up over the hood, his face slamming into the glass and spraying blood from his mouth in an ark across the windshield. I slam on the brakes and the car stops, the deer's body falling off the front of the hood as I breathe hard, my mind racing to register what just happened. As my pulse slows, I realize I just absolutely destroyed my car that I just paid over seven thousand dollars to have repaired.
"FUCK!"

I slam my hands on the steering wheel, closing my eyes as tears fall down my cheeks.
"FUCK! FUCK! FUCK!"

I catch my breath and decide to get off the road where I can be seen by anyone. I shift my car into reverse and back up to drive around the buck's body…that isn't there.

I push up, lifting off my seat to get a better view out of the windshield, but there is nothing on the ground besides a red stain from where the deer's body was just moments before. I start to look around frantically and stop when my eyes land on the rearview mirror. Standing twenty feet behind my car is the buck with blood dripping from it's bared teeth.

It opens it's mouth, a scream erupting from it's throat that I *know* is completely unnatural. It lowers it's head again, ready to attack and I grit my teeth in return; the god wrapped in the flesh of a beast bringing out my own animal from inside me.
"I know it's you, motherfucker."

I slam the car into reverse and press the gas pedal to the floor.
"COME ON THEN!"

He runs forward as I drive backwards as fast as I can. We collide even harder than the first time, his body slamming up onto my trunk. A short scream escapes me as his massive antlers break through my back glass, shattering it into tiny pieces. I turn around in my seat as I watch the deer try to move and free itself from my car. It raises its head and I see a large slice across it's throat, blood spilling out and down my back seats. A sound of pain comes from him as his eyes turn and meet mine. I watch the life finally leave his body as his head slumps down and his eyes become vacant. I take a long breath and exhale slowly, a shiver running up my spine. I turn my head to the left and gasp as every single deer that came out of the woods stands on the side of the road, staring at me and the dead buck. I quickly shift into drive and speed away, making the buck's body fall off the back of my car and hit the pavement with a wet slap.

CHAPTER SIXTEEN

I fly into my driveway, my tires kicking up gravel hard, spraying it into the road. As I pull into the garage, my car clunks and smokes, telling me that it is tired of belonging to me. I turn off the engine, yanking my keys from the ignition before closing my garage door and running up the steps. I toss my keys onto the counter and walk quickly across my living room to the glass sliding door. I slam it open, not bothering to close it behind me and walk with purpose down the deck stairs and across the backyard to the dock where the row boat still sits, tied up. When I get to the edge I yell out,

"Hey! I need to talk to you right now!"

No reply comes except for the gentle lapping of water against wood. I feel frustration fill me and yell out again, "MICHAEL!"

There is nothing. No gray bodies, no visions of Michael or Helen, no floating children or water puking corpses. I am completely alone. My legs suddenly feel weak and I sink down, collapsing onto the old boards of the dock that feel rough and worn underneath my back. I stare at the mountain looming on the other side of the water, it's peak blurry from the tears that fill my eyes.

I sit up suddenly as an idea presses it's way into my mind. I stand running back down the planks of the dock and up the grass back to the house. Once inside I open my laptop and log in. I open a ncw cmail and address it to *info@Cryptidhunter.com*.

It takes me a half hour to draft the email, telling D. everything that has happened and saying multiple times throughout the story that I know it all sounds crazy; a Blumhouse film, turned into reality. Once I've read through it three times, making the necessary adjustments, I move the mouse, letting it hover over the send button before clicking down, making my email shoot into the digital universe to find its recipient. I sit back, as I look around the wide expanse of my living room and kitchen thinking about how I can get proof of the cult's existence. My eyes grow large as a lightbulb clicks on inside my mind. I can't believe I haven't thought about this the entire time I've been here and I stand, running to my front door, throwing it open.

I scream and leap back as I look into the face of Sheriff Smith. He jumps back at my reaction and holds his hands up.
"Woah, woah, Ms. Monos! Easy!"

I regain my composure and not worried about pleasantries, say,
"What do you want, Sheriff?"

He takes a step forward, resuming his original stance and says,
"Someone reported seeing your car strike a deer out on the highway. I just wanted to make sure you were alright and that your weren't-"

I hold up a hand showing him to stop right there.
"I'm not drunk. I'm quitting in fact."

He nods slowly,
"Well, now that's good news, I suppose. I'm not against one having a nip here and there, but you know that drinking in excess is against the Bib-"

I lean forward interrupting him again.
"What I want to know is if anyone in this fucking town minds their own business."

His face turns sour.
"Well now, I don't think there's a reason for that kind of language."

My eyes glance behind the door and I curse at myself as I realize the shotgun is still upstairs, leaning against the side table in my bedroom. I step back, closing my door as I say, "I'm busy, Sheriff; please be so kind as to leave my property."

I hear the Sheriff step off my porch and head back towards his cruiser before starting it up and driving away slower than I wish he would. I pick up my purse with the gun still inside and head out the front door, trudging across my yard towards the tan storage unit dropped off in my front lawn before I arrived in Aima Island.

———

I drop my purse to the ground before sliding the key into the padlock and turning it, making the metal loop pop up and the lock free itself. I drop it on the ground before turning the metal handle of the unit towards me, then lifting up, and pulling forward to open the doors to the container.

280

Light from outside hits dust motes floating through the air as I stare at my father's pride and joy. The family car; a 1973 Oldsmobile Delta 88 Royale. I pick up my purse, walking into the container past a stack of boxes and an old red chainsaw before opening the heavy door and leaning inside, seeing exactly what I wanted to see. The keys are sitting on the driver's seat. I pick them up, sliding into the car and cranking it up. My dad loved this car and took care of it since he bought it off the lot. No computer chips, no back up camera; just gas and steel. After the accident, I had to find a new driver's side door, and get the rest fixed up, but I didn't hesitate, knowing I had to fix *one* broken thing in this whole fucked up situation.

I glance to the side out of the window and get out of the driver's seat, grabbing a box with Dad's Stuff written on the side, popping the trunk, throwing it inside before closing it and returning to the driver's seat. I press down on the gas pedal and the car comes growling out of the shipping container, into the grass. I turn the wheel, hitting the gravel driveway and turn out onto the road, headed back to Mount Aima.

CHAPTER SEVENTEEN

The familiar scenery fades into a blur as I drive with no regard for others on the road towards Mount Aima; towards the cult's meeting place. The sun has started to set as I pull up to the closed gate for the entrance to Mount Aima State Park. I leave the car running as I glance at the caution tape strung across the broken plank that marks the exit before I retrieve the bolt cutters from the trunk and walk to the gate. I place the blades around a link of the chain, pushing with all of my strength on the handles to make the jaws close and break the link. I strain, but when I let go, the chain still remains intact. I drop one of the handle grips, letting the heavy cutters rest against the ground. I try to think about my next move when I see that even though I didn't break the chain, I put a deep groove into it and decide to try again. The second time, I press half way through the thick metal and with one more go, I feel the chain give under the pressure of the cutters before it falls limp against the gate.

I pull on one end, making the chain clang and slink away from the metal gate before I drop it on the ground and return to the car. I toss the cutters on the passenger seat and pull through the open gate, getting out and closing it behind me in case any of the people of this town that like to watch and report things happen to drive by the state park after dark for some odd reason. I drive up the road, climbing the mountain and thinking about the audio tour the last time I was here. Finally I reach the lot that leads up to the caves. I pull into a spot and kill the engine, my heart pounding in my chest. Slowly, I exit the car and from the box in the trunk, retrieve my dad's polaroid camera, in lieu of mine, that got smashed when I ran into a tree, along with his old flashlight that flickers before turning on after a good smack on the side. With the light as my guide, I cross through the now familiar blocked off trail entrance and walk towards the caves.

_______________________   _______________________

This time, having been here before and not drunk, I am able to find the grouping of caves that Billy pulled me from just last night. The first two caves reveal nothing, but the third is a nightmare manifested right before my eyes. When I shine the light into the opening, I immediately spot blood, still wet, on a flat rock in the center of the chamber. I ease forward, glancing behind me a dozen times to make sure no one has followed me in here. I take the camera, snapping half a dozen photos of the rock and the surrounding area, covered in years of melted wax from excessive use of candles, before moving past the stone that has been set down as a table and deeper into the cave. Once I pass the first chamber, I find steps carved right into the rock leading down into another chamber. I, despite every fiber of my being telling me not to, venture down further into the cave. Once I get to the bottom, I swing my light out and my other hand shoots up to my mouth to stifle a scream. The walls are lined with human skeletons, all posed with their heads raised; their arms and hands up in the air as if in worship. There is another large stone in the center of the chamber, this one twice the size of the other. In the center is a human skull and the headdress I saw, who I assume belongs to the leader of the cult. The one I saw wearing it last night. I slowly raise the light. The ceiling is covered in symbols I do not recognize amongst pictures painted by hand. The "paint" is all the same deep red, almost brown color and I suspect it is not paint at all, but blood from animals or even worse; the skeletons surrounding me. I move the light around seeing that the pictures tell the story of Krotus and Mount Aima. There are pictures of Helen being sacrificed. The god coming out from the forest and devouring her. There are even pictures of hands sticking up out of the water of the lake, the mountain sitting behind them. I say to myself,

"They know what happens when they put people in the water."

I hear what sounds like voices and fear suddenly smacks into me, my brain telling me to run. I lift the camera, taking photos of everything I can, the flash illuminating the whole space and making me see purple and green circles when the light fades. I take all of the polaroids, shoving them into my jacket pocket before turning to leave. I lift the camera again, deciding to take one more picture of the entrance and when the flash goes off, I spot something on the ground. I pull my flashlight forward, and see Billy's hat; the same one he was wearing when I confronted him at Poseidon's Treasure, sitting on the ground, discarded. My heart almost leaps out of my chest. He was here, and not in the robes of the cult. I walk closer, bending down to inspect it further. A streak of blood on the brim tells me it is time to leave; right now. I stand up as the noise from above grows closer, definitely the voices of two men. I hear footsteps on the rock stairs and I move quickly, hiding behind a skeleton by the entrance, pressing my body into a hole that has been naturally formed from centuries of water erosion. The two men enter the room and one says to another,

"I don't know how I get put on body duty, I've got a god damn janky knee."

The other man says,

"Let's just get it over with, I'm already late for dinner. My wife's gonna have my ass."

I watch as they move across the room and into another hole walking down another set of stairs. As their footsteps fade, I react, pulling myself out of the hole and moving as fast as I can to get out. When I move past the skeleton in front of me, I don't notice the strap of the polaroid has snagged on one of the ribs until I turn and see the bones coming directly towards me. I jump out of the way, but when the skull hits the ground, the sound echoes through the entire cavern. From the next level below I hear the men question what the sound was and I break into a full run, hitting the stone steps and bursting out of the upper level into the woods.

I run back to wear I think the trail is, my mind starting to play tricks on me with every sound in the woods sounding one hundred times louder than it actually is. A branch breaks, making me turn to look and see a man in a park ranger's uniform, standing between the trees, watching me.

_______________   _______________

I turn back, running as hard as I can, my lungs burning from my recently relapsed nicotine habit. His steps get louder and I let out a shriek as I feel his hands latch onto my shoulders, stopping me suddenly and pulling me down to the ground. He climbs on top of me, holding me down, despite my efforts to buck him off. His hands latch around my throat, tightening and cutting off the air to my lungs. My eyes start to water as my hands search the ground for anything to fight him with. A sudden flash of realization breaks through and my right hand shoots to my side, sliding Billy's antler handled knife out of it's sheath. The corners of my vision start to go dark as I raise the blade and sink it into the man's leg. He screams out as I finally push him off me, gasping for air. I stand walking away as fast as I can as I watch him sit up and slowly slide the knife from his thigh.

———————————   ———————————

I roll over, finding my footing before standing to run as fast as I can, not sure how much the knife wound will slow him down. I find the path this time and move down it as quickly as I can, running to the car once I hit the parking lot. I'm five feet away when a body slams into mine, knocking me to the ground. I twist and turn, trying to free myself from the hands holding me down. I turn looking up into the face of the man from Mountain Grocery. He grits his teeth, pressing all of his weight down on top of me.

"I'm going to end this right now. Krotus can have you tonight and all of this can be over."

He pulls a pistol from the holster affixed to his belt and my eyes glance over at my purse laying on the ground, next to the polaroid camera. Images of him limping in the store pass through my mind. He was dependent on his-

My eyes go large as I rear back, making a fist. I buck my hips, punching him directly in his right knee, making him fall back as I take a second shot, slamming my fist directly into his balls. He lets out a sound of pain as I push him off my body and crawl towards my purse. I reach my hand out, but feel his fingers wrap around my ankle, throwing my mind back to when Helen grabbed my ankle in the lake. I can't think of that right now. I can't think of anything but survival. I turn, kicking my other foot up, connecting it with his jaw. I knock him back before rolling back over, grabbing my purse and sinking my hand inside. He lunges for me as I raise my own gun and pull the trigger, making a gunshot ring out as I watch the flash of the muzzle illuminate him fully before he falls to the ground. I pick myself up, limping to my car as my lungs still try to fill themselves fully, my neck sore from being squeezed. I open my car door and slide inside, cranking the engine and speed out, driving down the mountain as a red moon hangs high in the sky.

———————————   ———————————

I hit the freeway and my speed climbs higher and higher, the feeling of needing to escape, consuming me. I speed around other cars, weaving in and out of traffic, just

wanting to get home when blue lights come on behind me. My eyes shoot to my rearview mirror as I see the sheriff's car speeding up behind me, the siren coming on.
"SHIT. SHIT. SHIT!"

I press down harder on the gas, making the Delta pick up more speed as Sheriff Smith follows in tow. I blast through red lights and stop signs, needing to get away from everyone in this town. I almost lose control when I swing the heavy car onto my road, gripping the wheel hard and adjusting it, barely missing a sign that says SLOW DOWN. The memories of screams ring out in the car, passing through my mind as I swing the car away from the edge, back into the center of my lane. I turn into my driveway and the sheriff's car comes speeding in right behind me. I leave my purse in the car, getting out, ready to run when i hear,
"FREEZE!"

I don't have to turn around to know that Sheriff Smith has his gun on me. I raise my hands into the air as I hear him walking up quickly behind me, gravel crunching under his feet. He grabs my wrist, pulling it behind my back as I yell out,
"Let me go!"

I feel his hot breath hit the back of my ear as he says angrily to me,

"I am done with your bullshit, Ms. Monos. Youv'e been nothing but trouble since you got here and I'm ending it toni-"

Static blasts from the radio in his squad car, a woman's groan coming over the speaker, making us both look back. He grips my wrists hard as I try to wriggle away, knowing Helen is trying to help me. Suddenly, a massive cracking noise comes from the woods to our left, making both our heads turn. I don't know if the Sheriff is part of all this, but what I do know is that sound. It's Krotus, come to finish this under the light of the blood moon. I start to wriggle, trying to get myself free as Smith's grip tightens.
"LET ME GO! IT'S HIM!"

He yanks on my wrist and says low.
"Stop it right now. It's just a bear or somethi-"

I turn my head to look back and follow his eyes to my front door, illuminated by the flashing blue lights. There is a dead buck on my doorstep, one with broken antlers from crashing into my car multiple times. On the door is a massive symbol, painted in blood, of a circle with antlers sticking out of both sides. The Sheriff's grip loosens and I pull away, turning towards him with my hands raised. I take a risk and place my trust in someone.
"Sheriff, there are people who are trying to kill me."

Another crack comes from the woods and he pulls his gun from it's holster again. He turns his head trying to peer through the darkness before he turns back to me.

"Get inside and lock the doors!"

I don't need to be told twice and take off running towards my house. I run up the garage steps and through the door into the kitchen, breathing hard. I run down the steps into the basement, tripping on the last step and falling hard onto the cement floor, sliding a few feet. I lift my head, looking at the gun safe as I put down a hand, pushing myself up to a standing position. I enter the code and open the safe, looking at all the weapons sitting before me; then I take as many as I can carry.

———————————   ———————————

I run through the basement door, back into the kitchen where I unload everything onto the kitchen table. My eyes scan the room and find my laptop. I grab it, putting it on the counter before sinking my hands into my jacket and pulling out all of my polaroids from the cave. I drop them all on the countertop and type in my password to unlock the screen. My computer tells me I have entered the wrong password and with shaky fingers full of adrenaline, I attempt it again. The same error pops up and I slam my hands down on the keyboard.

"Come on!!"

I close my eyes and take a breath, opening them slowly and placing my fingers back on the keys. I type my password steadily this time and the screen unlocks. I open the main menu and activate my webcam before slowly and painstakingly using my laptop to take a photo of each print. I open up my email and see that I have a message from D, but before I can click it I hear the Sheriff's tires on gravel and run to the window to see his blue lights fade away as he leaves my property. Rage courses through me as I yell out,

"Fucking pussy!"

I whip around as a slam comes from my front door. I'm frozen, staring at where the sound came from as another sends me reeling into the living room and hiding bchind thc couch. Sweat rolls down my forehead while simultaneous tears crawl down my cheeks. I know it's him. I know it's Krotus, the god with deer legs and antlers. A god of the wild, come to kill me and trap my soul, just like the others. The door slams again, threatening to rip from its hinges and a howl; his howl, shrieks through the night air.

My mind fills with scenarios of what he will do to me. How my body will be torn and devoured; just another ghost for the lake. I don't know how long I've been sitting there when I suddenly realize the sounds have stopped. I slowly raise my head above the back of the couch and look around for any sign of the red irised creature looking through my windows. I see nothing and slowly stand, walking back to the window. The same one I watched the Sheriff leave from and then it dawns on me. The Sheriff should still be close. Even though he ran, if I call, he will have to come back. It's illegal for him not to, right?

I turn, walking into the kitchen, picking up my phone, looking down at the screen when the window behind me shatters. I scream, dropping my phone to the floor and grab the shotgun off the table, spinning, firing a shot at the window before running towards the front door, whipping it open and falling back as I see lights coming towards me, from my front yard.

_______________   _______________

Walking from the woods, holding lanterns in front of themselves, are the members of the cult, approaching my front door. They chant deeply and in unison over and over, their voices carrying through their bone masks.
"Érchetai o theós."

I find my footing, raising myself up as a cult member in the front drops their lantern to the ground, breaking into a run. I drop the gun, grabbing the handle of the door, slamming it closed, but stopping short as an antler comes pushing through the space between the door and the frame. I look down and see that the dead deer's head has slumped over, one of its points blocking the door from closing. I feel a slam as the weight of the cult member hits the door, knocking me back. I push against it with all of my weight as they try to force it open and get inside. My eyes glance down at the shotgun laying next to the door and I reach out a hand, my fingers straining to wrap around the grip.

Suddenly a knife comes flying through the gap, swinging wildly into the open space, making contact with my arm, slicing hard, sending blood dripping down off my elbow as I scream out in pain. I slam my weight into the door, making the antler break and the heavy wood crush their wrist as I jump to the side. The door flies open and I press the barrel of Billy's shotgun up under the chin of the mohawked check out girl from Super Everything. As recognition fills my eyes, I snarl, looking into her face.
"Saw my name on my I.D.; yeah, right. I knew that was bullshit."

She smiles at me despite the threat that lingers directly under her jaw.
"He will taste you tonight, pig."

She lunges forward, swinging her knife at me and I pull down on the trigger, releasing a full shell of buck shot directly into her head. The sound is deafening as her blood coats everything in the space of my foyer and her headless body falls onto my front porch next to the dead deer. I step out onto the porch pulling the fore-end back along the magazine tube, the empty shell flying out and landing on the wooden planks with a clack.

"I want all of you to get the fuck away from my hou-"

A hand flies out, grabbing the barrel of the gun and wrenching it from my grasp. I turn looking into dead eyes that reside behind another deer skull. They turn the gun on me as I dive through the open door, sound bursting into the night as a round of shot embeds itself into my door frame. I turn, kicking the door closed before standing and locking the dead bolt. Another shot is released into the door and I run to the kitchen table, grabbing the grenade. I shove it into my jacket as I reach my hand out to grab one of the pistols, when another shotgun blast slams into my door, before it's kicked open. I pick up the gun, aiming it at the cult member coming into my home and pull the trigger. Nothing happens and I pull it again; nothing. I remember from the videos that you have to turn the safety off, but it's too late as I drop the gun and dive out of the way, buckshot lodging itself in my counter and walls. I burst into a run climbing the stairs towards the second floor. Slamming into the wall at the top, I look down to see red robes following me. I run into my bedroom and slam the door, latching the lock, taking a couple steps back. I pull out the grenade, looking at it in my hand as the first boot slam comes from the other side of my bedroom door. I can't use it in this enclosed space because it will kill me too. I slide it back into my coat pocket and look around, trying to figure out what to do. I don't have a second to think as the door bursts open, the shotgun aimed directly at me. I jump sliding across the bed, falling off on the other side as a gunshot rings out, the window behind me breaking.

I look next to the bedside table, then turn my head, seeing if what I think is under my bed is still there. I see two robed figures walk slowly into the room and I reach under the bed grabbing the bottle of Crystal Head vodka. I hear one of them say,
"Just come out, Melissa. It's all over."

I grab a discarded sock off the floor and stuff it into the bottle's neck. Reaching into my jacket and finding my lighter, I light the white sock that instantly starts to burn and turn brown. I grit my teeth and with all my strength, I lob the bottle over the bed.

No crash comes and I stand to see the one not holding the shotgun, holding the bottle that was meant to explode. He turns his head to the side and says,
"Nice try."

I whip my arm up, revealing the shotgun that was next to my bedside table. This time I've made sure the safety is off as I pull the trigger, releasing a shell of buckshot that embeds into their flesh and shatters the glass bottle, making liquor touch flame and ignite, lighting both of them on fire.

Their screams fill my upstairs as I run out of the room, jumping over their smoldering bodies. Looking down into the downstairs, blurs of red move towards the stairs, their faces lifting and looking up at me. I run past the stairs and open a door, swinging myself inside, slamming it closed behind me. I move backwards, placing my back against the wall as I hear footsteps stop just outside the door. The door creaks open, light breaking through the darkness as I watch three cult members walk slowly into the room. I reach out my leg slowly, then kick the door making it slam as I turn, flipping on the red light sitting in the fixture of the darkroom. Startled, the robed figures look around, trying to figure out what's going on when I throw a tub of hydrochloric acid into the closest one's face. He releases a scream, his hands flying to his eyes as I reach out, flicking the switch again, making the room go into complete darkness. I hear the cult members scrambling around as I ease myself against the wall until my fingers touch the plug I am looking for. Light bursts out as I turn on my light box, making them turn towards me as I lift the box and bring it down on the head of the one rushing towards me, making the glass shatter. I choke, dropping what remains of the box as I feel a thick cord wrap around my neck, then go taut. I don't need to see who it is as I hear a man's voice say, "You shot me in the fucking leg. Time to die, bitch."

I look around for something to help me fight back against the man who tackled me in the parking lot outside of the cave. The room is wrapped in a warm glow from the light of the broken light box as my vision starts to go black at the

edges. I rasp out the last bit of air in my lungs, then finally see what I'm looking for and I slam my body backwards, making his grip on the power cord loosen for just a second; enough time for me to turn and kick him as hard as I can between the legs, his balls taking a beating. He screams out in pain, doubling over in front of me.
"YOU FUCKING BITCH!"

I grab him by his red hood, pushing his head towards the table and under my enlarger. I push his head against the baseboard and reach up behind the back of the neck, wrapping my fingers around the lock that holds it in place. When I feel it go loose, I let it drop, pushing down with my hand to give it more force, slamming it down on the skull of my attacker. He tries to get up and I bring my foot down on his right knee, hard, making him sink back to the ground. I lift the device with my hand and let go, letting it slam down again, making him go limp, his resistance fading. I let go of his hood and raise the printmaker again, holding it with both hands and this time force it down as hard as I can, slamming it into his skull that gives out a crack as the metal collides with fragile bone. I lift it again and again until his head releases a squelch and the body falls to the floor. I turn, grabbing the door handle and whip the door open, making my pupils shrink fast at the light coming from the hallway. I blink rapidly, helping my eyes adjust as I turn towards the stairs, running back to the kitchen. I slide to a stop at the counter, pressing send on my email to D before turning to run to the garage when I see a flash of red through a hole in the front door. I turn, grabbing the Ginsu knife from the countertop before running through the living room and whipping open the sliding glass door. I step out onto the porch and hit the red button affixed to the wall. The lights blast on, illuminating the whole back yard and I gasp as a mass of robed figures run across the grass towards the back porch. I jump back inside, closing the glass door and locking it right as a fist punches me in the face, making pain branch out instantly from my already broken nose as I see stars and fall to the ground. As my vision clears, I see a man, the hood of his robe pulled back standing over me. He smiles, cocking his head to the side as he raises a booted foot over my head. As his boot comes down, my hand shoots out to the side, grabbing the Ginsu knife from the floor and holding it straight up, the blade sliding cleanly through the bottom of his boot and out of the top, blood spurting from his foot encased inside the leather. He releases a scream, falling to the floor, his hands moving quickly around the blade and handle, not sure if he should leave the knife in or take it out. I stand, shaking my head, still trying to clear the daze from the pain branching out from my nose, burning through every nerve in my face. A loud crack comes from the front door and I turn my head, seeing more cult members come into my home. I move quickly through the kitchen to the garage door, running down the steps.

I turn my head just in time to see them try to back up at the sight of a live grenade sitting at the top of the stairs. It explodes, tearing through their bodies, but also through the stairs. When I am five steps from the bottom, the stairs release themselves from the wall, falling to the side and crashing hard to the ground. I push myself up again, my body screaming out in pain as I limp out of the garage and up the driveway.

There is no space for any other thought in my mind, except for escape. I hear another shot, this one from a pistol and I fall to the ground, the bullet hitting the cement next to me. I turn to look at where the shot came from and see a cult member, their robe on fire fall from a window hitting the ground hard. My legs feel like jelly as I try to get them back under me, crawling on my hands and knees back to the garage. I pull up on a shelf bolted into the wall, finally standing and planting my feet on the floor. I hear the sound of hooves on pavement and turn my head quickly to the right and see the silhouette of the creature walk out of the inky darkness, the dim garage light illuminating the tips of his horns. I press my body against the wall, sweat coating every inch of my clammy skin, nowhere to run. My eyes land on a shovel and I grip the handle, picking it up and swinging it in one swift movement. The blade arcs through the air, then stops as a giant hand shoots out grabbing the wooden shaft. The hand disappears back into the darkness as the shovel is ripped from my grasp, flying into the woods. I watch his giant furred leg as he takes a step forward, then a body comes running from the side of the house. In a flash of pale gray, Helen slams into him, knocking him past the garage, into the grass. I hear her gargled voice yell,
"RUN!"

I don't need to be told twice as a new burst of adrenaline pumps through me and I find my strength. As I run past my destroyed car, out through the garage door, I see Helen on top of the monster, struggling to hold him down. He lifts his head and an antler shoots through her back, making black blood and muck spray from her dead flesh. I turn, running towards the Delta still sitting in the gravel drive. A new set of footsteps make themselves heard as I turn just in time to see another red robe lunging for me. They tackle me, making us both roll on the ground; their hood falling back to show the woman from Mountain Top Liquor. I kick hard, my shoe connecting with her face, sending her falling back. I turn, trying to get away as I feel her fingers wrap around my ankle. My eyes land on the shipping container in the yard and I kick my foot back, making her grip slip from me. I stand, limping to the shipping container and stepping inside. Her voice comes from behind me, echoing off of the metal walls.

"Nowhere to run, bitch."

I keep my back to her until I hear her step inside the container. In one fluid motion I turn, pulling the starter cord of the chainsaw, making it come to life. I pull the trigger and shove the blade forward into her stomach. The chain spins, instantly cutting through fabric and flesh, mangling her insides as blood pours out of her mouth. She coughs, making dots of it fleck my face, adding to the blood of the checkout girl. I push harder, making her take two steps back as guts and bone catch in the chain, shooting out through the hole in her back. I let go of the handle and watch her body fall to the ground, the chainsaw protruding from her stomach.

I hear the heavy steps of hooves coming up the driveway and I turn, running to the car. I throw myself in behind the wheel and crank the engine, slamming it into reverse. I make a semi circle in the gravel, spinning the car around before shifting it back into drive. I look into the rearview mirror and scream as I see bright red eyes looking at me, as the giant monster holds my car, tires spinning and kicking up smoke. Its teeth grit as it stops me from leaving, hands gripped on my rear bumper. I glance down at my passenger seat and pull the gun from my purse. I click off the safety and turn my body, aiming it at Krotus. I release a shot that flies through the back glass lodging itself into his shoulder before I reach across, putting on my seatbelt.

I slam the shifter into reverse and slam into him, just like his buddy sitting dead on my front porch. The force knocks him to the side and I shift back into drive, slamming the pedal and making the car lurch forward. As I drive over gravel, I look in the mirror behind me. At first there is nothing, then I see him come out of the darkness, running towards me. I press down as hard as I can on the gas pedal, but two loud noises, like mini explosions, sound out, then two more, all making the car rattle and shake before coming to a stop. I look in my side mirror and see my tire is flat. My brake lights make everything glow red and I see that laying on the ground behind my wheel is a spike strip,

used to stop people from escaping; used to stop *me* from escaping. Krotus slams into the back of my car, making the back glass shatter and my scream ring out. I try to gas the car, but the rubber of my tires tears off, making the rims spin in the gravel. My driver's side window shatters and I feel a large hand wrap around my neck as another tears the seatbelt from the wall of the car before pulling me through the hole edged with broken glass. I reach out wrapping my hand around the gun, swinging it forward and squeezing off another shot, completely missing before Krotus grabs the pistol, pulling it from my hand and throwing it into the woods. I gasp and cough for air as I see the Mount Aima Antler Man clearly for the first time. The light from my brakes illuminates his whole frame in a sickly red hue. He has large teeth with incisors the size of quarters. Hair covers his body, but grows thicker when it reaches his waist, where he turns into a giant deer. I stare at his antlers, protruding from his forehead, huge and massive. My eyes drift over to my cabin, the top floor on fire, as I start to black out. Despite dying slowly, I think to myself,
"At least I'm not crazy."

He slams me against the car and I feel the last bit of oxygen left in my body fly from my lungs and leave me to die. I look around frantically, my eyes turning bloodshot as this ancient thing, this son of a god, kills me in my driveway. I see my only way out and swing my leg as hard as I can, my foot connecting with his massive balls hanging amongst his long, curled fur. He shrieks, his grip loosening, dropping me to the ground, gasping for air. I take two large gulps before I see him coming at me and roll underneath the car. I start to try and crawl out the other side, when I see his massive fingers come under the frame, turned upright, gripping the side.

One moment I am under a giant shield and the next I am exposed as the car flips through the air, landing on it's roof and then rolling one more time to land back on it's bare metal wheels. He grabs my ankle, pulling me back towards him and as I slide away, I see something tangled in one of the wheels of my car and turn my head, watching the spike strip slide by my face.

I reach out a hand grabbing it and feel searing pain shoot through my arm as the spikes puncture my skin. He turns me over, snarling in my face as I punch him in the nose, shattering the bones in my left hand, making me scream out. It takes him more by surprise than hurts him and I take the opportunity to sit up, wrapping the spike strip twice around his neck. I turn, finding my footing and launch myself towards the car. I slam into the side, smearing blood all over the doors before grabbing the handle and opening the driver's side door. I fall hard into the seat as I look over at Krotus. His red eyes flash as he stands and takes two steps towards me. I pray to whoever will listen to save me as I slam down the gas pedal and the wheels spin, rocks flying up behind them. The strip, caught in the wheel, starts to tighten, the slack sliding on the ground before pulling tight. I turn to look at this god of the wild and see the exact moment when he and I know the same thing. I fucking won.

———————————   ———————————

The strip pulls tight and sinks deep into his flesh, spraying blood and making him reach his hands up trying to free himself. He lets out a shrill scream that turns into a shrieking howl before his neck is sliced through and his head falls to the ground, released from the rest of his body. I let off the gas pedal too late as my bare rims catch, finding purchase, shooting the car forward, crashing directly into a tree next to the gravel drive, knocking me back and out of the open driver's side door, onto the ground. As I lay on the ground, broken, but not beaten, I turn my head, my eyes watching steam rise from the monster's neck as his body falls slowly, hitting the ground with a thud, next to his head. My body feels heavy as the blood drains from me, laying in the gravel, my eyes sliding closed until I hear someone call my name in the distance. I force my eyes open as the sheriff runs up.
"Ms. Monos! Ms. Monos!"

He drops to his knees and lifts my head.
"What happened?!"

I smile a bloody grin and a laugh bubbles free from my chest. The first laugh in a year.

"I fucking got him."

Sheriff Smith looks up and I watch his eyes grow two times their size as he takes in the dead god laying beside us. He looks back down at me and his face curls into a sneer. He drops my head to the ground and the sharp gravel sends more pain flowing through my body. I use the last of my strength to turn my head to look at him as he says,
"You stupid bitch. Do you have any idea what you've done?"
He pulls his gun from it's holster and says,
"Why couldn't you have just died like the rest of your family?"

He aims the gun at me and the last sound I hear before leaving this earth is three gunshots. A period to my story.

CHAPTER EIGHTEEN

My eyes shoot open, but I'm not laying on the gravel driveway. I'm standing in the middle of the lake. I look down at my feet placed on top of the water. My mind knows this shouldn't be possible, but isn't concerned about the unlikelihood of it either. I look up again and in front of me are all the dead bodies that were hidden under these waters for all these years, but now instead of gray and bloated, their skin has regained its color, their eyes no longer milky white, their insides not black and rotting. In the front of the group is Helen, now radiant that she is free from rot and bloat. She walks forward, each step making rings ripple through the water underneath her. She smiles, taking my hands in hers and says,

"Thank you, Melissa. We have been trapped here for so long."

She looks over her shoulder,
"Some of us, much longer than others."

My eyes follow hers and I look at a woman in a Victorian dress standing next to someone in bell bottoms, my eyes follow the crowd as I see every decade since the town was formed in people's clothes and hairstyles. Helen lets out a little sigh and my eyes move back to hers.
"There's someone else here to see you too."

She steps to the side as the crowd parts. My mother, father and brother, walk on the water towards me. A whimper breaks from my mouth, turning into a sob as tears roll down my face. They all hug me and pull back, smiling. My mother is the first to say,
"You did good honey."

My dad nods and my brother says,
"I can't believe my dorky sister killed a god."

A laugh breaks it's way through me and we all embrace again.
"Wait. How are you here? I went to your funeral. You weren't trapped in the lake."

My father rubs the back of his neck and says,

"The coffins in Ashton were empty, honey. They put us into the lake after the accident."

He looks past me at the house, not burnt or destroyed in this place, but exactly how it was when my whole family was here. He chuckles,
"We would like to stay here honestly, if you're able. Just not in the lake."

Helen steps forward,
"But now we all have to go, Melissa."

I look to my family, pleading with my eyes, but not telling them not to leave. I know they belong in another place now. I watch them walk back, the crowd closing in and following them. I look at Helen and ask,
"Will everyone be okay?"

She smiles and says,
"Melissa, wake up."

My eyebrows pull down in confusion as she says,
"Melissa, can you hear me? Melissa, wake up."

The lake and everyone in front of me are pulled away as I am yanked backwards, up into the air, high above Aima Island until I am floating in space. I see a light in front of me, a pinpoint in an endless sea of black and I swim towards it until I open my eyes, looking at a nurse with a smile very much like Helen's.

CHAPTER NINETEEN

My injuries were extensive, but for all its shortcomings, for some reason, the American healthcare system refuses to let me die. I had to stay at the hospital for a month before they released me and I was able to come home. The perfect amount of time for the top half of my house to be rebuilt due to fire damage. I'm still going to have to have some physical therapy, but the doctors are optimistic that I will regain all movement without any stiffness with enough patience and work.

I walk onto my porch, looking at my house, the feeling it has now, completely different than before. It no longer feels like a graveyard, but instead like a memorial, dedicated to

310

the people of the lake. Dedicated to my family. At least that's what the metal plate I had made and bolted next to my front door says that I touch as I walk through the repaired door frame into my home.

THIS HOUSE IS DEDICATED TO THE PEOPLE WHO WERE MURDERED IN AIMA ISLAND BY THE CULT OF THE ANTLER. MAY THEY FOREVER FIND PEACE.

I walk into the kitchen and set down the basket that was sitting on my front porch, along with the pizza box from my other hand. The smorgasbord wrapped in wicker is full of various types of liquor, cookies, cured meats and crackers. I look at the tag seeing it is from my lawyer with a handwritten note that says,

"Call me when you want to sue the town."

I pull the cellophane from the basket, taking a cookie from one of the boxes and popping it into my mouth before taking off the tops of all of the liquor bottles, setting them on my counter and dumping their contents down the drain one by one. There's no room in my life now for alcohol. I look over at one of the photographs I took after coming here, sitting on the table, waiting to be framed. Graffiti under the bridge to Aima that says, "Who Am I?". At this point, after everything, I'm not really sure who I am, but for the first time in a long time, I'm excited to find out.

I toss the empty glass bottles into the recycling bin and walk to the sliding glass door, opening it and walking out onto the porch. The sky is blue and dotted with puffy clouds like giant cotton balls floating in a beautiful sea. Mount Aima stands tall and proud, it's reflection in the lake, a work of art. By the dock are three headstones. My mother, my father and my brother. While I was still in the hospital, I had my lawyer lobby the town to allow me to bury my family on the property. Since it is my land and considering what I had just gone through, they approved my request and once their bodies were relinquished, they were placed here.

In the end, D whose name was actually Derrick saved my life. He replied to the email I sent with all the photos, an email I wouldn't read for weeks, where he told me he was in contact with his uncle, a police officer named Gil Griffin from Stadton City Police Department, and was having him look into the information I had given him. Apparently his uncle has always thought of him as a bit of a loon who needed a lesson in reality, until he had some odd experiences of his own in Aima Island. When he saw my email, full of pictures of skeletons and blood, he called in everyone he could and came immediately. The three gunshots I heard were not from the Sheriff shooting me, but from Gil shooting the sheriff, later found to be the leader of the cult. In the end, they had to call in the FBI, who found ninety-two bodies in the lake, but were certain this did not account for all of the victims. The Sheriff, who survived his wounds and the remaining members of the cult were arrested and are facing trial. When the cave was searched, the skeletons were taken and analyzed, later found to belong to past cult members, placed inside the cave to worship Krotus in death as they did in life. The one thing they didn't find was Krotus' body. When I woke up in the hospital, all I could talk about was the Mount Aima Antler Man, but the agent assigned to my case decided to omit it, and my lawyer later advised me not to talk about it. Derrick has promised to come visit me and I'm sure we will get plenty of time to talk about all the things that have happened on Aima Island.

Billy Walker's Chevy was found in the lake as well, on the opposite end from my home; dumped there after I saw it at the body shop, but his body was recovered elsewhere. Specifically, Sheriff Smith's backyard after the two men from the cave drove to his home to place the body in a pre dug hole, on his orders before joining the others to come kill me. Billy kept a journal found during the investigation that kept a detailed record of the goings on with the Aima Island cult and his part in everything. He apparently inherited the position of the one to sacrifice victims from his father, along with his father's truck, but always carried guilt over it. By the time I showed up, he abandoned his plan to run in a last ditch effort to scare me away, but the commotion I made outside of Poseidon's Treasure, plus seeing his knife on my belt made the sheriff catch on that he was trying to help me, so they killed him. They didn't sacrifice him though, not willing to do so to one of their own. The sheriff, while recovering from his gunshot wounds, confessed to everything and the FBI had a pretty easy time gathering up everyone involved, except for the ones that were killed at my home.

When I woke up in the hospital I told Detective Griffin that he had to check on Linda, that she had helped me and I hadn't heard from her, making me fear the worst. As soon as the name left my lips his face scrunched up, like he recognized it.

It turns out her name was Linda Mctaff and the reason the ghost walk stopped was because she had gone missing after filing a police report on an Aima Island woman that Linda said was trying to use witchcraft to raise her daughter from the dead. Her last known appearance before she disappeared was at a local restaurant named The Jade Dragon that shut down around years ago, after the owner didn't have the money to complete repairs from a kitchen fire.

Linda's sister shut down the ghost walk and closed the business that she never thought was a "real job" to begin with. I gaped at Gil Griffin not sure how to respond. I had seen this woman. I had talked with her and shared food with her. Now it made sense to me that she told me she had seen Helen, because she was a ghost herself. Another restless spirit trying to guide me. I asked him to tell me what happened, but he patted my arm and said,
"I think you've been through enough. Let's save that story for another time."

I walk back inside, closing the glass door behind me. I stand in awe, looking around my home that is so quiet and at peace, like blood was never spilt here; like people did not die here. I open my laptop and see that I have a new email. I click the icon and read the subject line.
DID YOU ACTUALLY SEE THE MOUNT AIMA ANTLER MAN???

I look to the left to see who has sent this and a smile breaks at the corner of my mouth as I see it is from *info@Cryptidhunter.com*. I reach out a hand gripping the corner of the pizza box featuring Nonno Pepperoni and close my eyes, spinning the box on the counter. When it stops, I lift the lid and pick up a piece. I open my eyes and my mouth forms into a line of disgust. Pineapple and anchovies.
"You got me again, Michael."

I laugh and take a huge bite.

EPILOGUE

"**A** year has passed since the night Krotus died. No, since the night he was murdered. I have fallen into darkness. I only have one thing left. Revenge."

Two hooves make clicking noises as they walk across the stone floor of a cave. A shadow is cast across Krotus' head atop a rock, surrounded by candles, part memorial, part altar. In the opening of the cave, a man appears. A man that has the legs and horns of a goat. The god of the wild; the ancient satyr, Pan. He takes another step forward, the warm sunlight crossing across his body as he looks down from the side of Mount Aima, at the little dot of a house that sits across the lake where Melissa Monos stands on her back porch.

ACKNOWLEDGEMENTS & APOLOGIES

When I first thought of this story, it was something very different. Inspired by where I live in North Carolina, it was originally titled, *The God of the Wild* and was going to feature Pan and a witch, but soon, his son, Krotus, a figure I thought I could take more liberties with, including his name, took his place. There are two main spellings of the gods name, the first being Crotus and the other Krotos. I liked the pronunciation of Crotus, but also really liked the K instead of the C, so I combined both of the spellings of his name and brought Krotus into PANIC. I also completely changed his appearance. Krotus, famously pictured as the zodiac symbol Sagittarius, traditionally has the lower body of a horse, the upper body of a man, a satyr's tail, and wings. As you know, all of this was changed as I wanted Krotus to be closer to his father Pan in appearance. I took away his horse body and gave him the legs of a deer and instead of satyr's horns, I placed antlers on his forehead. The only thing that stayed the same was his upper body. I believe gods can take many forms and this form is simply The Mount Aima Antler Man.

According to Krotus' story he led a relatively peaceful life spent around the muses. He was a master hunter and musician credited for things like inventing the bow, creating beats for music to be played by and even the creation of applause. There is no story that led me into making him something more sinister. It just worked out that way. Krotus did not deserve to be written in this way, but it is my hope that people will look him up because of this book and bring him more recognition. I'm sorry, Krotus, but damn did you kill the role. If you've gotten to this point, you know that Pan still made an appearance in the story and in the title as the word "panic" is derived from the god's name.

Thank you to my wife, Ruby Theyson, who listens to me talk about my stories for years before they are finished; who proofreads my work, and who endlessly supports me.

Thank you to Callie Dahl, for her quote on the cover of this book. Callie is an insanely talented independent author and

I knew I had to snag a quote by her for one of my books. When she expressed her excitement over this story, I knew for sure that I had something good in the making.

Thank you to paranormal investigator, Amanda Paulson for making sure I wrote the best ghosts I possibly could. Amanda fearlessly goes into the dark places we won't, always trying to solve the mysteries that surround us. You are the only ghost hunter I trust.

Thank you to Victoria Byers and Brittany Little of Reliquary Photo for the amazing photos you took of me and my wife, one of which is the author photo on this novel. I believe it is the two of you who inspired me to include my own photography in every iteration of this series. Special thanks must also be given to Victoria, who let me bounce the idea of killing someone with an enlarger in a dark room off of her, and if that would even be possible.

Thank you to the gods. It is you that protects and blesses my family and I am endlessly grateful.

And last, but certainly not least, thank you to you, the person reading this book and these acknowledgments. I loved writing this novel and taking photos of the landscapes and places that inspired it, that are included in each story. If I could go back in time and tell myself as a child that one day people would be reading books written by us, I would be giving that lonely child the greatest gift.

FROM THE WORLD OF *PANIC*

OUT OF THE DARKNESS

T.P. THEYSON

A LETTER FROM THE AUTHOR

Out of the Darkness was my first dive into the world of Aima Island. The story was inspired by an abandoned building I pass almost daily on the way to my log home, nestled in the woods of North Carolina. It was the perfect amount of creepy and I knew I wanted to base a story around it and the area I live in, combined with some of the odd and sensational things that you'll hear certain folks talk about happening in the South. When I started to write it however, the timing didn't feel right. I eventually put it to the side and concentrated all of my efforts on my modern mythological novel, War of the Pantheons. When I came back to the idea of basing a story in Aima, I decided to take some of my initial ideas and rework them, forming a very different story titled, PANIC.

As the completion of PANIC grew close, I felt a pull to revisit the original story that started it all, still sitting incomplete and untitled on my hard drive. I felt that there was more to be told about Aima Island, and this was an account I wanted to tell. I explored where the story, now given the title Out of the Darkness, would have led and wanted to take it even further, connecting it and the characters to my completed novel. I fell back into the story with fresh eyes, knowing more about Aima Island than ever before, from having spent a year writing about its people and landscapes.

I was able to link the two stories together, forming an even larger, ever growing tapestry of my fictional southern regions including places like Ashton, Aima Island, Stadton, Kolme, and Grande Gorge, based on the topography of North Carolina. I feel the novelette, although not necessary to understand the events of PANIC, really lends itself to the story, showing the types of things that can be expected from such a supernatural and ominous town. Included halfway through this book are more photos taken by myself of some of the inspirational places that this story and PANIC was formed from, including the abandoned building that started it all.

To be clear these events take place prior to the novel PANIC, I hope you enjoy Out of the Darkness and as always; thank you for reading.

INTRODUCTION

"Holy Shit…"

Brandon steps away from the body, shaking his head and putting distance between himself and the crime scene investigation crew, placing yellow, plastic placards and taking photos, one flash going off after the other like lightning in a dismal, dark sky. Gil watches him walk towards the police tape, lift it, ducking underneath, then head away from the crime scene. He has been working with James Brandon for years and knows that this is what he likes to do to give himself a cigarette break. He isn't truly shocked or disgusted by anything at this point. How could *either* of them be? Their purpose, hell, their entire existence consists of investigating the horrible things people do to each other. In a world built on blood and guts, laid on a foundation of the vile things people do to each other; it only takes so long before you become completely numb to it all, your stomach no longer twisting in knots at the sight of blood; your mind no longer screaming to run at the smell of a corpse.

As he watches the first plume of smoke rise from where Brandon has decided is a good spot to stand, under a dogwood tree, while he gets his nicotine fix, he turns to look at the victim again. True that they have seen a lot over the years and gag reflexes have been left behind long ago, but this victim; this was something truly fucked up and in a league of its own. Laying at the base of a tree is a burnt body, which would create enough work for Griffin and Brandon as it were, but that's far from the end of it. The body looks like it has run a marathon through a fire pit, every inch of skin up to the neck turned black, cracked and charred, but there are no burn marks on the ground or tree, which would suggest the body was dumped here. Not only that, but whoever killed this man, took their time. Each of the legs and arms were broken, making the limbs face the wrong direction and the head; well the head faces Gil, glassy eyes staring up into his. This wouldn't usually be out of the ordinary, but the body is laying on its stomach, ripples formed into twists in the skin, covered in bruising from whoever had snapped this man's neck so hard his head now sits backwards. What was once a living, breathing person; someone with feelings and emotions, someone who had favorite foods and hobbies, now sits at the base of this tree looking more like a creature of myth than anything close to human that Gil has ever seen.

Gil's eyes glance up, his senses taking in everything around him. The cold wind shaking the needles of the pine tree that stands Stadover this body like a protector, the smell of traffic driving by on the freeway, and the sounds of the hawks overhead, a sign that something below has died. He turns his head away from the bustle of people surrounding the scene and looks further out into the dense trees; the woods sitting silent, even the squirrels and cardinals keeping their distance. As he stares into the forest that grows so dense it chokes out the sunlight, creating pockets of darkness in the broad midday sun, Gil's mind can't help but ask himself, *"What kind of monster would do this to a person?"*

Before he can even begin to answer himself, a tractor trailer flies by on the road, making wind rush down the embankment to where the body was found at three a.m. that morning by a driver with a bit of bad luck, pulling over to change a flat tire. Gil stands as his eyes follow the truck driving over the speed limit down the freeway, headed across the bridge and towards Aima Island, thinking to himself that these truck drivers are going to kill someone, someday. His eyes trail back to the body and he sees the corpse's fingers twitch. He jumps back just as he feels a hand come down on his shoulder making him turn to look

directly into the face of his partner, James Brandon who points towards the bridge that crosses over the lake.
"It's gonna rain soon."

Gil turns back, looking at the body.
"Did you just see his hand move?"

The coroner looks up nonchalantly, pushing his glasses up the bridge of his nose.
"Oh yeah, it happens all the time."

He leans back on his crouched legs and pushes up his glasses.
"They've actually documented movements in corpses for up to seventeen months after death."

Brandon's voice comes from behind him.
"Well that's fucking terrifying. Anyways, we better wrap this up before Mother Nature decides to crash the party."

Gil looks at gray clouds forming over the water, threatening with every passing second to ruin any type of evidence they might find. As a tarp is stretched out, attached to metal stakes in a futile attempt to preserve the scene, Brandon says,
"Weatherman said it would be sunny all day, of course."

He looks down at the charred remains once more and says,
"Whelp, that's the south for you."

CHAPTER ONE

The windshield wipers of Gil's car drag across the glass, releasing a loud squeak, making him wince and fiddle with the controls. The rain is at that perfectly annoying point where you can't use the delayed setting on your wipers because they won't clear the windshield quick enough, but if you go to the next setting it's *too* quick and you'll hear nothing but screeching rubber, a noise Gil is fairly sure has been proven to drive people insane. The end result being that the driver has to constantly change the settings to try to accommodate the weather.

Brandon cracks his window, pulling out a brown BIC lighter, turning the striker wheel that has had the child proof metal strip popped off with a knife at some point. The lighter comes to life after three turns, sparking and igniting, providing what man has valued since he first walked the earth; the last thing their latest victim saw; fire.

———————————   ———————————

Gil's eyes drift over, watching Brandon suck flame into the tip of his cigarette and blow out smoke that sucks through the crack in the window and out into the world. He holds the cigarette in between his first and middle finger, tapping the end to make the ash fall out the window before taking another drag, talking as smoke flows out of his mouth.
"Any ideas what might have happened to that guy?"

Gil has been working alongside his partner for a long time and knows the question is rhetorical. He doesn't even attempt to answer, instead letting Brandon tell him what he thinks is going on.
"Looks like a hit to me. Bet the whole crew took a shot at him. That would account for all the broken bones. After that, tried to burn the evidence, but fucked it up. They'll find something on him. Case will be wrapped up before the end of the month."

Gil raises an eyebrow, his mouth moving to one side, not hiding the fact he thinks Brandon is completely off, but then James says,

"That head though; you ever seen anything like that?"
Gil stares forward, raindrops on the windshield lighting up red from the car's brake lights in front of him as midday traffic builds. Water starts to collect on the side of the road, the rain picking up and he turns the knob for the wipers to the first setting.
"No. Never."

Brandon flicks his cigarette out of the window and laughs,
"I didn't even know you could fucking do that to someone! It's like some Evil Dead shit!"

Gil, always uncomfortable at how Brandon talks about victims, licks his dry lips and says,
"Yeah."

They drive into the heart of Nattson County, Downtown Stadton, pulsing with its own heartbeat, people flowing through streets like blood cells through veins, keeping the city alive. They pass steakhouses and boutiques, the smell of fresh baked bagels from Fatal Bagel, creeping into the car, making Gil's stomach growl at the thought of smoked salmon and capers on an everything bagel with cream cheese. His eyes drift over to the neon sign of a poison symbol with a bagel replacing a skull, crossbones sticking out at either side, blazing bright in the gloomy, overcast day and he thinks about why anyone would buy food from a restaurant that has a name about their fare killing you, but ever since a year ago when two women with their hair in victory rolls and their arms and legs covered in tattoos opened shop, there has been a line around the block. People love it, including himself, admittedly. As far as he's concerned, good Lox is good Lox, regardless of what the name on the sign might be.

A horn blares behind them as they ease forward two feet before hitting the brakes again. Brandon scoffs saying something about how people who lay on their car horns in gridlocked traffic deserve to have a metal pipe taken to their knee caps. Gil tunes him out as he goes on saying they're the same kind of people who claim to be coffee drinkers, but then get nothing but nine dollar, syrupy, caramel bullshit from Siren's Song Coffee.

As his voice fades into the background, blending into all the other noises filling the city around them, they slowly stop at another red light at Trade and Main St., four giant figures watching over the square. Nicknamed The Guardians, decades ago, by the people living in Stadton, the statues, one placed on each corner, stand tall, looking down on all that pass by. The sculptures were donated by a group of anonymous philanthropists named The King's Council; people with more money than they know what to do with, but don't want it publicly known.

Now thought to guard the four wards of the city, the statues have become a staple of Stadton scenery, rumors springing up on conspiracy theory websites a couple times every decade that they are symbols of occult knowledge, placed purposefully at the center of the city to show all passersby that The King's Council are in fact a ruling class, working the gears and levers of all life in this megalopolis, placing themselves in complete control. Gil doesn't know what he believes. Hell, he's seen stranger things. A group of rich people seeking more power and money than what they already have is far less weird than a man with his head on backwards. The light turns green, then red again, a whole cycle passing with no movement of the car in front of him. His eyes stare out through the water dropped window, moving from one statue to the other.

The effigy of commerce wears a suit of armor, a gold sword in their hands and a knight's helmet covering their head. The representation of the future holds a bow in one hand while cradling a child in the crook of the opposite arm. The child feeds as the mother looks forward, her hair flowing all the way down her back. The third, The Judge, grips a mace with one hand and holds scales in the other. A blindfold covers his eyes; symbolism of justice being blind. The fourth, the one that Gil finds himself staring at every time he drives through this intersection, personifies transportation, the figure representing the workers who would spend centuries building up the city's roads, and not ironically the only one of a person of color, holding his hammer tight against his chest. As a mixed child growing up in the south, this was the guardian that Gil always felt closest to. The statue solemnly stares out across the square, always making Gil think of John Henry, his hammer at the ready. His grandfather loved to tell him the tall tale of the man who had a contest against a steam drill with only his

hammer and won. A story symbolizing the strength and endurance of their ancestors. When he was a kid, in his mind, all of the statues were of tales of heroes or even gods, placed to watch over everyone that walked underneath their gaze. Despite the fact that he felt like he was one of the only ones living here that knew the story behind the statues or even cared about the plaque that explained their origin and donation, inlaid into the sidewalk, it was still a small game for himself to imagine who or what they could be.
A horn sounds and Brandon says,
"Gil! Gil, go, man! It's green!"

Gil comes back to himself, stepping on the gas pedal too hard, making the car lurch forward before slowing back down to cross over the intersection. Brandon leans back, lighting another cigarette, his third of the drive, as he looks out the window at the steam rising off of the pavement from the rain hitting the hot asphalt, the city scenery of restaurants and businesses continuing to pass by. As he keeps looking out of the window he says to Gil,
"That body really has you spaced out, huh?"

Gil watches a woman run across the street, her high heels avoiding puddles, a copy of the Stadton Eye, the city's most popular newspaper, held high, guarding her hair from the rain.
"Yeah, guess it's just stuck in my head."

They turn into the lot of the S.C.P.D. building, standing high with a gaudy badge on the outside, like someone flexing their muscles for all to see. Brandon is the first out of the car and as Gil gets out he hears him say,

"We'll shake it loose. He's definitely not going to be the last body this week. This city has gone to shit."

Brandon starts to walk away, towards the station, still talking about how everyone is leaving the suburbs of Stadton to move out to places like Ashton and Kolme, but Gil hardly hears him. The gray of the sky has stolen his attention, rain falling and hitting him in the face. It feels cleansing after what he just witnessed, washing away the feeling of filth that has settled on his skin. He closes his eyes, seeing the scene they just left, the body laying at the base of that pine tree. He sees the black, charred fingers twitch, his mind's eye painting a picture of the body, left displayed for all to see. He imagines the face, looking up at him and then sees the mouth open, a garbled sound retching itself from the corpse's throat. The mouth opens wider as a bird's head pokes from the darkness, its feet gripping the bottom lip to pull itself free. Its head twists around like a snake, its beak opening as it releases, not a chirp, but a vicious sounding hiss. Gil's eyes shoot open, water stinging them as he looks back down. Brandon is standing under the overhang, another cigarette in hand.

"You done singing in the rain?"

Gil wonders quickly if Brandon has ever seen that movie and can't imagine his partner sitting down with a bowl of popcorn to watch a musical from 1952. He steps forward, walking around puddles that have formed in the parking lot, trying to not soak his shoes. Brandon has a shit eating grin on his face as Gil walks past, and for the 300th time tells himself that one day, he will wipe that stupid look off Brandon's face, but that day is not *today*.

———————————

Cold air hits him directly in the face as he pulls the handle of the door, opening a path to where he has spent most of his waking life for the last twenty years. He's seen ups and downs, corrupt cops, governors making back alley deals or passing laws inspired by bigotry in the middle of the night. He's seen this city betray and protect its own, countless times over. If he could give it all up for something else, if he could run away to one of the mountain towns a short drive away, he doesn't know if he would. He doesn't know if he could. This is what's familiar to him and sometimes what's familiar is the most comforting; even if it's rotted from the inside out. He finds his desk and sits, not wanting to interact with anyone, a wish that could never be fulfilled even if he thought about it as hard as he could when he blows out his birthday candles on the cake he buys for himself every year and eats alone.

He's not there for more than two minutes when a file is dropped on his desk, making him look up into deep, blue eyes. Grace Hanilley, a detective who all the boys besides Gil affectionately refer to as Handy Hanilley, a rumor

passing through the station that she performed "favors" to make detective, stands at his desk looking down at him. The issue is that everyone knows that she could beat their asses at solving a case or in a fist fight for that matter and this leads them to resort back to being little insecure boys on the playground, making fun of what they can't understand or compete with. Because of their inferiority complexes, she generally ends up running information for the other detectives instead of being out in the field, another thing she has proven herself to be quite adept at. Gil leans forward, flicking open the cover of the file.
"What's this?"

A man's face comes into view and Gil instantly recognizes the photo as a mugshot taken at the Stadton jail in the center of downtown. He glances at the name which reads: PHILLIP MAYSHEW.

His eyes flick back up and Grace smiles,
"That's your Vic."

Gil turns the page to read the rap sheet of the deceased when his eyes shoot back up to Grace's.
"How did you even know about the case? We literally just left the scene."

Grace smiles,
"Nothing travels faster than light, except gossip."

Gil glances back down at the file, then up again, a confused look painted on his face.

"One arrest for driving without a license in 1997?"

Grace's eyebrows move up, as her head twists slowly from side to side, showing she was surprised as well that someone with such a small criminal history would end up as a burnt human pretzel left at the base of a tree.

"Yup. Not much there at all."

Gil looks back down, turning the page to make sure he didn't miss anything.

"That's generally not the kind of person that ends up as a scorched and twisted fatality on the side of the freeway."

He flips back to the first page.

"Says here he was living in Aima Island back in '97. Was he-"

Grace cuts him off,

"Yup, he was still living there as far as we can tell. I called the sheriff already, mainly to make sure that there wasn't more information that was somehow missing from his file, but the sheriff is already headed out to his place. Apparently he knew him personally."

Gil looks up again,

"How's that?"

Grace purses her lips,

"Seems he was his nephew."

Gil's eyes close as he leans back in his chair, making it squeak loudly.
"Shit."

Grace looks up, seeing Brandon walking towards them and says,
"Well, good luck."

Gil with his eyes still closed, seeing nothing but black, burnt fingers twitching through his mind hears Brandon say,
"What were you talking to Handy about? She getting sweet on you?"

Gil opens his eyes and leans forward, standing and grabbing the file from his desk. As he walks by he says,
"Shut the fuck up, Brandon."

CHAPTER TWO

Gil and Brandon drive in silence, the familiar smell of Brandon's Camel Turkish Silvers filling the small space between them as they head back towards Aima Island, the rain washing away whatever was left of the body that laid beside the freeway just hours before. Gil thinks about the scene, an absolute horror sequence; the part of the movie where the soundtrack soars, a jump scare evolving. Something no one should ever have to lay eyes upon, gone now, while traffic passes by, no one even aware of what took place there until they watch their TVs tonight, sitting in their big ugly chairs in their meager living rooms, telling their partners that they drove by that exact spot earlier today, before shaking their heads and saying,

"This city has gone to shit."

A bump makes him come back to the present, the change of ground from pavement to the concrete of the bridge making a loud noise under the tires. He glances out of the window, the sun dancing off the lake as the choppy water passes underneath. On the shoreline, houses that Gil will never be able to afford, fly by. Houses with golf course access and private docks, pontoons and speed boats just sitting, waiting to be used, in gated neighborhoods with polo shirt block parties, where everyone is ignorant to the terror happening all around them, just outside of their private refuge.

A single fishing kayak floating in the middle of the lake catches his eye. He thinks to himself that the water is so close to Stadton and he should really get out here more, maybe take a day off and go fishing, but he knows he won't. Just another broken promise to himself. Another bump comes as they leave the bridge behind and drive past the WELCOME TO AIMA ISLAND sign. Gil hears Brandon mutter,

"More like shithole island."

He chooses to ignore the comment. He likes Aima and knows Brandon is just pissy because he told him to shut the fuck up about Grace Hannilley back at the station.

No longer on the lake, the scenery takes a drastic change, turning from brick mansions to a mix of homes that pass

by. Everything from double wides to two story moderns, split levels, cabins and condemned wooden shacks left long ago, the properties still trying to be bought by developers who want to build things like luxury apartments or cookie cutter homes to maximize profits. Further down the road and a couple of turns later, a small white outbuilding built from concrete blocks comes into view. As they drive closer they can see a main house once stood beside it, but has been long ago knocked down, nothing remaining except the river rock chimney. Gil says under his breath,
"Must be the wrong address."

Brandon leans forward, squinting through the windshield and says,
"Nahhh, I think this is the spot, alright. Sheriff is already here."

They see a man in a brown uniform come out of the outbuilding, a screen door slamming open and then closed with a loud *whap* sound of wood on wood. A second later the door flies open again, a woman storming from the building, yelling at the sheriff and waving her hands in the air. He stops, starting to turn before deciding against it and walking the rest of the way to his car. The woman runs across the dead grass with bare feet, knowing exactly where to step to not hurt herself on old pieces of brick or broken bottles. She reaches into the front of her apron that is tied securely around her waist and brings out a fist, lifting it above her head as the sheriff's car starts to pull away. She

slings her arm forward, opening her palm, salt flying from her hand, hitting the back of the car as she yells,
"Break your leg, you son of a bitch!"

The woman watches, with her hands on her hips as Gil turns the car into the dirt in front of the building after the sheriff pulls out, leaving. When they climb out of the car, she points a finger down the road towards where the sheriff's car just went and says,
"You with him?"

Gil looks at Brandon, then turns back to the woman.
"No ma'am. We're not from the Sheriff's department. I'm Gil Griffin and this is James Brandon. We're S.C.P.D."

They show their badges and she scoffs,
"Stadton City? Sheriffs, cops, you're all the same."

She removes her hand from her apron pocket and starts walking back towards the outbuilding. Gil takes two steps forward and says,
"We'd like to ask you about Phillip Mayshew."

Without turning around she says,
"Yeah, seems he's all anyone wants to talk about today."

She gets to the screen door and says,
"Well come on then."

As he steps on the porch, Gil raises his hand, wiping the sweat from his forehead as Brandon slaps his neck.
"Fucking mosquitos. I swear they survive year round now."

Just an hour ago the wind and rain were sending chills through his body, but now the sun is out, taking Nattson County towards a humid 74 degrees. They walk through the entrance, the door left open and let the screen door swing shut behind them.

―――――――――――――――――   ―――――――――――――――――

The inside is dark with small lines of sunlight creeping in from broken blinds that cover the windows, making it take a moment for their eyes to adjust. There are bundles of herbs hanging from the ceiling alongside unrolled tubes of fly paper, melted candles strewn about the makeshift home, along with symbols drawn all over the windows and walls in paint and permanent marker. Gil glances at Brandon who wearily whispers to him,
"Is that a dead cat?"

Gil looks to the wall to the right of them to see something hanging in front of one of the windows inside; the dried carcass of some animal, tied at the feet with twine. Gil thinks to himself that it could very well be a cat, but it could just as well be a skunk or a fox. Without answering he turns to the woman who has her back to them. She's digging through a crate, bottles clinking together as she looks for something. He takes a step towards her.

"So ma'am, like we were saying, we wanted to ask you about Phillip Mayshew. This was listed as his last known address. I assume you already found out from the sheriff that he is-"

Gil's eyes catch a jar of brine sitting on top of the fridge full of entrails with a metal railroad spike stuck through the center. A fly lands on the jar, then takes off again, hitting one of the fly paper rolls and buzzing as it struggles for its life. He coughs, clearing his throat.

"-dead."

Without turning around, she says,

"Yeah, I heard. And before you ask, he's not my husband."

Brandon reaches out a hand hesitantly touching a small pile of bones on a table that fall over. He yanks his hand back, wiping his palm off on his pants, then clearing his throat.

"You are Bridget Mayshew, is that correct?"

"That's what they call me."

"And you weren't married to Phillip Mayshew?"

"I didn't say that. I said he wasn't my husband. We split six years ago."

"And when was the last time you saw Mr. Mayshew?"

She finally turns from the table.
"Comes by once a month."

Gil cuts in.
"And why is that?"

She turns back to the table.
"Because we have a child together."

Gil looks around.
"And do the two of you…live here?"

Finally she gets tired of answering questions and slams something on the table before turning around.
"Look, if all you want to do is judge me, why don't you go talk to his uncle. I'm sure he will be willing to tell you all kinds of things about me, since you are all in the business of oppression and control. I'm busy though and you need to leave."

The air inside the building suddenly feels thick and hard to breathe, like being under a wet blanket, making Gil sweat harder, pulling at his collar that suddenly feels tight. He pulls a card from his jacket pocket and sets it on the corner of the table.
"If you think of anything you'd like to tell us, feel free to give us a call."

Bridget doesn't answer and the two detectives turn, leaving the hot outbuilding. As soon as they are outside, the breeze

cools the sweat on their foreheads making them feel refreshed. Brandon looks at Gil and says,
"What the fuck was that?"

Gil looks back at the building, seeing Sarah through the screen door still at the table. His hand instinctively comes up to his neck, rubbing the front of his throat. He felt like he was being choked in there, a feeling of suffocation, unable to get a full breath of air. He's never felt anything like that in his entire life and hopes he never will again. He walks away and gets back in the car.

Sarah stops what she's doing, standing still at the table as she listens to the second door close and the car pull away. Her hand shoots out, grabbing the card Gil left on the table. She lifts it to her nose, inhaling the scent. She lowers it, holding it over a lit candle. The card lights, burning quickly as she drops it to the floor. As the rest of the card burns, it curls in on itself, the orange embers burning out, leaving nothing but gray ash. Turning to the left, she grips a broom and turns back, sweeping the floor where the detectives just walked. As she holds open the screen door, sweeping the dust outside she mutters under her breath,
"You are not welcome here."

She turns, letting the screen slam shut behind her as she looks back into the dark room, her eyes focusing on a corner by the back door.
"Don't worry; he won't hurt you, baby."

CHAPTER THREE

Gil pulls out onto the road, his want to get away from that outbuilding feeling overwhelming. Something wasn't right back there. Something shifted when she told them to leave. That wasn't just some poor woman living in an old cinder block shack; she was something more, something sinister. Gil feels lost in his thoughts, something in his mind tainted when he suddenly looks up as he sees a child stumble onto the freeway, hobbling barefoot across the pavement.
"SHIT!"

He slams his foot on the brakes, making the tires lock up and squeal as the back of the car fishtails, finally bringing

the two men to a stop. Brandon whips his head towards Gil and yells,
"WHAT THE FUCK IS WRONG WITH YOU!?"

A car flys by, laying on the horn the whole time and Gil eases forward, pulling to the side of the road. Brandon immediately opens his door, walking over to Gil's side. Gil straightens up in his seat, with closed eyes that shoot open when he hears the car door open, feeling both of Brandon's hands grip his jacket, pulling him out of the car hard. He slams Gil against the side of the car and yells,
"YOU COULD HAVE KILLED US, GRIFFIN!"

Gil, not paying any mind to Brandon's anger, looks to the side, cars flying by.
"The kid! Where's the kid?"

Brandon lets go of Gil's jacket, running his hands through his hair. He inhales deeply, letting out a sigh.
"What are you talking about?"

Gil looks around.
"There was a kid in the road. Didn't you see her?"

Brandon leans against the car, his anger extinguished. He lights a cigarette, inhaling then blowing out a cloud of smoke.
"You need a fucking vacation, my friend. There wasn't anything in the road."

Gil knows what he saw, but then again; maybe Brandon is right. Maybe he needs a break. He hasn't even had a day off in nine weeks. He glances over at his partner.
"Can I have one of those?"

Brandon looks up from the spot on the ground he's staring at.
"I thought you quit like four years ago."

Gil nods.
"Five. Just give me one, okay?"

Brandon pulls out his pack, opening the top of the box and sliding out a cigarette. He hands it to Gil and passes him his brown lighter. Gil takes both, placing the filter of the cigarette between his lips and sparking the lighter, touching the flame to the end. He inhales, the first time nicotine has entered his body in half a decade. It flows through him, triggering a brain response he had all but forgotten. The first couple puffs don't taste good, but then his body falls back into his addiction like he never stopped, a buzz filling his head as every fiber in him starts to crave more. He takes another drag and blows out smoke.
"I'm sorry about that, man. I don't know what I saw."

Brandon laughs,
"You're probably creeped out by the fact that in one day we've seen a burnt body with its head on backwards and then had to go to some she-demon's horror house to ask about it.

352

He takes another drag of his cigarette and chuckles, "Don't worry, I'm not gonna tell anyone you're losing it."

Gil looks at Brandon with disdain and then they both laugh, the feeling rising between them that they used to have when they first got partnered up. The good times, before Brandon's divorce and Gil's wife dying three years ago. A time before they were jaded and resentful towards the whole world around them; when they still thought they could make a difference. As the tension dissipates, they put out their smokes and climb back into the car, Brandon sliding another out of the pack, chain smoking them back to back as Gil puts on his turn signal and pulls back out into traffic.

CHAPTER FOUR

Brandon was right when he said Mayshew wouldn't be the last homicide that week. By the time they got back to the station, there wasn't even time for them to sit down before they got called out on an open and shut murder, the wife, covered in blood, bawling next to the body of her husband, crying about killing him. She told them that she was the one who called the police after shooting him six times when he broke the news to her that he wanted a divorce. When he told her it was over, she held back her tears, walked to the closet and returned with his gun, taking aim and unloading all six chambers into his chest.

Even as Gil watches handcuffs get placed on her wrists to take her back to the station to sign a confession, he knows the wheels of justice will turn as slow as ever. In the end, he's sure she will probably hire a high priced lawyer who will concoct a way to get her off on temporary insanity, place her in a leisurely penal institution that will release her in a year, a slap on the wrist and a record she will lobby to have expunged. As they walk her out, Gil stares at the body, laying on the floor of the upscale Stadton Heights mansion, a pool of blood staining the pristine white carpet of the bedroom. Photo bulbs snap as people rush around the scene, like if they don't get it handled quick enough the body is going to get up and walk away, but all Gil can do is stare. His eyes narrow as he sees something move beside the body; little fingers sliding out from the puddle of blood on the floor. The hand leading to an arm that grips the dry carpet, pulling a shoulder, then a head out of the slough of gore. He stands frozen, unable to react as the small body spider walks, on all fours, directly out of the floor and in his direction, a creature more than a person. As the child leaps off the bloody carpet towards him, his hands instinctively fly up in front of his face, making him wake up in his bed. As he sits up, rubbing his eyes, trying to pull himself from the false reality he was just in, he can almost swear he can hear something scuttling down the hallway directly outside the bedroom door.

The next morning couldn't come fast enough. It's been three days since being called out to the scene where the opulent wife admitted to murdering her husband. She has been processed, placing her in others custody, freeing himself and Brandon up, able to concentrate on the Mayshew case once again. Gil sits at his desk, typing and jotting down notes. He looks over at Brandon working his way through a fourteen inch sandwich despite it only being 8 AM. Gil takes a sip of bitter coffee, the freeze dried they keep around the station as Brandon slides over on his wheeled desk chair, pastrami hanging at a dangerous angle out of the side of his sub.

"What you doing there, Inspector Gadget?"

Gil looks up.

"I found out some info on Mayshew's ex wife."

He clicks a key and a screen comes up, showing a mug shot of the woman living in the outbuilding that they talked to three days ago, the name Bridget Mayshew sitting over the photo in dark bold letters.

"She definitely has more priors than Phillip did. Drunk and disorderly, DUI, grand theft auto, larceny, assault, and a whole bunch of others from when she was living in Grande Gorge."

Brandon sinks his teeth into his sandwich, tearing off a huge bite, talking through meat and cheese.

"Yeah, man. She's a crazy broad. I could have told you that without running it through NCIC. She look good for our suspect?"

Gil nods slowly.
"With her priors and being split from Phillip, she definitely does and there's something else."

"What?"

Gil inhales, letting out his breath in a slow sigh.
"Bridget told us Phillip came there once a month because of their child."

Brandon nods and then scrunches his eyebrows together as Gil turns the screen towards him.
"Their daughter died when she was four; six years ago."

They sit for a moment in silence thinking about this information before Brandon says,
"I think we should go talk to that sheriff, see what he knows before we try and get a warrant."

They stand, putting on their jackets and walking away from their desks. Halfway out of the room, Brandon doubles back, grabbing the rest of his paper wrapped sub and jogs back to the door.

CHAPTER FIVE

The weather has turned again, a prominent feature of the south; dumping heaps of rain on the car as they drive to Aima Island for the third time in a week. After finishing his sandwich in the car, Brandon convinces Gil to stop off at a Poseidon's Treasure fast food restaurant, so he can get a Trident sized Cheerwine soda, because his giant hoagie has inevitably made him thirsty. Gil glances over at the thirty ounces of corn syrup and carbonated water sitting in a plastic cup featuring the Greek god of the sea holding up his famed mythological weapon, a cheese burger stuck onto each one of the prongs of the trident. His eyebrows raise as he shakes his head.

"I really don't know how you drink that stuff."

Brandon laughs,

"Wife never let me have junk food. I'm just making up for lost time."

They drive over the bridge into Aima Island, passing Mountain Top Liquor, a line of customers already waiting for the building to open, even though it is only nine in the morning. An inflatable Yodeler waves at people as they drive by, beckoning them to come in and feed their addiction. Gil comes to a stop, a road crew delaying them. A man in a dayglow vest and hardhat turns his sign from STOP to SLOW as they pull past Nattson County construction workers filling in potholes that constantly form on the seventy year old road. They finally pull into the Sheriff's station, parking next to a small group of squad cars.

The inside of the building is small and musty smelling. A time portal back to the eighties, the last time the county put any funding into upgrading the meager station. Wooden benches line the walls and a bulletin board displays black and white pictures of people with the word MISSING above their heads. A woman in her mid twenties sits at the front desk, the only person in the room, looking at her phone, her bright acrylic nails tapping on the screen, no doubt seeing if she has more followers on social media from posting a cat video, rather than using the super computer with access to the world's information that she holds in the palm of her hand to actually learn something of merit. Gil and Brandon walk up to the desk and stand

waiting as she keeps typing away, little synthetic clicks sounding out through the deadly silent room. Finally Gil clears his throat and she sets down her phone, an annoyed look painted across her face.
"Help you?"

Brandon leans forward,
"Well, how kind of you to ask."

He motions to Gil and then himself.
"We're officers Griffin and Brandon from the S.C.P.D.. We're kind of in the middle of solving a murder and need a minute of the Sheriff's time. If you could get him for us, that would be great."

His plasters an award winning smile on his face and the woman rolls her eyes, sliding out of her chair and walking back towards a door that has SHERIFF painted on the glass. She opens it just enough for her head to fit through, saying something that they can't make out before pulling her head back out and closing the door. She walks back up to the desk and says,
"You two can go on back."

They walk around the desk, their footfalls echoing in the deadly silent station before they stop at the closed door. Gil looks at Brandon.
"You shouldn't have told her that we're on assignment."

Brandon laughs,

"Like she could give a shit."

He reaches out, turning the knob and they walk inside. The sheriff sits at his desk that has a nameplate that says A. Smith, typing on his laptop that he closes and sets his hands on top of, his fingers interlaced as he says,
"Have a seat gentlemen. What can I do for you?"

As they sit in the chairs facing the desk, Brandon opens his mouth to speak, but Gil cuts him off,
"We're working the Phillip Mayshew case."

The sheriff's face goes flat.
"Well, I'll make it easy for you boys. Bridget Mayshew did it."

Gil pulls out his notebook and pen.
"And what makes you believe that?"

The sheriff lets out a sarcastic laugh.
"Because she's a witch! Everyone knows it. She always has been. At least since-"

He trails off, looking up at the men in front of him, then quickly clears his throat.
"Anyhow, Phillip got wrapped up with her right after they both got out of highschool and then they had Sadie."

Gil writes down the daughter's name, looking back up as the sheriff continues.

"Terrible thing that happened to that girl. Was sick her whole life. I've tried to nail her momma for it for years, but I can't get it to stick. She died in the hospital, but I know she was doing something to her. Poisoning her or some shit. I can't get enough to put her away, but this business with my nephew, that's the final straw. We don't take kindly to witches in our community."

Gil looks up from his notepad.
"We talked to Bridget, actually. She said Phillip would come see her once a month because of-"

He looks down referencing his fresh notes.
"Sadie."

The sheriff leans forward, his elbows on his desk.
"Sadie has been dead for six years."

Gil nods.
"We saw that too. So if Sadie isn't alive, why was Phillip going over there once a month?"

The sheriff sits back up.
"Hell if I know. Booty call most likely. You know women like that, always trying to-"

Gil cuts him off, not interested in his opinions on "women like that".
"Were they maintaining a sexual relationship?"

The sheriff's face starts to grow aggravated,
"Now boys, I respect the fact that you're trying to solve this case. I'm thankful and I'll go ahead and speak for my sister and say she's thankful too for you trying to figure out who would do such a terrible thing to her boy, but I'm not going to sit here and pretend to know why my nephew was still fucking around with that woman."

He straightens up, leaning back in his chair.
"Now, I'd suggest you go make an arrest before something happens to her."

Brandon finally gets a chance to talk,
"And what's that supposed to mean?"

The sheriff holds up his hands.
"No threats are being made here, boys. It's like I told you, Aima Island doesn't take kindly to witchcraft. This is a powder keg and I'm trying to help you avoid the match being struck."

Gil looks at Brandon then back and says,
"Well thanks for your time, Sheriff."

The sheriff nods,
"I'll see you boys out."

He turns in his chair, retrieving a crutch that's propped up against the wall behind his desk chair, bracing himself, putting his weight on it as he stands and hobbles around the

desk. Gil and Brandon look down at his leg that is in a cast and Brandon asks,
"What happened there?"

The sheriff looks down at his own leg then back up.
"I told you, she is a witch, This is her doing."

He hobbles out of his office as Gil and Brandon turn to look at each other, Brandon raising his eyebrows before his partner puts up a hand to stop him. There is no way Gil is about to entertain a conversation about if Bridget cursed the sheriff and made him break his leg.

The three of them walk past the girl at the counter who is leaning back in her chair. She has now inserted airpods that blast a deep baseline into her ears. Outside Brandon turns to Gil.
"I'm telling you, the people of Aima Island are fucking weirdos, man. We saw her throw that salt at his car and tell him to break his leg!"

He spreads his arms as he keeps talking.
"All kinds of crazy shit happens around here. You ever hear about all the disappearances up on the mountain? The people here are nuts and if we don't act fast, I'll bet you they're gonna kill that woman and make it look like another one of their mountain accidents."

Gil looks up at the mountain looming in the distance. *Everyone* has heard of people going missing up there, but that's what happens when you decide to place yourself into the wilderness and contend with the wild things that reside there. Humans can be so strong, but they are also so fragile. Movement flashes out in his peripherie, a small body rushing in between cars, darting from the protection of one vehicle to another. He turns his head, nothing meeting his gaze. He squints, taking a step to the side to see in between the parked cruisers. Brandon follows his line of vision and says,

"What is it?"

Gil rubs his hands over his face, feeling like this investigation is making him lose his mind.

"Nothing. This case is just making me bug out."

Brandon starts rambling again about how being on Aima Island will do that to you and when he was a kid, his father wouldn't even let his family cross the bridge to come to the lake because of the "strange things" that happen here, as they both get in the car and drive out of the lot, back towards Stadton.

CHAPTER SIX

Brandon is long gone from the station, probably slinging back three dollar beers at the Stadton Reapers hockey game while Gil pours through information, trying to figure out Bridget's role in Phillip Mayshew's murder. Brandon seemed quite concerned about what could happen to her when they were in Aima, but by the time they got back, that sentiment had faded. He slapped a hand on Gil's shoulder and said,

"You gotta clock out sometime, buddy."

He invited Gil to come along, but he declined. If what the sheriff is saying contains any grain of truth, then the clock is ticking down before the people of Aima Island take matters into their own hands; villagers with torches and pitchforks, marching to the monster's tower to serve justice.

Gil can feel the frustration in him building. There has to be something they are missing; a slip up that's just waiting to be found. Something about this case doesn't feel right and he can't for the life of him place a finger on it. He leans back, his eyes feeling tired from staring at the screen. His desk lamp is the only light in the room, casting out a circle of illumination around him, the only people working the station now on the lower levels while every desk in investigation sits abandoned. A rustle comes from a row of desks in the corner of the room and he squints, trying to peer through the darkness. Last year they had to bring in an exterminator when they found rats breeding in the building's basement. He makes a mental note to tell maintenance that they're going to have to call pest control again and turns back to his work, but another noise comes from the same corner, this time something falling and breaking, the sound of glass shattering on the old, tiled floor. He stands, walking towards where the sound came from, trying to see in the dark, his eyes adjusting slowly from the light of his lamp. This time when he hears the rustle, he thinks he sees something move and its silhouette shows that it is much larger than a rat. He reaches into his pocket, pulling out a flashlight and clicking it on. He slowly moves the light along the floor then feels his blood turn to ice as the light illuminates little feet, then legs, a nightgown and then the whole body of a little girl curled up in the corner, her face hidden behind jet black hair. He takes a slow step forward.

"Hey there. How did you get in here?"

She says nothing and he takes another step forward.

"Are you alright? I can help you."

As he gets closer and closer he can see that she is shaking, a whimper escaping from her mouth.

"You don't have to be afraid. I'm a police offi-"

His words stop as the girl turns quickly, her milky eyes full of malice. Her mouth opens, a scream erupting from behind her dark, chapped lips as she runs on all fours at him like a wild animal, her chipped nails scraping against the tiled floor. He drops the flashlight that rolls on the ground as he turns and runs towards the doors. Weight slams onto his back, knocking him forward as he can feel her sharp nails digging into the skin of his neck and shoulders, drawing blood. He reaches back trying to pull her off, tripping over a chair leg and slamming down onto his desk, scattering papers across the floor. The weight is suddenly gone and he sits up, looking around frantically, his hand reaching down to unsnap the strap on his gun holster. A scuffle comes from behind a desk three rows away, then another from his left. He pulls his gun, turning his head, trying to figure out where the girl is at, when a glob of something wet drips onto the top of his head. He looks up slowly to see the little girl perched on top of his desk, the light illuminating her gaunt features. She bares her teeth, saliva dripping out of her mouth as she stares at him, an animal about to devour its prey. His eyes drift down, seeing that she is holding something in her right hand. She grasps it tightly and Gil can see it is an old, dirty baby doll. His eyes move back to hers as a low growl crawls up from her throat. Before he can raise his weapon, she lets out another scream and jumps from the desk, landing on him hard, sending his gun sliding across the floor, into the darkness. He gets the wind knocked out of him while she moves her hands fast, her nails cutting into the skin of his face and forearms as he tries to cover himself. He lifts his leg, wedging his foot between the two of them, pushing hard and kicking her off of him. She flies through the air, slamming into Brandon's desk, her spine making a sickening crack as she hits the metal side, falling to the floor, laying still. Gil finds his footing, standing slowly. He cocks his head, looking at her body that is folded the wrong way, her spine snapped in half. He shoves his hand into his pocket, looking for his phone to call help when he sees her hand twitch. He lowers the phone from his ear as he watches the rest of her body slowly stir. His mouth goes dry as he watches her stand, her bones making cracking noises as they shift back into place and she stands up straight. Her gaze rises slowly as she starts to growl again and he wastes no time, turning to run across the room as she jumps from desk to desk, knocking laptops and files to the floor. He runs down the stairwell as a scream comes from above him, ripping through the silence. The back doors to the station slam open as he breaks through hard, running across the parking lot into the woods next to the station. He hides behind a tree, his breath coming hard, making him regret the cigarettes he's been bumming from Brandon ever since he saw the little girl; *this* little girl, in the middle of the road. He leans to the side to peek around the tree as she flies through the air, hitting him hard and knocking him to the ground. She grabs his head with both hands, lifting it then smacking it into a rock. Pain radiates through his skull as she leans close and whispers,

"Stay away."

Her nails dig into the sides of his head as she lifts it again, slamming it back down, making everything turn dark.

CHAPTER SEVEN

Gil wakes up, the sunlight coming in between the trees, blinding him. He holds up his hand to shade his face, his eyes adjusting as he looks around, seeing faces staring down at him; then hears Brandon say,
"Okay, okay, give him some room!"

The people surrounding him back up as a medic walks through the crowd, crouching down and helping Gil sit up before taking out a flashlight and examining the back of his head. He comes back around to face him, shining a light into his eyes. Gil pushes the medic out of the way, looking over at Brandon who crouches down next to the medic.
"Gil, who did this to you?"

Gil scrunches his face, the pain still radiating from the attack. Brandon speaks slowly.

"Gil, it's me, Brandon.

He groans,
"I know who you are. Help me up."

Brandon steps back, offering a hand that Gil takes. He gets his feet under him and raises to full height, onlookers already becoming disinterested and heading towards the station to start their day. The medic steps behind Gil, still trying to examine his wound. He whips around and says,
"Will you get the fuck off me? I'm fine."

He turns, limping across the parking lot as Brandon follows close behind him. Gil opens the front door, heading up the stairs to investigations, his appearance garnering more looks as he heads towards the locker room. Brandon asks,
"Gil, what happened?"

Gil turns around, holding a single finger in front of his mouth then motions his head to the side to tell him silently to follow him into the locker room. Once inside, Gil walks to his locker, opening it and pulling out his spare clothes he keeps at the station. He unbuttons his shirt, torn and bloody, tossing it on the bench. He removes his socks and shoes and walks around the corner to the showers with spare clothes in hand. Brandon leans on the outside wall as he hears the water turn on and three minutes later turn off. Gil

comes back around the corner, now wearing S.C.P.D. sweatpants with a matching hoodie. He towels off his wet hair and tosses it into the used bin. Brandon stands silent, eyebrows raised, waiting for an answer. Gil turns to him.
"It was a kid."

Brandon can't help but laugh.
"The fuck you mean? A kid did this to you?"

Gil tells him about the girl in the corner of the room that attacked him and Brandon looks concerned.
"I mean, you know how crazy that sounds right? If it wasn't for the scratches all over you, I'd call you batshit."

Gil pulls his hood up, trying his best to not show his face.
"I'll tell you what's even crazier. It was the same kid that I saw in the road and I'm pretty sure I saw her in the sheriff's parking lot. She might have even been in my house the other night. It's Sadie Mayshew."

Brandon looks around, making sure no one else is hearing this as he rubs the back of his neck and sighs,
"Gil, maybe you should talk to someone, man. Ever since we saw that body, I don't know. Something is going on with you."

Gil's face turns to one of anger and he grabs Brandon by his suit's lapels, pulling him close.
"I'm telling you. She looked like she had come back from the dead, but it was her. I didn't imagine this!"

Brandon holds up his hands in surrender, looking at the scratches, dried lines of blood, streaked across Gil's face.
"Okay, okay. Let's say it was. Let's just say a dead kid came into the police station and attacked you. What for?"

Gil lets go of him and takes a deep breath.
"I found something last night."

Brandon sighs,
"Gil last night was Sunday, you've been missing since Saturday night."

His hand trails back to his neck,
"We've been looking for you since Sunday morning. Someone finally checked the woods. I don't know what's going on, but you're lucky to be alive."

Gil takes this in before shaking his head and pulling the drawstring tight on his sweatpants. They walk out of the locker room to their desks where Gil opens up what he was looking at before he was attacked. On the screen is a police report filed by a woman named Linda Mctaff last year. Brandon asks,
"What's this?"

Gil sits down and says,
"Linda Mctaff called the police last year and filed a report that Bridget and Phillip Mayshew were doing witchcraft behind the outbuilding Bridget lives in. No one took her

seriously because she told us that she thought they were trying to talk to their dead daughter."

Brandon looks at Gil.
"Wait are you saying that-"

Gil stares back at Brandon who looks back at the screen, then says,
"Well, let's go talk to her then."

Gil turns back to the screen, clicking the mouse and making another screen expand. Brandon's eyes close as Gil says,
"We can't. Linda Mctaff disappeared three weeks after she filed the report. Her body was never fou-"

He doesn't finish his sentence before a bellowing voice carries out across the room.
"GRIFFIN! BRANDON! GET IN HERE!"

They look over at the captain's office and then at each other as they stand up, walking past everyone casting eyes on them before opening his office door and stepping inside. He stares at them as they sit down in chairs and then for a beat more before he says,
"Do the two of you want to tell me what the fuck is going on here?"

Gil spots his gun that was knocked from his hands, sitting on the captain's desk. He opens his mouth to speak, but is stopped as a hand is held up showing him that the question was rhetorical.

"Rumor around the station is you two are hunting dead little girls and a witch from Aima Island."

Brandon shakes his head. Someone else must have been in the locker room. He leans forward, cutting in,

"Sir, Griffin was attacked Saturday night. I mean, look at him! Someone is obviously trying to stop us from solving this case!"

The captain's eyes move to Gil and he sighs.

"I don't know what is going on with you, Griffin, but we already looked at the footage of you being attacked. There was no one in there with you. I watched you do a number on yourself though."

Gil's mouth closes slowly and both continue to sit in silence. The captain leans back in his chair,

"I'm putting you on leave. After what you said you saw in the middle of the road and then this. I have no choice. You can come back in two months after getting a clean psych eval."

Gil nods and stands, turning and walking out of the room as Brandon follows. When they're both outside of the office Brandon calls out,

"Gil, hold up!"

380

Gil turns, swinging a fist that connects with Brandon's jaw, making him fall to the ground like a bag of rocks. The whole room stops what they're doing, watching what is unfolding. Gil looks down at Brandon rubbing his jaw and says,

"I can't believe you told the captain I saw something in the road. We're done."

He turns, letting all the eyes of the people he's worked with for decades follow him as he walks out of the station.

CHAPTER EIGHT

Gil gets in his car and puts his key in the ignition. The passenger side door opens and Brandon slides into the seat. Gil shakes his head then stares forward out of the windshield.

"Get out."

Brandon pulls a cigarette from his pack, lighting it and blowing out smoke before looking over at his partner.

"I know what you're going to do and you're not doing it alone."

Gil stares out of the windshield and says,

"I don't trust you anymore and without that-"

Brandon slams his hand on the dashboard.

"I was worried about you, okay?! I wasn't ratting you out. You saw a kid in the road that wasn't there! But no matter what's happening, I know you're about to go see that woman and you're not going there alone. We've worked together for far too long to be bickering about shit like this, so shut up and let's go."

Gil turns the key, then sits, waiting for the car to heat up. "You could lose your badge."

Brandon opens up the glove box in front of him, reaching in and pulling out Gil's backup pistol, handing it to him. He flicks his spent cigarette out of the window, pulling two more from his pack and lighting them before handing one to Gil. He leans back, blowing out smoke. "What's new?"

They peel out of the parking lot, merging into morning traffic, headed back to the outbuilding; back to Aima Island.

Gil looks over at Brandon.
"Call the sheriff. Have him meet us there. We're going to need local on this."

Brandon shifts in his seat as he pulls out his phone, dialing and holding it to his ear. After a few moments he says,
"This is Officer James Brandon of the S.C.P.D. We are headed to question a suspect in the Phillip Mayshew case. We need Sheriff Smith to report to-"

He stops talking and lowers the phone. Gil looks over at him.
"What? What is it?"

Brandon sighs,
"The sheriff is missing."

Gil presses down on the gas pedal, picking up speed as the car crosses over the bridge.

CHAPTER NINE

They pull onto the dirt, putting the car into park and getting out. They stop as Brandon motions to the side of the building. They walk over, seeing the Sheriff's squad car parked on the side of the outbuilding, covered in pine branches and leaves. Brandon looks back at Gil who nods and they both unlatch their holsters, slowly drawing their weapons, making sure to keep their fingers off their triggers until proven necessary. They walk slowly towards the front door, stepping up onto the porch, trying not to, make any noise. Gil winces as he steps on a old, loose board that lets out a creek. He looks up, giving two quick nods of his head and Brandon places his back against the wall next to the

entrance as Gil opens the screen, using his free hand to knock hard on the wood door.
"S.C.P.D., OPEN THE DOOR!"

No noise comes from inside and Gil calls out again,
"MS. MAYSHEW, THIS IS OFFICER GIL GRIFFIN, OPEN THE DOOR OR WE WILL BE FORCED TO ENTER!"

The inside of the house remains silent and Gil looks to Brandon, both nodding in acknowledgment. Gil takes a step back, Brandon reaching over and holding the screen door as he centers himself in front of the entryway before raising his foot and kicking the door hard. Nothing happens and he kicks it again, the old door resisting his breach. Finally with another kick the old wood shreds from the hinges, the whole door falling onto the floor. They enter the house, guns raised, keeping watch on the corners as they clear the room. They look around, taking in everything they saw the first time. Brandon reaches down, lifting something from the table and Gil turns to look, his eyes growing wide. Brandon is holding up the babydoll Sadie Mayshew had in the police station Saturday night. He reaches out his free hand, yelling,
"BRANDON, NO!"

From the shadow, a body erupts, bursting forward, knocking a chair out of the way and jumping on the table then back off onto Brandon as bones and bowls of herbs go scattering onto the floor. He drops the doll, lifting his gun and trying to fire off shots at whatever has attacked him. As bullets fly, Gil dives to the ground. He sees Sadie biting and clawing at Brandon as he spins around trying to get her off. She bares her teeth before sinking them into the flesh of Brandon's neck, making him drop his gun, grabbing onto her, pulling at her with both hands to get her off his back. Gil rolls over, laying on his belly, taking aim and yells, "SADIE!"

She lifts her head, red blood dripping from her mouth down her pail chin. Brandon gets a hold of her, pulling her off and throwing her onto the kitchen table. As she rises back up to attack again, Gil fires three shots, all hitting their mark in the girl's body, the third one directly in her forehead, making her fall off the table onto the floor. He stands, running over, looking at the body on the ground leaking black blood out of its shriveled skin. He looks up at Brandon and says,
"Believe me now?"

Brandon, a hand on his neck, covered in his own blood, winces at the pain.
"Yeah, I fucking believe you. You happy?."

Gil looks around the room.
"Let's see if we can find Bridget."

Brandon pulls a handkerchief from his pocket, bunching it up and holding it to his neck wound. He crouches down, picking up his gun before following Gil to check under the bed and in the bathroom, but finding no one. Back in the main room, Gil nods towards the back door and Brandon nods back in acknowledgement. They walk slowly towards it and Gil reaches a hand out, wrapping his fingers around the handle, turning it and pulling the door open. There is a fire pit, surrounded by old chairs and a carcass covered in flies next to it. On the other side of the pit is the Sheriff, tied up and unconscious, lying in the dirt next to a live goat tied to a stake. They glance at each other and walk out of the door slowly.

Their heads turn to the side as Bridget yells out, "MURDERER!"

She lunges from the cinder block wall with a pitchfork in her hands, shoving it towards Brandon. He jumps out of the way and the three prongs sink into Gil's stomach, making him scream out as he drops to his knees. Brandon turns back, taking aim at Bridget, but stops as she lifts a hand, opening it flat in front of her mouth and blows a powder into his face. Gil watches as his partner stands frozen, his pistol raised. Bridget takes a step to the side out of the line of fire as she raises a single finger. She looks at Gil on the ground, and smiles.
"You'd be surprised at the wonderful things you can concoct out of simple household herbs."

She turns her attention back to Brandon, muttering something inaudible as she moves her finger in a counterclockwise circle. Gil writhes on the ground as he

watches Brandon lower the gun, his face devoid of any emotion. He calls out,
"Brandon!"

Bridget turns to Gil and snarls,
"You cops always have to stick your noses where they don't belong, don't you?! We had a good thing going. Phillip would bring me goats once a month and we would trade their lives for my daughter to have hers back. But men are weak. He had guilt that she wasn't laid to rest. Told me we had to stop. Now *you* want to make me stop. EVERYONE IS TRYING TO KEEP MY CHILD FROM ME!"

She regains her composure, tears sliding down her cheeks.
"Well, I'm done having monthly visits with her. I want something more permanent."

She nods towards the Sheriff on the ground.
"I'm going to trade him for her and make her come back for good."

Gil, one hand wrapped around the handle of the pitchfork and another held out towards Bridget says,
"Your daughter is dead, Bridget."

She grabs the handle of the pitchfork and pulls hard, yanking it from Gil's body as he screams out in pain, his hoodie soaked in blood.
"No! She can come back. I can bring anyone back! I can reach in and pull her soul out of the darkness."

She turns her head and looks at Brandon.
"But not while you two are around."

She holds her finger out again and Brandon stiffens, under her control. She then lifts a second finger, turning her hand upside down so that her fingers mimic legs. She moves her fingers back and forth and Brandon walks forward stepping into the fire pit and standing in the center. She turns her hand back up, lowering the second finger and keeping one raised. She points to the gas can and Brandon bends over picking it up. She makes a half circle motion and he lifts the can, turning it upside down and letting the contents flow over his head. She points at his pocket and he drops the can, reaching into his pants and pulling out his lighter. She lowers her finger and raises her thumb, making the motion of a lighter striking as Gil yells,
"NO!"

Brandon rolls his thumb on the striker wheel, making sparks catch gas. He instantly erupts into flames, his face remaining stoic, making no sound as his body burns. Gil looks around, seeing his gun on the ground and starts to crawl towards it while Bridget watches his partner burn alive. He reaches out, then feels pain shoot through him as she slams the prongs of the pitchfork down through his leg. Brandon regains consciousness now that she is distracted and screams erupt from his mouth as he tries to put the flames out. Bridget and Gil both look at him as he reaches behind his coat, pulling out his back up firearm, raising it to his temple and pulling the trigger. His body hits the ground, a burning black heap and Bridget smiles as she pushes down harder on the handle of the pitchfork. She turns her head slowly back to Gil and says,

"One down, one to-"

She looks down the barrel of the gun as Gil squeezes the trigger and a bullet flies past her head, a complete miss. His strength gone, he drops the gun and Bridget starts to laugh. She pulls a knife from a sheath at her side and leans down towards Gil as another shot rings out, the bullet ripping through her stomach, sending her falling back towards the fire pit. She stumbles, her hand reaching down to cover her wound as she falls down in the grass. Gil looks behind him at Grace Hannilley holding a smoking revolver. Gil reaches down, pulling the pitchfork from his leg, spurts of blood flowing down his skin. He uses the rest of his strength to crawl towards Bridget, his consciousness quickly fading. When he is almost to her she sits up, holding the knife in the air, ready to strike. She tries to lunge forward, but stops as the Sheriff grabs ahold of her with his hands, tied at the wrist. Gil scoots back to a safe distance as Bridget looks around quickly from Gil to Grace, and back at the Sheriff. Grace calls out,

"Drop the weapon!"

In a last moment of desperation she turns to the side, slitting the throat of the goat before she turns the blade on herself, shoving the knife into her own neck, falling back dead, as the goat bleats, bleeding out slowly next to her.

CHAPTER TEN

Gil stares at himself in the bathroom mirror, his whole body in pain. He survived Bridget's attack, being found by Grace Hannilley who came to question Bridget after the case was given to her directly after Gil and Brandon left the station. He was told he's going to have permanent pain and nerve damage to deal with as a result of being stuck through with a pitchfork twice, but that he's lucky to be alive. Doctors love using that phrase, *"lucky to be alive"*, but really, it just depends on who you ask. Sheriff Smith survived, having only minor injuries. He said he had come to see her earlier in the day to ask some questions and she had surprised him, getting the drop on him. Gil doesn't know if this is true or if he was there to "handle" the problem, but since Bridget is dead, there's only one side to the story now. If they had been just a few minutes later, they would have been too late, the sheriff sacrificed to bring Sadie back from the dead; at least that's what Bridget believed and after what he's seen, Gil is pretty sure he believes it too.

He was released from the hospital after two weeks, given a "good job" by the captain, next to the news that because of his injuries, he would be riding a desk for the rest of his life. He was told he would receive a medal for his part in the case, but all he was interested in was seeing Brandon. He took a car directly from Stadton Medical to the cemetery with one stop on the way. Sitting in the grass, he had a smoke, a second lit cigarette resting on top of Brandon's tombstone as he talked to him, saying his goodbyes. He guesses that this case was the one to end it on; by far the weirdest thing either of them had ever been involved in. He misses Brandon and can admit that to himself, but he's thankful that they got to finish it together, that they got to put an end to it side by side.

Now, back in his apartment, staring at himself in the bathroom mirror, he reaches up, touching the scar on his face. He thinks about the one thing that has bothered him the entire time and still does. Why did Bridget slice that goat's throat before killing herself? As he stares into the mirror, thinking about that question, one he has thought about every day in the hospital during his slow recovery, his eyes suddenly grow wide as he remembers her telling him that a life could be traded for a life. Something in the mirror catches his eye behind him, coming out of the darkness and as he tries to turn, a hand reaches out, grasping the back of his skull, slamming his face forward into the glass of the bathroom mirror.